SUPERMIND

Originally published in 1963

By Randall Garrett
and
Laurence Janifer

And the Special Bonus Story
AND NOW A MESSAGE . . .
By Greg Fowlkes

SUPERMIND

© 2011 Resurrected Press
www.ResurrectedPress.com

Published by Resurrected Press

This classic book was handcrafted by Resurrected Press. Resurrected Press is dedicated to bringing high quality classic books back to the readers who enjoy them. These are not scanned versions of the originals, but, rather, quality checked and edited books meant to be enjoyed!

Please visit ResurrectedPress.com to view our entire catalogue!

ISBN 13: 978-1-935774-54-9

Printed in the United States of America

OTHER RESURRECTED PRESS
SCIENCE FICTION

And more!
Visit ResurrectedPress.com
to see our entire catalogue!

FOREWORD

Supermind is the conclusion of the series featuring that paragon of the FBI, agent Kenneth Malone as he confronts yet another psychic enemy of the United States. This novel is an expanded version of the story "Occasion for Disaster" that appeared in the November 1960 through February 1961 issues of *Analog Science Fact & Fiction* magazine.

In this adventure it becomes apparent that some outside agent is causing chaos and confusion at all levels of government by inducing inefficiency, ineptness, and downright incompetence. It sounds hard to believe, doesn't it, but the effect is traced down to bursts of psychic static that are affecting the minds of those in positions of authority. At first it appears to be the work of the Kremlin, and Malone travels to Russia in the company of Queen Elizabeth the First (Rose Thompson) and the beautiful Luba Garbitsch. But, on discovering that the Soviet Union is as messed up as the United States, Malone realizes he is facing a much deeper conspiracy.

Garrett and Janifer take all the clichés of the period, Russian spies, government incompetence, world-wide conspiracies to take over the world, and stand them on their heads. After applying mass quantities of alcohol, and copious amounts of tobacco products (this was the early 60's) Malone finally is able to penetrate to the heart of the conspiracy behind all the problems of the world.

Supermind is a product of its time, those days of paranoia and fun known as the sixties. It was written in the same spirit that brought us the movies The President's Analyst and Dr. Strangelove, and serves as a fitting conclusion to the trilogy of novels featuring agent Malone; *Brain Twister, The Impossibles,* and *Supermind.*

Resurrected Press is proud to bring these three novels to you for your enjoyment.

About the Author

Mark Phillips

Mark Phillips was the pen named used b Randall Garrett and Laurence Janifer for the three novels, *Brain Twister, The Impossibles,* and *Supermind.* The pair was nominated for a Hugo for best novel for Brain Twister in 1960. They also collaborated on the novel *Pagan Passions.*

Randall Garrett

Gordon Randall Garrett (December 16, 1927-December 31, 1987) was a prolific author of science fiction and fantasy. He was a regular contributor to Astounding and other magazines during the 50's and 60's. He is best known for his alternate reality stories featuring the detective Lord Darcy who lives in a world where the Plantagenates still rule an Anglo-French empire and magic works. He wrote under a number of pseudonyms including David Gordon, John Gordon, Ivar Jorgensen, Darrel T. Langart, Gerald Vance and others. He collaborated on several works with Laurence Janifer and with Robert Silverberg as Robert Randall. He was a founding member of the Society for Creative Anachronism.

Laurence M. Janifer

Laurence M. Janifer (March 17, 1933-July 10, 2002) was born in Brooklyn, New York. Originally named Laurence M. Harris, he changed his name to Janifer, which was the name of his Polish grandfather. Starting with the publication of a story in 1959 his writing career spanned three decades. Many of his early stories were published under the name Larry M. Harris. He collaborated on a number of stories and novels with

Randall Garrett, often using the pseudonym Mark Phillips. In addition to his career as a writer, he served as an editor for various magazines and literary agencies.

Greg Fowlkes
Editor-In-Chief
Resurrected Press
www.ResurrectedPress.com

1

In 1914, it was enemy aliens.

In 1930, it was Wobblies.

In 1957, it was fellow travelers.

In 1971, it was insane telepaths.

And, in 1973:

"We don't know *what* the hell it is," said Andrew J. Burris, Director of the FBI. He threw his hands in the air and looked baffled and confused.

Kenneth J. Malone tried to appear sympathetic. "What what is?" he asked.

Burris frowned and drummed his fingers on his big desk. "Malone," he said, "make sense. And don't stutter."

"Stutter?" Malone said. "You said you didn't know what it was. What the hell it was. And I wanted to know what it was."

"That's just it," Burris said. "I don't know."

Malone sighed and repressed an impulse to scream. "Now wait a minute, Chief—" he started.

Burris frowned again. "Don't call me Chief," he said.

Malone nodded. "Okay," he said. "But if you don't know what it is, you must have some idea of what you don't know. I mean, is it larger than a breadbox? Does it perform helpful tasks? Is it self-employed?"

"Malone," Burris sighed, "you ought to be on television."

"But—"

"Let me explain," Burris said. His voice was calmer now, and he spoke as if he were enunciating nothing but the most obvious and eternal truths. "The country," he said, "is going to hell in a handbasket."

Malone nodded again. "Well, after all, Chief—"

"Don't call me Chief," Burris said wearily.

"Anything you say," Malone agreed peacefully. He eyed the Director of the FBI warily. "After all, it isn't anything new," he went on. "The country's always been going to hell in a handbasket, one way or another. Look at Rome."

"Rome?" Burris said.

"Sure," Malone said. "Rome was always going to hell in a handbasket, and finally it—" He paused. "Finally it did, I guess," he said.

"Exactly," Burris said. "And so are we. Finally." He passed a hand over his forehead and stared past Malone at a spot on the wall. Malone turned and looked at the spot, but saw nothing of interest. "Malone," Burris said, and the FBI agent whirled around again.

"Yes, Ch—Yes?" he said.

"This time," Burris said, "it isn't the same old story at all. This time it's different."

"Different?" Malone said.

Burris nodded. "Look at it this way," he said. His eyes returned to the agent. "Suppose you're a congressman," he went on, "and you find evidence of inefficiency in the government."

"All right," Malone said agreeably. He had the feeling that if he waited around a little while everything would make sense, and he was willing to wait. After all, he wasn't on assignment at the moment, and there was nothing pressing waiting for him. He was even between romances.

If he waited long enough, he told himself, Andrew J. Burris might say something worth hearing. He looked attentive and eager. He considered leaning over the desk a little, to look even more eager, but decided against it; Burris might think he looked threatening. There was no telling.

"You're a congressman," Burris said, "and the government is inefficient. You find evidence of it. What do you do?"

Malone blinked and thought for a second. It didn't take any longer than that to come up with the old, old answer. "I start an investigation," he said. "I get a committee and I talk to a lot of newspaper editors and magazine editors and maybe I go on television and talk some more, and my committee has a lot of meetings—"

"Exactly," Burris said.

"And we talk a lot at the meetings," Malone went on, carried away, "and get a lot of publicity, and we subpoena famous people, just as famous as we can get, except governors or presidents, because you can't—they tried that back in the Fifties, and it didn't work very well—and that gives us some more publicity, and then when we have all the publicity we can possibly get—"

"You stop," Burris said hurriedly.

"That's right," Malone said. "We stop. And that's what I'd do."

"Of course, the problem of inefficiency is left exactly where it always was," Burris said. "Nothing's been done about it."

"Naturally," Malone said. "But think of all the lovely publicity. And all the nice talk. And the subpoenas and committees and everything."

"Sure," Burris said wearily. "It's happened a thousand times. But, Malone, that's the difference. It isn't happening this time."

There was a short pause. "What do you mean?" Malone said at last.

"This time," Burris said, in a tone that sounded almost awed, "they want to keep it a secret."

"A secret?" Malone said, blinking. "But that's—that's not the American way."

Burris shrugged. "It's un-congressman-like, anyhow," he said. "But that's what they've done. Tiptoed over to me and whispered softly that the thing has to be investigated quietly. Naturally, they didn't give me any orders—but only because they know they can't make one stick. They suggested it pretty strongly."

"Any reasons?" Malone said. The whole idea interested him strangely. It was odd—and he found himself almost liking odd cases, lately. That is, he amended hurriedly, if they didn't get *too* odd.

"Oh, they had reasons, all right," Burris said. "It took a little coaxing, but I managed to pry some loose. You see, every one of them found inefficiency in his own department. And every one knows that other men are investigating inefficiency."

"Oh," Malone said.

"That's right," Burris said. "Every one of them came to me to get me to prove that the goof-ups in his particular department weren't his fault. That covers them in case one of the others happens to light into the department."

"Well, it must be *somebody's* fault," Malone said.

"It isn't theirs," Burris said wearily, "I ought to know. They told me. At great length, Malone."

Malone felt a stab of honest pity. "How many so far?" he asked.

"Six," Burris said. "Four representatives, and two senators."

"Only two?" Malone said.

"Well," Burris said, "the Senate is so much smaller. And, besides, we may get more. As a matter of fact, Senator Lefferts is worth any six representatives all by himself."

"He is?" Malone said, puzzled. Senator Lefferts was not one of his favorite people. Nor, as far as he knew, did the somewhat excitable senator hold any place of honor in the heart of Andrew J. Burris.

"I mean his story," Burris said. "I've never heard anything like it— at least, not since the Bilbo days. And I've only heard about those," he added hurriedly.

"What story?" Malone said. "He talked about inefficiency—"

"Not exactly," Burris said carefully. "He said that somebody was out to get him—him, personally. He said somebody was trying to discredit him by sabotaging all his legislative plans."

"Well," Malone said, feeling that some comment was called for, "three cheers."

"That isn't the point," Burris snapped. "No matter how we feel about Senator Lefferts or his legislative plans, we're sworn to protect him. And he says 'they' are out to get him."

"They?" Malone said.

"You know," Burris said, shrugging. "The great 'they.' The invisible enemies all around, working against him."

"Oh," Malone said. "Paranoid?" He had always thought Senator Lefferts was slightly on the batty side, and the idea of real paranoia didn't come as too much of a surprise. After all, when a man was batty to start out with ... and he even *looked* like a vampire, Malone thought confusedly.

"As far as paranoia is concerned," Burris said, "I checked with one of our own psych men, and he'll back it up. Lefferts has definite paranoid tendencies, he says."

"Well, then," Malone said, "that's that."

Burris shook his head. "It isn't that simple," he said. "You see, Malone, there's some evidence that somebody *is* working against him."

"The American public, with any luck at all," Malone said.

"No," Burris said. "An enemy. Somebody sabotaging his plans. Really."

Malone shook his head. "You're crazy," he said.

Burris looked shocked. "Malone, I'm the Director of the FBI," he said. "And if you insist on being disrespectful—"

"Sorry," Malone murmured. "But—"

"I am perfectly sane," Burris said slowly. "It's Senator Lefferts who's crazy. The only trouble is, he has evidence to show he's not."

Malone thought about odd cases, and suddenly wished he were somewhere else. Anywhere else. This one showed sudden signs of developing into something positively bizarre. "I see," he said, wondering if he did.

"After all," Burris said, in a voice that attempted to sound reasonable, "a paranoid has just as much right to be persecuted as anybody else, doesn't he?"

"Sure," Malone said. "Everybody has rights. But what do you want me to do about that?"

"About their rights?" Burris said. "Nothing, Malone. Nothing."

"I mean," Malone said patiently, "about whatever it is that's going on."

Burris took a deep breath. His hands clasped behind his head, and he looked up at the ceiling. He seemed perfectly relaxed. That, Malone knew, was a bad sign. It meant that there was a dirty job coming, a job nobody wanted to do, and one Burris was determined to pass off on him. He sighed and tried to get resigned.

"Well," the FBI director said, "the only actual trouble we can pinpoint is that there seem to be a great many errors occurring in the paperwork. More than usual."

"People get tired," Malone said tentatively.

"But computer-secretary calculating machines don't," Burris said. "And that's where the errors are, in the computer-secretaries down in the Senate Office Building. I think you'd better start out there."

"Sure," Malone said sadly.

"See if there's any mechanical or electrical defect in any of those computers," Burris said. "Talk to the computer technicians. Find out what's causing all these errors."

"Yes, sir," Malone said. He was still trying to feel resigned, but he wasn't succeeding very well.

"And if you don't find anything—" Burris began.

"I'll come right back," Malone said instantly.

"No," Burris said. "You keep on looking."

"I do?"

"You do," Burris said. "After all, there has to be *something* wrong."

"Sure," Malone said, "if you say so. But—"

"There are the interview tapes," Burris said, "and the reports the Congressmen brought in. You can go through those."

Malone sighed. "I guess so," he said.

"And there must be thousands of other things to do," Burris said.

"Well—" Malone began cautiously.

"You'll be able to think of them," Burris said heartily. "I know you will. I have confidence in you, Malone. Confidence."

"Thanks," Malone said sadly.

"You just keep me posted from time to time on what you're doing, and what ideas you get," Burris said. "I'm leaving the whole thing in your hands, Malone, and I'm sure you won't disappoint me."

"I'll try," Malone said.

"I know you will," Burris said warmly. "And no matter how long it takes, I know you'll succeed."

"No matter how long it takes?" Malone said hesitantly.

"That's right!" Burris said. "You can do it, Malone! You can do it."

Malone nodded slowly. "I hope so," he said. "Well, I— Well, I'll start out right away, then."

He turned. Before he could make another move Burris said, "Wait!"

Malone turned again, hope in his eyes. "Yes, sir?" he said.

"When you leave—" Burris began, and the hope disappeared. "When you leave," he went on, "please do one little favor for me. Just one little favor, because I'm an old, tired man and I'm not used to things any more."

"Sure," Malone said. "Anything, Chief."

"Don't call me—"

"Sorry," Malone said.

Burris breathed heavily. "When you leave," he said, "please, please use the door."

"But—"

"Malone," Burris said, "I've tried. I've really tried. Believe me. I've tried to get used to the fact that you can teleport. But—"

"It's useful," Malone said, "in my work."

"I can see that," Burris said. "And I don't want you to, well, to stop doing it. By no means. It's just that it sort of unnerves me, if you see what I mean. No matter how useful it is for the FBI to have an agent who can go instantaneously from one place to another, it unnerves me." He sighed. "I can't get used to seeing you disappear like an overdried soap bubble, Malone. It does something to me, here." He placed a hand directly over his sternum and sighed again.

"I can understand that," Malone said. "It unnerved me, too, the first time I saw it. I thought I was going crazy, when that kid—Mike Fueyo—winked out like a light. But then we got him, and some FBI agents besides me have learned the trick." He stopped there, wondering if he'd been tactful. After all, it took a latent ability to learn teleportation, and some people had it, while others didn't. Malone, along with a few other agents, did. Burris evidently didn't, so he couldn't teleport, no matter how hard he tried or how many lessons he took.

"Well," Burris said, "I'm still unnerved. So please, Malone, when you come in here, or go out, use the door. All right?"

"Yes, sir," Malone said. He turned and went out. As he opened the door, he could almost hear Burris' sigh of relief. Then he banged it shut behind him and, feeling that he might as well continue with his spacebound existence, walked all the way to the elevator, and rode it downstairs to the FBI laboratories. The labs, highly efficient and divided into dozens of departments, covered several floors. Malone passed through the Fingerprint section, filled with technicians doing strange things to great charts and slides, and frowning over tiny pieces of material and photographs. Then came Forgery Detection, involving many more technicians, many more slides and charts and tiny pieces of things and photographs, and even a witness or two sitting on the white bench at one side and looking lost and somehow civilian. Identification Classified was next, a great barn of a room filled with index files. The real indexes were in the sub-basement; here, on microfilm, were only the basic divisions. A man was standing in front of one of the files, frowning at it. Malone went on by without stopping.

Cosmetic Surgery Classification came next. Here there were more indexes, and there were also charts and slides. There was an agent sitting on a bench looking bored while two female technicians— classified as O&U for Old and Ugly in Malone's mind—fluttered around him, deciding what disguises were possible, and which of those was indicated for the particular job on hand. Malone waved to the agent, whom he knew very slightly, and went on. He felt vaguely regretful that the FBI couldn't hire prettier girls for Cosmetic Surgery, but the trouble was that pretty girls fell for the Agents, and vice versa, and this led to an unfortunate tendency toward only handsome and virile-looking disguises. The O&U division was unfortunate, he decided, but a necessity.

Chemical Analysis (III) was next. The Chemical Analysis Section was scattered over several floors, with the first stages up above. Division III, Malone remembered, was devoted to nonpoisonous substances, like clay or sand found in boots or trouser cuffs, cigar ashes and such. They were placed on the same floor as

Fingerprints to allow free and frequent passage between the sections on the problems of plastic prints, made in putty or like substances, and visible prints, made when the hand is covered with a visible substance like blood, ketchup or glue.

Malone found what he was looking for at the very end of the floor. It was the Computer Section, a large room filled with humming, clacking and buzzing machines of an ancient vintage, muttering to themselves as they worked, and newer machines which were smaller and more silent. Lights were lighting and bells were ringing softly, relays were relaying and the whole room was a gigantic maze of calculating and control machines. What space wasn't filled by the machines themselves was filled by workbenches, all littered with an assortment of gears, tubes, spare relays, transistors, wires, rods, bolts, resistors and all the other paraphernalia used in building the machines and repairing them. Beyond the basic room were other, smaller rooms, each assigned to a particular kind of computer work.

The narrow aisles were choked here and there with men who looked up as Malone passed by, but most of them gave him one quick glance and went back to work. A few didn't even do that, but went right on concentrating on their jobs. Malone headed for a man working all alone in front of a workbench, frowning down at a complicated-looking mechanism that seemed to have neither head nor tail, and prodding at it with a long, thin screwdriver. The man was thin, too, but not very long; he was a little under average height, and he had straight black hair, thick-lensed glasses and a studious expression, even when he was frowning. He looked as if the mechanism were a student who had cut too many classes, and he was being kind but firm with it.

Malone managed to get to the man's side, and coughed discreetly. There was no response.

"Fred?" he said.

The screwdriver waggled a little. Malone wasn't quite sure that the man was breathing.

"Fred Mitchell," he said.

Mitchell didn't look up. Another second passed.

"Hey," Malone said. Then he closed his eyes and took a deep breath. "Fred," he said in a loud, reasonable-sounding voice, "the State Department's translator has started to talk pig-Latin."

Mitchell straightened up as if somebody had jabbed him with a pin. The screwdriver waved wildly in the air for a second, and then pointed at Malone. "That's impossible," Mitchell said in a flat, precise voice. "Simply impossible. It doesn't have a pig-Latin circuit. It can't possibly—" He blinked and seemed to see Malone for the first time. "Oh," he said. "Hello, Malone. What can I do for you?"

Malone smiled, feeling a little victorious at having got through the Mitchell armor, which was almost impregnable when there was a job in hand. "I've been standing here talking to you for some time."

"Oh, have you?" Mitchell said. "I was busy." That, obviously, explained that. Malone shrugged.

"I want you to help me check over some calculators, Fred," he said. "We've had some reports that some of the government machines are out of kilter, and I'd like you to go over them for me."

"Out of kilter?" Fred Mitchell said. "No, you can forget about it. It's absolutely unnecessary to make a check, believe me. Absolutely. Forget it." He smiled suddenly. "I suppose it's some kind of a joke, isn't it?" he said, just a trifle uncertainly. Fred Mitchell's world, while pleasant, did not include much humor, Malone knew. "It's supposed to be funny," he said in the same flat, precise voice.

"It isn't funny," Malone said.

Fred sighed. "Then they're obviously lying," he said, "and that's all there is to it. Why bother me with it?"

"Lying, Fred?" Malone said.

"Certainly," Fred said. He looked at the machinery with longing.

Malone took a breath. "How do you know?" he said.

Fred sighed. "It's perfectly obvious," he said in a patient tone. "Since the State Department translator has no pig-Latin circuit, it can't possibly be talking pig-Latin. I will admit that such a circuit would be relatively easy to build, though it would have no utility as far as I can see. Except, of course, for a joke." He paused. "Joke?" he said, in a slightly uneasy tone.

"Sure," Malone said. "Joke."

Mitchell looked relieved. "Very well, then," he began. "Since—"

"Wait a minute," Malone said. "The pig-Latin is a joke. That's right. But I'm not talking about the pig-Latin."

"You're not?" Mitchell asked, surprised.

"No," Malone said.

Mitchell frowned. "But you said—" he began.

"A joke," Malone said. "You were perfectly right. The pig-Latin is a joke." He waited for Fred's expression to clear, and then added: "But what I want to talk to you about isn't."

"It sounds very confused," Fred said after a pause. "Not at all the sort of thing that—that usually goes on."

"You have no idea," Malone said. "It's about the political machines, all right, but it isn't anything as simple as pig-Latin." He explained, taking his time over it.

When he had finished, Fred was nodding his head slowly. "I see," he said. "I understand just what you want me to do."

"Good," Malone said.

"I'll take a team over to the Senate Office Building," Fred said, "and check the computer-secretaries there. That way, you see, I'll be able to do a full running check on them without taking any one machine out of operation for too long."

"Sure," Malone said.

"And it shouldn't take long," Fred went on, "to find out just what the trouble is." He looked very confident.

"How long?" Malone asked.

Fred shrugged. "Oh," he said, "five or six days."

Malone repressed an impulse to scream. "Days?" he said. "I mean—well, look, Fred, it's important. Very important. Can't you do the job any faster?"

Fred gave a little sigh. "Checking and repairing all those machines," he said, "is an extremely complex job. Sometimes, Malone, I don't think you realize quite how complex and how delicate a job it is to deal with such a high-order machine. Why—"

"Wait a minute," Malone said. "Check and repair them?"

"Of course," Fred said.

"But I don't want them repaired," Malone said. Seeing the look of horror on Fred's face, he added hastily, "I only want a report from you on what's wrong, whether they are actually making errors or not. And if they are making errors, just what's making them do it. And just what kind of errors. See?"

Fred nodded very slowly. "But I can't just leave them there," he said piteously. "In pieces and everything. It isn't right, Malone. It just isn't right."

"Well, then," Malone said with energy, "you go right ahead and repair them, if you want to. Fix 'em all up. But you can do that after you make the report to me, can't you?"

"I—" Fred hesitated. "I had planned to check and repair each machine on an individual basis."

"The Congress can allow for a short suspension," Malone said. "Anyhow, they can now, or as soon as I get the word to them. Suppose you check all the machines first, and then get around to the repair work."

"It's not the best way," Fred demurred.

Malone discovered that it was his turn to sigh. "Is it the fastest?" he said.

Fred nodded.

"Then it's the best," Malone said. "How long?"

Fred rolled his eyes to the ceiling and calculated silently for a second. "Tomorrow morning," he announced, returning his gaze to Malone.

"Fine," Malone said. "Fine."

"But—"

"Never mind the buts," Malone said hurriedly. "I'll count on hearing from you tomorrow morning."

"All right."

"And if it looks like sabotage," Malone added, "if the errors aren't caused by normal wear and tear on the machines, you let me know right away. Phone me. Don't waste an instant."

"I'll—I'll start right away," Fred said heavily. He looked sadly at the mechanism he had been working on, and put his screwdriver down next to it. It looked to Malone as if he were putting flowers on the grave of a dear departed. "I'll get a team together," Fred added. He gave the mechanism and screwdriver one last fond parting look, and tore himself away.

Malone looked after him for a second, thinking of nothing in particular, and then turned in the opposite direction and headed back toward the elevator. As he walked, he began to feel more and more pleased with himself. After all, he'd gotten the investigation started, hadn't he?

And now all he had to do was go back to his office and read some reports and listen to some interview tapes, and then he could go home.

The reports and the interview tapes didn't exactly sound like fun, Malone thought, but at the same time they seemed fairly innocent. He would work his way through them grimly, and maybe he would even indulge his most secret vice and smoke a cigar or two to make the work pass more pleasantly. Soon enough, he told himself, they would be finished.

Sometimes, though, he regretted the reputation he'd gotten. It had been bad enough in the old days, the pre-1971 days when Malone had thought he was just lucky. Burris had called him a Boy Wonder then, when he'd cracked three difficult cases in a row. Being just lucky had made it a little tough to live with the Boy Wonder label. After all, Malone thought, it wasn't actually as if he'd done anything.

But since 1971 and the case of the Telepathic Spy, things had gotten worse. Much worse. Now Malone wasn't just lucky any more. Instead, he could teleport and he could even foretell the future a little, in a dim sort of way. He'd caught the Telepathic Spy that way, and when the case of the Teleporting Juvenile Delinquents had come up he'd been assigned to that one too, and he'd cracked it. Now Burris seemed to think of him as a kind of God, and gave him all the tough dirty jobs.

And if he wasn't just lucky any more, Malone couldn't think of himself as a fearless, heroic FBI agent, either. He just wasn't the type. He was ... well, talented. That was the word, he told himself: talented. He had all these talents and they made him look like something spectacular to Burris and the other FBI men. But he wasn't, really. He hadn't done anything really tough to get his talents; they'd just happened to him.

Nobody, though, seemed to believe that. He heaved a little sigh and stepped into the waiting elevator.

There were, after all, he thought, compensations. He'd had some good times, and the talents did come in handy. And he did have his pick of the vacation schedule lately. And he'd met some lovely girls...

And besides, he told himself savagely as the elevator shot upward, he wasn't going to do anything except return to his office and read some reports and listen to some tapes. And then he was going to go home and sleep all night, peacefully. And in the morning Mitchell was going to call him up and tell him that the computer-secretaries needed nothing more than a little repair. He'd say they were getting old, and he'd be a little pathetic about it; but it wouldn't be anything serious. Malone would send out orders to get the machines repaired, and that would be that. And then the next case would be something both normal and exciting, like a bank robbery or a kidnapping involving a gorgeous blonde who would be so grateful to Malone that...

He had stepped out of the elevator and gone down the corridor without noticing it. He pushed at his own office door and walked into the outer room. The train of thought he had been following was very nice, and sounded very attractive indeed, he told himself.

Unfortunately, he didn't believe it. His prescient ability, functioning with its usual efficient aplomb, told Malone that things would not be better, or simpler, in the morning. They would be worse, and more complicated.

They would be quite a lot worse.

And, as usual, that prescience was perfectly accurate.

2

The telephone, Malone realized belatedly, had had a particularly nasty-sounding ring. He might have known it would be bad news.

As a matter of fact, he told himself sadly, he had known.

"Nothing at all wrong?" he said into the mouthpiece. "Not with any of the computers?" He blinked. "Not even one of them?"

"Not a thing," Mitchell said. "I'll be sending a report up to you in a little while. You read it; we put them through every test, and it's all detailed there."

"I'm sure you were very thorough," Malone said helplessly.

"Of course we were," Mitchell said. "Of course. And the machines passed every single test. Every one. Malone, it was beautiful."

"Goody," Malone said at random. "But there's got to be something—"

"There is, Malone," Fred said. "There is. I think there's definitely something odd going on. Something funny. I mean peculiar, not humorous."

"I thought so," Malone put in.

"Right," Fred said. "Malone, try and relax. This is a hard thing to say, and it must be even harder to hear, but—"

"Tell me," Malone said. "Who's dead? Who's been killed?"

"I know it's tough, Malone," Fred went on.

"Is everybody dead?" Malone said. "It can't be just one person, not from that tone in your voice. Has somebody assassinated the entire senate? Or the president and his cabinet? Or—"

"It's nothing like that, Malone," Fred said, in a tone that implied that such occurrences were really rather minor. "It's the machines."

"The machines?"

"That's right," Fred said grimly. "After we checked them over and found they were in good shape, I asked for samples of both the input and the output of each machine. I wanted to do a thorough job."

"Congratulations," Malone said. "What happened?"

Fred took a deep breath. "They don't agree," he said.

"They don't?" Malone said. The phrase sounded as if it meant something momentous, but he couldn't quite figure out what. In a minute, he thought confusedly, it would come to him. But did he want it to?

"They definitely do not agree," Fred was saying. "The correlation is erratic; it makes no statistical sense. Malone, there are two possibilities."

"Tell me about them," Malone said. He was beginning to feel relieved. To Fred, the malfunction of a machine was more serious than the murder of the entire Congress. But Malone couldn't quite bring himself to feel that way about things.

"First," Fred said in a tense tone, "it's possible that the technicians feeding information to the machines are making all kinds of mistakes."

Malone nodded at the phone. "That sounds possible," he said. "Which ones?"

"All of them," Fred said. "They're all making errors— and they're all making about the same number of errors. There don't seem to be any real peaks or valleys, Malone; everybody's doing it."

Malone thought of the Varsity Drag and repressed the thought. "A bunch of fumblebums," he said. "All fumbling alike. It does sound unlikely, but I guess it's possible. We'll get after them right away, and—"

"Wait," Fred said. "There is a second possibility."

"Oh," Malone said.

"Maybe they aren't mistakes," Fred said. "Maybe the technicians are deliberately feeding the machine with wrong answers."

Malone hated to admit it, even to himself, but that answer sounded a lot more probable. Machine technicians weren't exactly picked off the streets at random; they were highly trained for their work, and the idea of a whole crew of them starting to fumble at once, in a big way, was a little hard to swallow.

The idea of all of them sabotaging the machines they worked on, Malone thought, was a tough one to take, too. But it had the advantage of making some sense. People, he told himself dully, will do nutty things deliberately. It's harder to think of them doing the same nutty things without knowing it.

"Well," he said at last, "however it turns out, we'll get to the bottom of it. Frankly, I think it's being done on purpose."

"So do I," Fred said. "And when you find out just who's making the technicians do such things—when you find out who gives them their orders—you let me know."

"Let you know?" Malone said. "But—"

"Any man who would give false data to a perfectly innocent computer," Fred said savagely, "would—would—" For a second he was apparently lost for comparisons. Then he finished: "Would kill his own mother." He paused a second and added, in an even more savage voice, "And then lie about it!"

The image on the screen snapped off, and Malone sat back in his chair and sighed. He spent a few minutes regretting that he hadn't chosen, early in life, to be a missionary to the Fiji Islands, or possibly simply a drunken bum without any troubles, but then the report Mitchell had mentioned arrived. Malone picked it up without much eagerness, and began going through it carefully.

It was beautifully typed and arranged; somebody on Mitchell's team had obviously been up all night at the job. Malone admired the work, without being able to get enthusiastic about the contents. Like all technical reports, it tended to be boring and just a trifle obscure to someone who wasn't completely familiar with the field involved. Malone and cybernetics were not exactly bosom buddies, and by the time he finished reading through the report he was suffering from an extreme case of ennui.

There were no new clues in the report, either; Mitchell's phone conversation had covered all of the main points. Malone put the sheaf of papers down on his desk and looked at them for a minute as if he expected an answer to leap out from the pile and greet him with a glad cry. But nothing happened. Unfortunately, he had to do some more work.

The obvious next step was to start checking on the technicians who were working on the machines. Malone determined privately that he would give none of his reports to Fred Mitchell; he didn't like the idea of being responsible for murder, and that was the least Fred would do to someone who confused his precious calculators.

He picked up the phone, punched for the Records Division, and waited until a bald, middle-aged face appeared. He asked the face to send up the dossiers of the technicians concerned to his office. The face nodded.

"You want them right away?" it said in a mild, slightly scratchy voice.

"Sooner than right away," Malone said.

"They're coming up by messenger," the voice said.

Malone nodded and broke the connection. The technicians had, of course, been investigated by the FBI before they'd been hired, but it wouldn't do any harm to check them out again. He felt grateful that he wouldn't have to do all that work himself; he would just go through the dossiers and assign field agents to the actual checking when he had a picture of what might need to be checked.

He sighed again and leaned back in his chair. He put his feet up on the desk, remembered that he was entirely alone, and swung them down again. He fished in a private compartment in his top desk drawer, drew out a cigar and unwrapped it. Putting his feet back on the desk, he lit the cigar, drew in a cloud of smoke, and lapsed into deep thought.

Cigar smoke billowed around him, making strange, fantastic shapes in the air of the office. Malone puffed away, frowning slightly and trying to force the puzzle he was working on to make some sense.

It certainly looked as though something were going on, he thought. But, for the life of him, he couldn't figure out just what it was. After all, what could be anybody's purpose in goofing up a bunch of calculators the way they had? Of course, the whole thing could be a series of accidents, but the series was a pretty long one, and made Malone suspicious to start with. It was easier to assume that the goof-ups were being done deliberately.

Unfortunately, they didn't make much sense as sabotage, either.

Senator Deeds, for instance, had sent out a ten-thousand-copy form letter to his constituents, blasting an Administration power bill in extremely strong language, and asking for some comments on the Deeds-Hartshorn Air Ownership Bill, a pending piece of legislation that provided for private, personal ownership, based on land title, to the upper stratosphere, with a strong hint that rights of passage no longer applied without some recompense to the owner of the air. Naturally, Deeds had filed the original with a computer-secretary to turn out ten thousand duplicate copies, and the machine had done so, folding the copies, slipping them into addressed envelopes and sending them out under the Senator's franking stamp.

The addresses on the envelopes, however, had not been those of the Senator's supporters. The letter had

been sent to ten thousand stockholders in major airline
companies, and the Senator's head was still ringing from
the force of the denunciatory letters, telegrams and
telephone calls he'd been getting.

And then there was Representative Follansbee of
South Dakota. A set of news releases on the proposed
Follansbee Waterworks Bill contained the statement that
the artificial lake which Follansbee proposed in the Black
Hills country "be formed by controlled atomic power
blasts, and filled with water obtained from collecting the
tears of widows and orphans."

Newsmen who saw this release immediately checked
the bill. The wording was exactly the same. Follansbee
claimed that the "widows and orphans" phrase had
appeared in his speech on the bill, and not in the
proposed bill itself. "It's completely absurd," he said, with
commendable calm, "to consider this method of filling an
artificial lake." Unfortunately, the absurdity was now
contained in the bill, which would have to go back to
committee for redefinition, and probably wouldn't come
up again in the present session of Congress. Judging from
the amount of laughter that had greeted the error when it
had come to light, Malone privately doubted whether any
amount of redefinition was going to save it from a
landslide defeat.

Representative Keller of Idaho had made a speech
which contained so many errors of fact that newspaper
editorials, and his enemies on the floor of Congress, cut
him to pieces with ease and pleasure. Keller complained
of his innocence and said he'd gotten his facts from a
computer-secretary, but this didn't save him. His reelection was a matter for grave concern in his own party,
and the opposition was, naturally, tickled. They would
not, Malone thought, dare to be tickled pink.

And these were not the only casualties. They were the
most blatant foul-ups, but there were others, such as the
mistake in numbering of a House Bill that resulted in a
two-month delay during which the opposition to the bill

raised enough votes to defeat it on the floor. Communications were diverted or lost or scrambled in small ways that made for confusion—including, Malone recalled, the perfectly horrible mixup that resulted when a freshman senator, thinking he was talking to his girlfriend on a blanked-vision circuit, discovered he was talking to his wife.

The flow of information was being blocked by bottlenecks that suddenly existed where there had never been bottlenecks before.

And it wasn't only the computers, Malone knew. He remembered the reports the senators and representatives had made. Someone forgot to send an important message here, or sent one too soon over there. Both courses were equally disturbing, and both resulted in more snarl-ups. Reports that should have been sent in weeks before arrived too late; reports meant for the eyes of only one man were turned out in triplicate and passed all over the offices of Congress.

Each snarl-up was a little one. But, together, they added up to inefficiency of a kind and extent that hadn't been seen, Malone told himself with some wonder, since the Harding administration fifty years before.

And there didn't seem to be anyone to blame anything on.

Malone thought hopefully of sabotage, infiltration and mass treason, but it didn't make him feel much better. He puffed out some more smoke and frowned at nothing.

There was a knock at the door of his office.

Speedily and guiltily, he swung his feet off the desk and snatched the cigar out of his mouth. He jammed it into a deep ashtray and put the ashtray back into his desk drawer. He locked the drawer, waved ineffectively at the clouds of smoke that surrounded him, and said in a resigned voice: "Come in."

The door opened. A tall, solidly-built man stood there, wearing a fringe of beard and a cheerful expression. The man had an enormous amount of muscle distributed more or less evenly over his chunky body, and a pot-belly that looked as if he had swallowed a globe of the world. In addition, he was smoking a cigarette and letting out little puffs of smoke, rather like a toy locomotive.

"Well, well," Malone said, brushing feebly at the smoke that still wreathed him faintly. "If it isn't Thomas Boyd, the FBI's answer to Nero Wolfe."

"And if the physique holds true, you're Sherlock Holmes, I suppose," Boyd said.

Malone shook his head, thinking sadly of his father and the cigar. "Not exactly," he said. "Not ex—" And then it came to him. It wasn't that he was ashamed of smoking cigars like his father, exactly, but cigars just weren't right for a fearless, dedicated FBI agent. And he had just thought of a way to keep Boyd from knowing what he'd been doing. "That's a hell of a cigarette you're smoking, by the way," he said.

Boyd looked at it. "It is?" he said.

"Sure is," Malone said, hoping he sounded sufficiently innocent. "Smells like a cigar or something."

Boyd sniffed the air for a second, his face wrinkled. Then he looked down at his cigarette again. "By God," he said, "you're right, Ken. It *does* smell like a cigar." He came over to Malone's desk, looked around for an ashtray and didn't find one, and finally went to the window and tossed the cigarette out into the Washington breeze. "How are things, anyhow, Ken?" he said.

"Things are confused," Malone said. "Aren't they always?"

Boyd came back to the desk and sat down in a chair at one side of it. He put his elbow on the desk. "Sure they are," he said. "I'm confused myself, as a matter of fact. Only I think I know where I can get some help."

"Really?" Malone said.

Boyd nodded. "Burris told me I might be able to get some information from a certain famous and highly respected person," he said.

"Well, well," Malone said. "Who?"

"You," Boyd said.

"Oh," Malone said, trying to look disappointed, flattered and modest all at the same time. "Well," he went on after a second, "anything I can do—"

"Burris thought you might have some answers," Boyd said.

"Burris is getting optimistic in his old age," Malone said. "I don't even have many questions."

Boyd nodded. "Well," he said, "you know this California thing?"

"Sure I do," Malone said. "You're looking into the resignation out there, aren't you?"

"Senator Burley," Boyd said. "That's right But Senator Burley's resignation isn't all of it, by any means."

"It isn't?" Malone said, trying to sound interested.

"Not at all," Boyd said. "It goes a lot deeper than it looks on the surface. In the past year, Ken, five senators have announced their resignations from the Senate of the United States. It isn't exactly a record—"

"It sounds like a record," Malone said.

"Well," Boyd said, "there was 1860 and the Civil War, when a whole lot of senators and representatives resigned all at once."

"Oh," Malone said. "But there isn't any Civil War going on now. At least," he added, "I haven't heard of any."

"That's what makes it so funny," Boyd said. "Of course, Senator Burley said it was ill health, and so did two others, while Senator Davidson said it was old age."

"Well," Malone said, "people do get old. And sick."

"Sure," Boyd said. "The only trouble is—" He paused. "Ken," he said, "do you mind if I smoke? I mean, do you mind the smell of cigars?"

"Mind?" Malone said. "Not at all." He blinked. "Besides," he added, "maybe this one won't smell like a cigar."

"Well, the last one did," Boyd said. He took a cigarette out of a pack in his pocket, and lit it. He sniffed. "You know," he said, "you're right. This one doesn't."

"I told you," Malone said. "Must have been a bad cigarette. Spoiled or something."

"I guess so," Boyd said vaguely. "But about these retirements—the FBI wanted me to look into it because of Burley's being mixed up with the space program scandal last year. Remember?"

"Vaguely," Malone said. "I was busy last year."

"Sure you were," Boyd said. "We were both busy getting famous and well known."

Malone grinned. "Go on with the story," he said.

Boyd puffed at his cigarette. "Anyhow, we couldn't find anything really wrong," he said. "Three senators retiring because of ill health, one because of old age. And Farnsworth, the youngest, had a nervous breakdown."

"I didn't hear about it," Malone said.

Boyd shrugged "We hushed it up," he said. "But Farnsworth's got delusions of persecution. He apparently thinks somebody's out to get him. As a matter of fact, he thinks *everybody's* out to get him."

"Now that," Malone said, "sounds familiar."

Boyd leaned back a little more in his chair. "Here's the funny thing, though," he said. "The others all act as if they're suspicious of everybody who talks to them. Not anything obvious, you understand. Just worried, apprehensive. Always looking at you out of the corners of their eyes. That kind of thing."

Malone thought of Senator Lefferts, who was also suffering from delusions of persecution, delusions that had real evidence to back them up. "It does sound funny," he said cautiously.

"Well, I reported everything to Burris," Boyd went on. "And he said you were working on something similar, and we might as well pool our resources."

"Here we go again," Malone said. He took a deep breath, filling his nostrils with what remained of the cigar odor in the room, and felt more peaceful. Quickly, he told Boyd about what had been happening in Congress. "It seems pretty obvious," he finished, "that there is some kind of a tie-up between the two cases."

"Maybe it's obvious," Boyd said, "but it is just a little bit odd. Fun and games. You know, Ken, Burris was right."

"How?" Malone said.

"He said everything was all mixed up," Boyd went on. "He told me the country was going to Rome in a handbasket, or something like that."

Wondering vaguely if Burris had really been predicting mass religious conversions, Malone nodded silently.

"And he's right," Boyd said. "Look at the newspapers. Everything's screwy lately."

"Everything always is screwy," Malone said.

"Not like now," Boyd said. "So many big-shot gangsters have been killed lately we might as well bring back Prohibition. And the labor unions are so busy with internal battles that they haven't had time to go on strike for over a year."

"Is that bad?" Malone said.

Boyd shrugged. "God knows," he said. "But it's sure confusing as all hell."

"And now," Malone said, "with all that going on—"

"The Congress of the United States decides to go off its collective rocker," Boyd finished. "Exactly." He stared down at his cigarette for a minute with a morose and pensive expression on his face. He looked, Malone thought, like Henry VIII trying to decide what to do about all these here wives.

Then he looked up at Malone. "Ken," he said in a strained voice, "there seem to be a lot of nutty cases lately."

Malone considered. "No," he said at last. "It's just that when a nutty one comes along, we get it."

"That's what I mean," Boyd said. "I wonder why that is."

Malone shrugged. "It takes a thief to catch a thief," he said.

"But these aren't thieves," Boyd said. "I mean, they're just nutty." He paused. "Oh," he said.

"And two thieves are better than one," Malone said.

"Anyhow," Boyd said with a small, gusty sigh, "it's company."

"Sure," Malone said.

Boyd looked for an ashtray, failed again to find one, and walked over to flip a second cigarette out onto Washington. He came back to his chair, sat down, and said, "What's our next step, Ken?"

Malone considered carefully. "First," he said finally, "we'll start assuming something. We'll start assuming that there is some kind of organization behind all this, behind all the senators' resignations and everything like that."

"It sounds like a big assumption," Boyd said.

Malone shook his head. "It isn't really," he said. "After all, we can't figure it's the work of one person: it's too widespread for that. And it's silly to assume that everything's accidental."

"All right," Boyd said equably. "It's an organization."

"Trying to subvert the United States," Malone went on. "Reducing everything to chaos. And that brings in everything else, Tom. That brings in the unions and the gang wars and everything."

Boyd blinked. "How?" he said.

"Obvious," Malone said. "Strife brought on by internal confusion, that's what's going on all over. It's the same pattern. And if we assume an organization trying to jam up the United States, it even makes sense." He leaned back and beamed.

"Sure it makes sense," Boyd said. "But who's the organization?"

Malone shrugged.

"If I were doing the picking," Boyd said, "I'd pick the Russians. Or the Chinese. Or both. Probably both."

"It's a possibility," Malone said. "Anyhow, if it's sabotage, who else would be interested in sabotaging the United States? There's some Russian or Chinese organization fouling up Congress, and the unions, and the gangs. Come to think of it, why the gangs? It seems to me that if you left the professional gangsters strong, it would do even more to foul things up."

"Who knows?" Boyd said. "Maybe they're trying to get rid of American gangsters so they can import some of their own."

"That doesn't make any sense," Malone said, "but I'll think about it. In the meantime, we have one more interesting question."

"We do?" Boyd said.

"Sure we do," Malone said. "The question is: how?"

Boyd said: "Mmm." Then there was silence for a little while.

"How are the saboteurs doing all this?" Malone said. "It just doesn't seem very probable that *all* the technicians in the Senate Office Building, for instance, are spies. It makes even less sense that the labor unions are composed mostly of spies. Or, for that matter, the Mafia and the organizations like it. What would spies be doing in the Mafia?"

"Learning Italian," Boyd said instantly.

"Don't be silly," Malone said. "If there were that many spies in this country, the Russians wouldn't have to fight at all. They could *vote* the Communists into power, and by a nice big landslide, too."

"Wait a minute," Boyd said. "If there aren't so many spies, then how is all this getting done?"

Malone beamed. "That's the question," he said. "And I think I have an answer."

"You do?" Boyd said. After a second he said: "Oh, no."

"Suppose you tell me," Malone said.

Boyd opened his mouth. Nothing emerged. He shut it. A second passed and he opened it again. "Magic?" he said weakly.

"Not exactly," Malone said cheerfully. "But you're getting warm."

Boyd shut his eyes. "I'm not going to stand for it," he announced. "I'm not going to take any more."

"Any more what?" Malone said. "Tell me what you have in mind."

"I won't even consider it," Boyd said. "It haunts me. It gets into my dreams. Now, look, Ken, I can't even see a pitchfork any more without thinking of Greek letters."

Malone took a breath. "Which Greek letter?" he said.

"You know very well," Boyd said. "What a pitchfork looks like. *Psi.* And I'm not even going to think about it."

"Well," Malone said equably, "you won't have to. If you'd rather start with the Russian-spy end of things, you can do that."

"What I'd rather do," Boyd said, "is resign."

"Next year," Malone said instantly. "For now, you can wait around until the dossiers come up—they're for the Senate Office Building technicians, and they're on the way. You can go over them, and start checking on any known Russian agents in the country for contacts. You can also start checking on the dossiers, and in general for any hanky-panky."

Boyd blinked. "Hanky-panky?" he said.

"It's a perfectly good word," Malone said, offended. "Or two words. Anyhow, you can start on that end, and not worry about anything else."

"It's going to haunt me," Boyd said.

"Well," Malone said, "eat lots of ectoplasm and get enough sleep, and everything will be fine. After all, I'm going to have to do the real end of the work, the psionics end. I may be wrong, but—"

He was interrupted by the phone. He flicked the switch and Andrew J. Burris' face appeared on the screen.

"Malone," Burris said instantly, "I just got a complaint from the State Department that ties in with your work. Their translator has been acting up."

Malone couldn't say anything for a minute.

"Malone," Burris went on. "I said—"

"I heard you," Malone said. "And it doesn't have one."

"It doesn't have one what?" Burris said.

"A pig-Latin circuit," Malone said. "What else?"

Burris' voice was very calm. "Malone," he said, "what does pig-Latin have to do with anything?"

"You said—"

"I said one of the State Department translators was acting up," Burris said. "If you want details—"

"I don't think I can stand them," Malone said.

"Some of the Russian and Chinese releases have come through with the meaning slightly altered," Burris went on doggedly. "And I want you to check on it right away. I—"

"Thank God," Malone said.

Burris blinked. "What?"

"Never mind," Malone said. "Never mind. I'm glad you told me, Chief. I'll get to work on it right away, and—"

"You do that, Malone," Burris said. "And for God's sake stop calling me Chief! Do I look like an Indian? Do I have feathers in my hair?"

"Anything," Malone said grandly, "is possible." He broke the connection in a hurry.

3

The summer sun beat down on the white city of Washington, D. C, as if it had mistaken its instructions slightly and was convinced that the city had been put down somewhere in the Sahara. The sun seemed confused, Malone thought. If this were the Sahara, obviously there was no reason whatever for the Potomac to be running through it. The sun was doing its best to correct this small error, however, by exerting even more heat in a valiant attempt to dry up the river.

Its attempt was succeeding, at least partially. The Potomac was still there, but quite a lot of it was not in the river bed any more. Instead, it had gone into the air, which was so humid by now that Malone was willing to swear that it was splashing into his lungs at every inhalation. Resisting an impulse to try the breaststroke, he stood in the full glare of the straining sun, just outside the Senate Office Building. He looked across at the Capitol, just opposite, squinting his eyes manfully against the glare of its dome in the brightness.

The Capitol was, at any rate, some relief from the sight of Thomas Boyd and a group of agents busily grilling two technicians. That was going on in the Senate Office Building, and Malone had come over to watch the proceedings. Everything had been set up in what Malone considered the most complicated fashion possible. A big room had been turned into a projection chamber, and films were being run off over and over. The films, taken by hidden cameras watching the computer-secretaries, had caught two technicians red-handed punching errors into the machines. Boyd had leaped on this evidence, and he and his crew were showing the movies to the technicians and questioning them under bright lights in an effort to break down their resistance.

But it didn't look as though they were going to have any more success than the sun was having, turning Washington into the Sahara. After all, Malone told himself, wiping his streaming brow, there were no Pyramids in Washington. He tried to discover whether that made any sense, but it was too much work. He went back to thinking about Boyd.

The technicians were sticking to their original stories that the mistakes had been honest ones. It sounded like a sensible idea to Malone; after all, people did make mistakes. And the FBI didn't have a single shred of evidence to prove that the technicians were engaged in deliberate sabotage. But Boyd wasn't giving up. Over and over he got the technicians to repeat their stories, looking for discrepancies or slips. Over and over he ran off the films of their mistakes, looking for some clue, some shred of evidence.

Even the sight of the Capitol, Malone told himself sadly, was better than any more of Boyd's massive investigation techniques.

He had come out to do some thinking. He believed, in spite of a good deal of evidence to the contrary, that his best ideas came to him while walking. At any rate, it was a way of getting away from four walls and from the prying eyes and anxious looks of superiors. He sighed gently, crammed his hat onto his head and started out.

Only a maniac, he reflected, would wear a hat on a day like the one he was swimming through. But the people who passed him as he trudged onward to no particular destination didn't seem to notice; they gave him a fairly wide berth, and seemed very polite, but that wasn't because they thought he was nuts, Malone knew. It was because they knew he was an FBI man.

That was the result of an FBI regulation. All agents had to wear hats. Malone wasn't sure why, and his thinking on the matter had only dredged up the idea that you had to have a hat in case somebody asked you to keep something under it. But the FBI was firm about its rulings. No matter what the weather, an agent wore a hat. Malone thought bitterly that he might just as well wear a red, white and blue luminous sign that said *FBI* in great winking letters, and maybe a hooting siren too. Still, the Federal Bureau of Investigation was not supposed to be a secret organization, no matter what occasional critics might say. And the hats, at least as long as the weather remained broiling, were enough proof of that for anybody.

Malone could feel water collecting under his hat and soaking his head. He removed the hat quickly, wiped his head with a handkerchief and replaced the hat, feeling as if he had become incognito for a few seconds. The hat was back on now, feeling official but terrible, and about the same was true of the fully-loaded Smith & Wesson .44 Magnum revolver which hung in his shoulder holster. The harness chafed at his shoulder and chest and the weight of the gun itself was an added and unwelcome burden.

But even without the gun and the hat, Malone did not feel exactly chipper. His shirt and undershirt were no longer two garments, but one, welded together by seamless sweat and plastered heavily and not too skillfully to his skin. His trouser legs clung damply to calves and thighs, rubbing as he walked, and at the knees each trouser leg attached and detached itself with the unpleasant regularity of a wet bastinado. Inside Malone's shoes, his socks were completely awash, and he seemed to squish as he walked. It was hard to tell, but there seemed to be a small fish in his left shoe. It might, he told himself, be no more than a pebble or a wrinkle in his sock. But he was willing to swear that it was swimming upstream.

And the forecast, he told himself bitterly, was for continued warm.

He forced himself to take his mind off his own troubles and get back to the troubles of the FBI in general, such as the problem at hand. It was an effort, but he frowned and kept walking, and within a block he was concentrating again on the *psi* powers.

Psi, he told himself, was behind the whole mess. In spite of Boyd's horrified refusal to believe such a thing, Malone was sure of it. Three years ago, of course, he wouldn't have considered the notion either. But since then a great many things had happened, and his horizons had widened. After all, capturing a double handful of totally insane, if perfectly genuine telepaths, from asylums all over the country, was enough by itself to widen quite a few stunned horizons. And then, later, there had been the gang of juvenile delinquents. They had been perfectly normal juvenile delinquents, stealing cars and bopping a stray policeman or two. It happened, though, that they had solved the secret of instantaneous teleportation, too. This made them just a trifle unusual.

In capturing them, Malone, too, had learned the teleportation secret. Unlike Boyd, he thought, or Burris, the idea of psionic power didn't bother him much. After all, the psionic spectrum (if it was a spectrum at all) was just as much a natural phenomenon as gravity or magnetism.

It was just a little hard for some people to get used to.

And, of course, he didn't fully understand *how* it worked, or *why*. This put him in the position, he told himself, of an Australian aborigine. He tried to imagine an Australian aborigine in a hat on a hot day, decided the aborigine would have too much sense, and got back off the subject again.

However, he thought grimly, there was this Australian aborigine. And he had a magnifying glass, which he'd picked up from the wreck of some ship. Using that—assuming that experience, or a friendly missionary, taught him how—he could manage to light a fire, using the sun's thermonuclear processes to do the job. Malone doubted that the aborigine knew anything about thermonuclear processes, but he could start a fire with them.

As a matter of fact, he told himself, the aborigine didn't understand oxidation, either. But he could use that fire, when he got it going. In spite of his lack of knowledge, the aborigine could use that nice, hot, burning fire...

Hurriedly, Malone pried his thoughts away from aborigines and heat, and tried to focus his mind elsewhere. He didn't understand psionic processes, he thought; but then, nobody did, really, as far as he knew. But he could use them.

And, obviously, somebody else could use them too.

Only what kind of force was being used? What kind of psionic force would it take to make so many people in the United States goof up the way they were doing?

That, Malone told himself, was a good question, a basic and an important question. He was proud of himself for thinking of it.

Unfortunately, he didn't have the answer.

But he thought he knew a way of getting one.

It was perfectly true that nobody knew much about how psionics worked. For that matter, nobody knew very much about how gravity worked. But there was still some information, and, in the case of psionics, Malone knew where it was to be found.

It was to be found in Yucca Flats, Nevada.

It was, of course, true that Nevada would probably be even hotter than Washington, D. C. But there was no help for that, Malone told himself sadly; and, besides, the cold chill of the expert himself would probably cool things off quite rapidly. Malone thought of Dr. Thomas O'Connor, the Westinghouse psionics expert and frowned. O'Connor was not exactly what might be called a friendly man.

But he did know more about psionics than anyone else Malone could think of. And his help had been invaluable in solving the two previous psionic cases Malone had worked on.

For a second he thought of calling O'Connor, but he brushed that thought aside bravely. In spite of the heat of Yucca Flats, he would have to talk to the man personally. He thought again of O'Connor's congealed personality, and wondered if it would really be effective in combating the heat. If it were, he told himself, he would take the man right back to Washington with him, and plug him into the air-conditioning lines.

He sighed deeply, thought about a cigar and decided regretfully against it, here on the public street where he would be visible to anyone. Instead, he looked around him, discovered that he was only a block from a large, neon-lit drugstore and headed for it. Less than a minute later he was in a phone booth.

The operators throughout the country seemed to suffer from heat prostration, and Malone was hardly inclined to blame them. But, all the same, it took several minutes for him to get through to Dr. O'Connor's office, and a minute or so more before he could convince a security-addled secretary that, after all, he would hardly blow O'Connor to bits over the long-distance phone.

Finally the secretary, with a sigh of reluctance, said she would see if Dr. O'Connor were available. Malone waited in the phone booth, opening the door every few seconds to breathe. The booth was air-conditioned, but remained for some mystical reason an even ten degrees above the boiling point of Malone's temper.

Finally Dr. O'Connor's lean, pallid face appeared on the screen. He had not changed since Malone had last seen him. He still looked, and acted, like one of Malone's more disliked law professors.

"Ah," the scientist said in a cold, precise voice. "Mr. Malone. I am sorry for our precautions, but you understand that security must be served."

"Sure," Malone said.

"Being an FBI man, of course you would," Dr. O'Connor went on, his face changing slightly and his voice warming almost to the boiling point of nitrogen. It was obvious that the phrase was Dr. O'Connor's idea of a little joke, and Malone smiled politely and nodded. The scientist seemed to feel some friendliness toward Malone, though it was hard to tell for sure. But Malone had brought him some fine specimens to work with— telepaths and teleports, though human, being no more than specimens to such a very precise scientific mind— and he seemed grateful for Malone's diligence and effort in finding such fascinating objects of study.

That Malone certainly hadn't started out to find them made, it appeared, very little difference.

"Well, then," O'Connor said, returning to his normal, serious tone. "What can I do for you, Mr. Malone?"

"If you have the time, Doctor," Malone said respectfully, "I'd like to talk to you for a few minutes." He had the absurd feeling that O'Connor was going to tell him to stop by after class, but the scientist only nodded.

"Your call is timed very well," he said. "As it happens, Mr. Malone, I do have a few seconds to spare just now."

"Fine," Malone said.

"I should be glad to talk with you," O'Connor said, without looking any more glad than ever.

"I'll be right there," Malone said. O'Connor nodded again, and blanked out. Malone switched off and took a deep, superheated breath of phone booth air. For a second he considered starting his trip from outside the phone booth, but that was dangerous—if not to Malone, then to innocent spectators. Psionics was by no means a household word, and the sight of Malone leaving for Nevada might send several citizens straight to the wagon. Which was not a place, he thought judiciously, for anybody to be on such a hot day.

He closed his eyes for a fraction of a second. In that time he reconstructed from memory a detailed, three-dimensional, full-color image of Dr. O'Connor's office in his mind. It was perfect in detail; he checked it over mentally and then, by a special effort of will, he gave himself the psychic push that made the transition possible.

When he opened his eyes, he was in O'Connor's office, standing in front of the scientist's wide desk. He hoped nobody had been looking into the phone booth at the instant he had disappeared, but he was reasonably sure he'd been unobserved. People didn't go around peering into phone booths, after all, and he had seen no one.

O'Connor looked up without surprise. "Ah," he said. "Sit down, Mr. Malone." Malone looked around for the chair, which was an uncomfortably straight-backed affair, and sat down in it gingerly. Remembering past visits to O'Connor, he was grateful for even the small amount of relaxation the hard wood afforded him. O'Connor had only recently unbent to the point of supplying a spare chair in his office for visitors, and, apparently, especially for Malone. Perhaps, Malone thought, it was more gratitude for the lovely specimens.

Malone still felt uncomfortable, but tried bravely not to show it. He felt slightly guilty, too, as he always did when he popped into O'Connor's office without bothering to stay space-bound. By law, after all, he knew he should check in and out at the main gate of the huge, ultra-top-secret Government reservation whenever he visited Yucca Flats. But that meant wasting a lot of time and going through a lot of trouble. Malone had rationalized it out for himself that way, and had gotten just far enough to do things the quick and easy way and not quite far enough to feel undisturbed about it. After all, he told himself grimly, anything that saved time and trouble increased the efficiency of the FBI, so it was all to the good.

He swallowed hard. "Dr. O'Connor—" he began.

O'Connor looked up again. "Yes?" he said. He'd had plenty of practice in watching people appear and disappear, between Malone and the specimens Malone had brought him; he was beyond surprise or shock by now.

"I came here to talk to you," Malone began again.

O'Connor nodded, a trifle impatiently. "Yes," he said. "I know that."

"Well—" Malone thought fast. Presenting the case to O'Connor was impossible; it was too complicated, and it might violate governmental secrecy somewhere along the line. He decided to wrap it up in a hypothetical situation. "Doctor," he said, "I know that all the various manifestations of the *psi* powers were investigated and named long before responsible scientists became interested in the subject."

"That," O'Connor said with some reluctance, "is true." He looked sad, as if he wished they'd waited on naming some of the psionic manifestations until he'd been born and started investigating them. Malone tried to imagine a person doing something called O'Connorizing, and decided he was grateful for history.

"Well, then—" he said.

"At least," O'Connor cut in, "it is true in a rather vague and general way. You see, Mr. Malone, any precise description of a psionic manifestation must wait until a metalanguage has grown up to encompass it; that is, until understanding and knowledge have reached the point where careful and accurate description can take place."

"Oh," Malone said helplessly. "Sure." He wondered if what O'Connor had said meant anything, and decided that it probably did, but he didn't want to know about it.

"While we have not yet reached that point," O'Connor said, "we are approaching it in our experiments. I am hopeful that, in the near future—"

"Well," Malone cut in desperately, "sure. Of course. Naturally."

Dr. O'Connor looked miffed. The temperature of the room seemed to drop several degrees, and Malone swallowed hard and tried to look ingratiating and helpful, like a student with nothing but A's on his record.

Before O'Connor could pick up the thread of his sentence, Malone went on: "What I mean is something like this. Picking up the mental activity of another person is called telepathy. Floating in the air is called levitation. Moving objects around is psychokinesis. Going from one place to another instantaneously is teleportation. And so on."

"The language you use," O'Connor said, still miffed, "is extremely loose. I might go so far as to say that the statements you have made are, essentially, meaningless as a result of their lack of rigor."

Malone took a deep breath. "Dr. O'Connor," he said, "you know what I mean, don't you?"

"I believe so," O'Connor said, with the air of a king granting a pardon to a particularly repulsive-looking subject in the lowest income brackets.

"Well, then," Malone said. "Yes or no?"

O'Connor frowned. "Yes or no what?" he said.

"I—" Malone blinked. "I mean, the things have names," he said at last. "All the various psionic manifestations have names."

"Ah," O'Connor said. "Well. I should say—" He put his fingertips together and stared at a point on the white ceiling for a second. "Yes," he said at last.

Malone breathed a sigh of relief. "Good," he said. "That's what I wanted to know." He leaned forward. "And if they all do have names," he went on, "what is it called when a large group of people are forced to act in a certain manner?"

O'Connor shrugged. "Forced?" he said.

"Forced by mental power," Malone said.

There was a second of silence.

"At first," O'Connor said, "I might think of various examples: the actions of a mob, for example, or the demonstrations of the Indian Rope Trick, or perhaps the sale of a useless product through television or through other advertising." Again his face moved, ever so slightly, in what he obviously believed to be a smile. "The usual name for such a phenomenon is 'mass hypnotism,' Mr. Malone," he said. "But that is not, strictly speaking, a *psi* phenomenon at all. Studies in that area belong to the field of mob psychology; they are not properly in my scope." He looked vastly superior to anything and everything that was outside his scope. Malone concentrated on looking receptive and understanding.

"Yes?" he said.

O'Connor gave him a look that made Malone feel he'd been caught cribbing during an exam, but the scientist said nothing to back up the look. Instead he went on: "I will grant that there may be an amplification of the telepathic faculty in the normal individual in such cases."

"Good," Malone said doubtfully.

"Such an amplification," O'Connor went on, as if he hadn't heard, "would account for the apparent—ah— mental linkage that makes a mob appear to act as a single organism during certain periods of—ah— stress." He looked judicious for a second, and then nodded. "However," he said, "other than that, I would doubt that there is any psionic force involved."

Malone spent a second or two digesting O'Connor's reply.

"Well," he said at last, "I'm not sure that's what I meant. I mean, I'm not sure I meant to ask that question." He took a breath and decided to start all over. "It's not like a mob," he said, "with everybody all doing the same thing at the same time. It's more like a group of men, all separated, without any apparent connections between any of the men. And they're all working toward a common goal. All doing different things, but all with the same objective. See?"

"Of course I do," O'Connor said flatly. "But what you're suggesting—" He looked straight at Malone. "Have you had any experience of this ... phenomenon?"

"Experience?" Malone said.

"I believe you have had," O'Connor said. "Such a concept could not have come to you in a theoretical manner. You must be involved with an actual situation very much like the one you describe."

Malone swallowed. "Me?" he said.

"Mr. Malone," O'Connor said. "May I remind you that this is Yucca Flats? That the security checks here are as careful as anywhere in the world? That I, myself, have top-security clearance for many special projects? You do not need to watch your words here."

"It's not security," Malone said. "Anyhow, it's not only security. But things are pretty complicated."

"I assure you," O'Connor said, "that I will be able to understand even events which you feel are complex."

Malone swallowed again, hard. "I didn't mean—" he started.

"Please, Mr. Malone," O'Connor said. His voice was colder than usual. Malone had the feeling that he was about to take the extra chair away. "Go on," O'Connor said. "Explain yourself."

Malone took a deep breath. He started with the facts he'd been told by Burris, and went straight through to the interviews of the two computer-secretary technicians by Boyd and Company.

It took quite awhile. By the time he had finished, O'Connor wasn't looking frozen any more; he'd apparently forgotten to keep the freezer coils running. Instead, his face showed frank bewilderment, and great interest. "I never heard of such a thing," he said. "Never. Not at any time."

"But—"

O'Connor shook his head. "I have never heard of a psionic manifestation on that order," he said. It seemed to be a painful admission. "Something that would make a random group of men co-operate in that manner—why, it's completely new."

"It is?" Malone said, wondering if, when it was all investigated and described, it might be called O'Connorizing. Then he wondered how anybody was going to go about investigating it and describing it, and sank even deeper into gloom.

"Completely new," O'Connor said. "You may take my word." Then, slowly, he began to brighten again, with all the glitter of newly-formed ice. "As a matter of fact," he said, in a tone more like his usual one, "as a matter of fact, Mr. Malone, I don't think it's possible."

"But it happened," Malone said. "It's still happening. All over."

O'Connor's lips tightened. "I have given my opinion," he said. "I do not believe that such a thing is possible. There must be some other explanation."

"All right," Malone said agreeably. "I'll bite. What is it?"

O'Connor frowned. "Your levity," he said, "is uncalled-for."

Malone shrugged. "I didn't mean to be—" He paused. "Anyhow, I didn't mean to be funny," he went on. "But I would like to have another idea of what's causing all this."

"Scientific theories," O'Connor said sternly, "are not invented on the spur of the moment. Only after long, careful thought."

"You mean you can't think of anything," Malone said.

"There must be some other explanation," O'Connor said. "Naturally, since the facts have only now been presented to me, it is impossible for me to display at once a fully-constructed theory."

Malone nodded slowly. "Okay," he said. "Have you got any hints, then? Any ideas at all?"

O'Connor shook his head. "I have not," he said. "But I strongly suggest, Mr. Malone, that you recheck your data. The fault may very well lie in your own interpretations of the actual facts."

"I don't think so," Malone said.

O'Connor grimaced. "I do," he said firmly.

Malone sighed, very faintly. He shifted in the chair and began to realize, for the first time, just how uncomfortable it really was. He also felt a little chilly, and the chill was growing. That, he told himself, was the effect of Dr. O'Connor. He no longer regretted wearing his hat. As a matter of fact, he thought wistfully for a second of a small, light overcoat.

O'Connor, he told himself, was definitely not the warm, friendly type.

"Well, then," he said, conquering the chilly feeling for a second, "maybe there's somebody else. Somebody who knows something more about psionics, and who might have some other ideas about—"

"Please, Mr. Malone," O'Connor said. "The United States Government would hardly have chosen me had I not been uniquely qualified in my field."

Malone sighed again. "I mean, maybe there are some books on the subject," he said quietly, hoping he sounded tactful. "Maybe there's something I could look up."

"Mr. Malone." The temperature of the office, Malone realized, was definitely lowering. O'Connor's built-in freezer coils were working overtime, he told himself. "The field of psionics is so young that I can say, without qualification, that I am acquainted with everything written on the subject. By that, of course, I mean scientific works. I do not doubt that the American Society for Psychical Research, for instance, has hundreds of crackpot books which I have never read, or even heard of. But in the strictly scientific field, I must say that—"

He broke off, looking narrowly at Malone with what might have been concern, but looked more like discouragement and boredom.

"Mr. Malone," he said, "are you ill?"

Malone thought about it. He wasn't quite sure, he discovered. The chill in the office was bothering him more and more, and as it grew he began to doubt that it was all due to the O'Connor influence. Suddenly a distinct shudder started somewhere in the vicinity of his shoulders and rippled its way down his body.

Another one followed it, and then a third.

"Mr. Malone," O'Connor said.

"Me?" Malone said. "I'm—I'm all right."

"You seem to have contracted a chill," O'Connor said.

A fourth shudder followed the other three.

"I—guess so," Malone said. "I d-d—I do s-seem to be r-r-rather chilly."

O'Connor nodded. "Ah," he said. "I thought so. Although a chill is certainly odd at seventy-two degrees Fahrenheit." He looked at the thermometer just outside the window of his office, then turned back to Malone. "Pardon me," he said. "Seventy-one point six."

"Is—is that all it is?" Malone said. Seventy-one point six degrees, or even seventy-two, hardly sounded like the broiling Nevada desert he'd expected.

"Of course," O'Connor said. "At nine o'clock in the morning, one would hardly expect great temperatures. The desert becomes quite hot during the day, but cools off rapidly; I assume you are familiar with the laws covering the system."

"Sure," Malone said. "S-sure."

The chills were not getting any better. They continued to travel up and down his body with the dignified regularity of Pennsylvania Railroad commuter trains.

O'Connor frowned for a second. It was obvious that his keen scientific eye was sizing up the phenomenon, and reporting events to his keen scientific brain. In a second or less, the keen scientific brain had come up with an answer, and Dr. O'Connor spoke in his very keenest scientific voice.

"I should have warned you," he said, without an audible trace of regret. "The answer is childishly simple, Mr. Malone. You left Washington at noon."

"Just a little before noon," Malone said. Remembering the burning sun, he added: "High noon. Very high."

"Just so," O'Connor said. "And not only the heat was intense; the humidity, I assume, was also high."

"Very," Malone said, thinking back. He shivered again.

"In Washington," O'Connor said, "it was noon. Here it is nine o'clock, and hardly as warm. The atmosphere is quite arid, and about twenty degrees below that obtaining in Washington."

Malone thought about it, trying to ignore the chills. "Oh," he said at last. "And all the time I thought it was you."

"What?" O'Connor leaned forward.

"Nothing," Malone said hastily. "Nothing at all."

"My suggestion," O'Connor said, putting his fingertips together again, "is that you take off your clothes, which are undoubtedly damp, and—"

Naturally, Malone had not brought any clothes to Yucca Flats to change into. And when he tried to picture himself in a spare suit of Dr. O'Connor's, the picture just wouldn't come. Besides, the idea of doing a modified striptease in, or near, the O'Connor office was thoroughly unattractive.

"Well," he said slowly, "thanks a lot, Doctor, but no thanks. I really have a better idea."

"Better?" O'Connor said.

"Well, I—" Malone took a deep breath and shut his eyes.

He heard Dr. O'Connor say: "Well, Mr. Malone, goodbye. And good luck."

Then the office in Yucca Flats was gone, and Malone was standing in the bedroom of his own apartment, on the fringes of Washington, D.C.

4

He walked over to the wall control and shut off the air-conditioning in a hurry. He threw open a window and breathed great gulps of the hot, humid air from the streets. In a small corner at the back of his mind, he wondered why he was grateful for the air he had suffered under only a few minutes before. But that, he reflected, was life. And a very silly kind of life, too, he told himself without rancor.

In a few minutes he left the window, somewhat restored, and headed for the shower. When it was running nicely and he was under it, he started to sing. But his voice didn't sound as much like the voice of Lauritz Melchior as it usually did, not even when he made a brave, if foolhardy stab at the Melchior accent. Slowly, he began to realize that he was bothered.

He climbed out of the shower and started drying himself. Up to now, he thought, he had depended on Dr. Thomas O'Connor for edifying, trustworthy and reasonably complete information about psionics and *psi* phenomena in general. He had looked on O'Connor as a sort of living version of an extremely good edition of the Britannica, always available for reference.

And now O'Connor had failed him. That, Malone thought, was hardly fair. O'Connor had no business failing him, particularly when there was no place else to go.

The scientist had been right, of course, Malone knew. There was no other scientist who knew as much about psionics as O'Connor, and if O'Connor said there were no books, then that was that: there were no books.

He reached for a drawer in his dresser, opened it and pulled out some underclothes, humming tunelessly under his breath as he dressed. If there was no one to ask, he thought, and if there were no books...

He stopped with a sock in his hand, and stared at it in wonder. O'Connor hadn't said there were no books. As a matter of fact, Malone realized, he'd said exactly the opposite.

There were books. But they were "crackpot" books. O'Connor had never read them. He had, he said, probably never even heard of many of them.

"Crackpot" was a fighting word to O'Connor. But to Malone it had all the sweetness of flattery. After all, he'd found telepaths in insane asylums, and teleports among the juvenile delinquents of New York. "Crackpot" was a word that was rapidly ceasing to have any meaning at all in Malone's mind.

He realized that he was still staring at the sock, which was black with a pink clock. Hurriedly, he put it on, and finished dressing. He reached for the phone and made a few fast calls, and then teleported himself to his locked office in FBI Headquarters, on East 69th Street in New York. He let himself out, and strolled down the corridor. The agent-in-charge looked up from his desk as Malone passed, blinked, and said, "Hello, Malone. What's up now?"

"I'm going prowling," Malone said. "But there won't be any work for you, as far as I can see."

"Oh?"

"Just relax," Malone said. "Breathe easy."

"I'll try to," the agent-in-charge said, a little sadly. "But every time you show up, I think about that wave of red Cadillacs you started. I'll never feel really secure again."

"Relax," Malone said. "Next time it won't be Cadillacs. But it might be spirits, blowing on ear-trumpets. Or whatever it is they do."

"Spirits, Malone?" the agent-in-charge said.

"No, thanks," Malone said sternly. "I never drink on duty." He gave the agent a cheery wave of his hand and went on out to the street.

The Psychical Research Society had offices in the Ravell Building, a large structure composed mostly of plate glass and anodized aluminum that looked just a little like a bright blue transparent crackerbox that had been stood on end for purposes unknown. Having walked all the way down to this box on 56th Street, Malone had recovered his former sensitivity range to temperature and felt pathetically grateful for the coolish sea breeze that made New York somewhat less of an unbearable Summer Festival than was normal.

The lobby of the building was glittering and polished, as if human beings could not possibly exist in it. Malone took an elevator to the sixth floor, stepped out into a small, equally polished hall, and hurriedly looked off to his right. A small door stood there, with a legend engraved in elegantly small letters. It said:

The Psychical Research Society   Push

Malone obeyed instructions. The door swung noiselessly open, and then closed behind him.

He was in a large square-looking room which had a couch and chair set at one corner, and a desk at the far end. Behind the desk was a brass plate, on which was engraved:

The Psychical Research Society   Main Offices

To Malone's left was a hall that angled off into invisibility, and to the left of the desk was another one, going straight back past doors and two radiators until it ran into a right-angled turn and also disappeared.

Malone took in the details of his surroundings almost automatically, filing them in his memory just in case he ever needed to use them.

One detail, however, required more than automatic attention. Sitting behind the desk, her head just below the brass plaque, was a redhead. She was, Malone thought, positively beautiful. Of course, he could not see the lower two-thirds of her body, but if they were half as interesting as the upper third and the face and head, he was willing to spend days, weeks or even months on their investigation. Some jobs, he told himself, feeling a strong sense of duty, were definitely worth taking time over.

She was turned slightly away from Malone, and had obviously not heard him come in. Malone wondered how best to announce himself, and regretfully gave up the idea of tiptoeing up to the girl, placing his hands over her eyes, kissing the back of her neck and crying: "Surprise!" It was elegant, he felt, but it just wasn't *right*.

He compromised at last on the old established method of throat-clearing to attract her attention. He was sure he could take it from there, to an eminently satisfying conclusion.

He tiptoed on the deep-pile rug right up to her desk. He took a deep breath.

And the expected happened.

He sneezed.

The sneeze was loud and long, and it echoed through the room and throughout the corridors. It sounded to Malone like the blast of a small bomb, or possibly a grenade. Startled himself by the volume of sound he had managed to generate, he jumped back.

The girl had jumped, too, but her leap had been straight upward, about an inch and a half. She came down on her chair and reached up a hand. The hand wiped the back of her neck with a slow, lingering motion of complete loathing. Then, equally slowly, she turned.

"That," she said in a low, sweet voice, "was a hell of a dirty trick."

"It was an accident," Malone said. "The Will of God."

"God has an exceedingly nasty mind," the girl said. "Something, by the way, which I have often suspected." She regarded Malone darkly. "Do you always do that to strangers? Is it some new sort of perversion?"

"I have never done such a thing before," Malone said sternly.

"Oh," the girl said. "An experimenter. Avid for new sensations. Probably a jaded scion of a rich New York family." She paused. "Tell me," she said, "is it fun?"

Malone opened his mouth, but nothing came out. He shut it, thought for a second and then tried again. He got as far as: "I—" before Nemesis overtook him. The second sneeze was even louder and more powerful than the first had been.

"It must be fun," the girl said acidly, producing a handkerchief from somewhere and going to work on her face. "You just can't seem to wait to do it again. Would it do any good to tell you that the fascination with this form of greeting is not universal? Or don't you care?"

"Damn it," Malone said, goaded, "I've got a cold."

"And you feel you should share it with the world," the girl said. "I quite understand. Tell me, is there anything I can do for you? Or has your mission been accomplished?"

"My mission?" Malone said.

"Having sneezed twice at me," the girl said, "do you feel satisfied? Will you vanish softly and silently away? Or do you want to sneeze at somebody else?"

"I want the president of the Society," Malone said. "According to my information, his name is Sir Lewis Carter."

"And if you sneeze at him," the girl said, "yours is going to be mud. He isn't much on novelty."

"I—"

"Besides which," she said, "he's extremely busy. And I don't think he'll see you at all. Why don't you go and sneeze at somebody else? There must be lots of people who would consider themselves honored to be noticed, especially in such a startling way. Why don't you try and find one somewhere? Somewhere very far away."

Malone was beyond speech. He fumbled for his wallet, flipped it open and showed the girl his identification.

"My, my," she said. "And hasn't the FBI anything better to do? I mean, can't you go and sneeze at counterfeiters in their lairs, or wherever they might be?"

"I want to see Sir Lewis Carter," Malone said doggedly.

The girl shrugged and picked up the phone on the desk. It was a blank-vision device, of course; many office intercoms were. She dialed, waited and then said, "Sir Lewis, please." Another second went by. Then she spoke again. "Sir Lewis," she said, "this is Lou, at the front desk. There's a man here named Malone, who wants to see you."

She waited a second. "I don't know what he wants," she told the phone. "But he's from the FBI." A second's pause. "That's right, the FBI," she said. "All right, Sir Lewis. Right away." She hung up the phone and turned to watch Malone warily.

"Sir Lewis," she said, "will see you. I couldn't say why. But take the side corridor to the rear of the suite. His office has his name on it, and I won't tell you you can't miss it because I have every faith that you will. Good luck."

Malone blinked. "Look," he said. "I know I startled you, but I didn't mean to. I—" He started to sneeze, but this time he got his own handkerchief out in time and muffled the explosion slightly.

"Good work," the girl said approvingly. "Tell me, Mr. Malone, have you been toilet-trained, too?"

There was nothing at all to say to that remark, Malone reflected as he wended his way down the side corridor. It seemed endless, and kept branching off unexpectedly. Once he blundered into a large open room filled with people at desks. A woman who seemed to have a great many teeth and rather bulbous eyes looked up at him. "Can I help you?" she said in a fervent whine.

"I sincerely hope not," Malone said, backing away and managing to find the corridor once more. After what seemed like a long time, and two more sneezes, he found a small door which was labeled in capital letters:

THE PSYCHICAL RESEARCH SOCIETY
SIR LEWIS CARTER
PRESIDENT

Malone sighed. "Well," he muttered, "they certainly aren't hiding anything." He pushed at the door, and it swung open.

Sir Lewis was a tall, solidly-built man with a kindly expression. He wore grey flannel trousers and a brown tweed jacket, which made an interesting color contrast with his iron-grey hair. His teeth were clenched so firmly on the bit of a calabash pipe with a meerschaum bowl that Malone wondered if he could ever get loose. Malone shut the door behind him, and Sir Lewis rose and extended a hand.

Malone went to the desk and reached across to take the hand. It was firm and dry. "I'm Kenneth Malone," Malone said.

"Ah, yes," Sir Lewis said. "Pleased to meet you. Always happy, of course, to do whatever I can for your FBI. Not only a duty, so to speak, but a pleasure. Sit down. Please do sit down."

Malone found a chair at the side of the desk, and sank into it. It was soft and comfortable. It provided such a contrast to O'Connor's furnishings that Malone began to wish it was Sir Lewis who was employed at Yucca Flats. Then he could tell Sir Lewis everything about the case.

Now, of course, he could only hedge and try to make do without stating very many facts. "Sir Lewis," he said, "I trust you'll keep this conversation confidential."

"Naturally," Sir Lewis said. He removed the pipe, stared at it, and replaced it.

"I can't give you the full details," Malone went on, "but the FBI is presently engaged in an investigation which requires the specialized knowledge your organization seems to have."

"FBI?" Sir Lewis said. "Specialized investigation?" He seemed pleased, but a trifle puzzled. "Dear boy, anything we have is at your disposal, of course. But I quite fail to see how you can consider us—"

"It's rather an unusual problem," Malone said, feeling that that was the understatement of the year. "But I understand that your records go back nearly a century."

"Quite true," Sir Lewis murmured.

"During that time," Malone said, "the Society investigated a great many supposedly supernatural or supernormal incidents."

"Many of them," Sir Lewis said, "were discovered to be fraudulent, I'm afraid. The great majority, in fact."

"That's what I'd assume," Malone said. He fished in his pockets, found a cigarette and lit it. Sir Lewis went on chewing at his unlit pipe. "What we're interested in," Malone said, "is some description of the various methods by which these frauds were perpetrated."

"Ah," Sir Lewis said. "The tricks of the trade, so to speak?"

"Exactly," Malone said.

"Well, then," Sir Lewis said. "The luminous gauze, for instance, that passes for ectoplasm; the various methods of table-lifting; control of the Ouija board—things like that?"

"Not quite that elementary," Malone said. He puffed on the cigarette, wishing it was a cigar. "We're pretty much up to that kind of thing. But had it ever occurred to you that many of the methods used by phony mind-reading acts, for instance, might be used as communication methods by spies?"

"Why, I believe some have been," Sir Lewis said. "Though I don't know much about that, of course; there was a case during the First World War—"

"Exactly," Malone said. He took a deep breath. "It's things like that we're interested in," he said, and spent the next twenty minutes slowly approaching his subject. Sir Lewis, apparently fascinated, was perfectly willing to unbend in any direction, and jotted down notes on some of Malone's more interesting cases, murmuring: "Most unusual, most unusual," as he wrote. The various types of phenomena that the Society had investigated came into the discussion, and Malone heard quite a lot about the Beyond, the Great Summerland, Spirit Mediums and the hypothetical existence of fairies, goblins and elves.

"But, Sir Lewis—" he said.

"I make no claims personally," Sir Lewis said. "But I understand that there is a large and somewhat vocal group which does make rather solid-sounding claims in that direction. They say that they have seen fairies, talked with goblins, danced with the elves."

"They must be very unusual people," Malone said, understating heavily.

"Oh," Sir Lewis said, without a trace of irony, "they certainly are."

Talk like this passed away nearly a half-hour, until Malone finally felt that it was the right time to introduce some of his real questions. "Tell me, Sir Lewis," he said. "Have you had many instances of a single man, or a small group of men, controlling the actions of a much larger group? And doing it in such a way that the larger group doesn't even know it is being manipulated?"

"Of course I have," Sir Lewis said. "And so have you. They call it advertising."

Malone flicked his cigarette into an ashtray. "I didn't mean exactly that," he said. "Suppose they're doing it in such a way that the larger group doesn't even suspect that manipulation is going on?"

Sir Lewis removed his pipe and frowned at it. "I may be able to give you a little information," he said slowly, "but not much."

"Ah?" Malone said, trying to sound only mildly interested.

"Outside of mob psychology," Sir Lewis said, "and all that sort of thing, I really haven't seen any record of a case of such a thing happening. And I can't quite imagine anyone faking it."

"But you have got some information?" Malone said.

"Certainly," Sir Lewis said. "There is always spirit control."

"Spirit control?" Malone blinked.

"Demoniac intervention," Sir Lewis said. "'My name is Legion,' you know."

Sir Lewis Legion, Malone thought confusedly, was a rather unusual name. He took a breath and caught hold of his revolving mind. "How would you go about that?" he said, a little hopelessly.

"I haven't the foggiest," Sir Lewis admitted cheerfully. "But I will have it looked up for you." He made a note. "Anything else?"

Malone tried to think. "Yes," he said at last. "Can you give me a condensed report on what is known—and I mean *known*—on telepathy and teleportation?"

"What you want," Sir Lewis said, "are those cases proven genuine, not the ones in which we have established fraud, or those still in doubt."

"Exactly," Malone said. If he got no other use out of the data, it would provide a measuring-stick for the Society. The general public didn't know that the Government was actually using psionic powers, and the Society's theories, checked against actual fact, would provide a rough index of reliability to use on the Society's other data.

But spirits, somehow, didn't seem very likely. Malone sighed and stood up.

"I'll have copies made of all the relevant material," Sir Lewis said, "from our library and research files. Where do you want the material sent? I do want to warn you of its bulk; there may be quite a lot of it."

"FBI Headquarters, on 69th Street," Malone said. "And send a statement of expenses along with it. As long as the bill's within reason, don't worry about itemizing; I'll see that it goes through Accounting myself."

Sir Lewis nodded. "Fine," he said. "And, if you should have any difficulties with the material, please let me know. I'll always be glad to help."

"Thanks for your co-operation," Malone said. He went to the door, and walked on out.

He blundered back into the same big room again, on his way through the corridors. The bulbous-eyed woman, who seemed to have inherited a full set of thirty-two teeth from each of her parents, gave him a friendly if somewhat crowded smile, but Malone pressed on without a word. After awhile, he found the reception room again.

The girl behind the desk looked up. "How did he react?" she said.

Malone blinked. "React?" he said.

"When you sneezed at him," she said. "Because I've been thinking it over, and I've got a new theory. You're doing a survey on how people act when encountering sneezes. Like Kinsey."

This girl—Lou something, Malone thought, and with difficulty refrained from adding "Gehrig"—had an unusual effect, he decided. He wondered if there were anyone in the world she couldn't reduce to paralyzed silence.

"Of course," she went on, "Kinsey was dealing with sex, and you aren't. At least, you aren't during business hours." She smiled politely at Malone.

"No," he said helplessly, "I'm not."

"It is sneezing, then," she said. "Will I be in the book when it's published?"

"Book?" Malone said, feeling more and more like a rather low-grade moron.

"The book on sneezing, when you get it published," she said. "I can see it now: *The Case of Miss X, a Receptionist.*"

"There isn't going to be any book," Malone said.

She shook her head. "That's a shame," she said. "I've always wanted to be a Miss X. It sounds exciting."

"X," Malone said at random, "marks the spot."

"Why, that's the sweetest thing that's been said to me all day," the girl said. "I thought you could hardly talk, and here you come out with lovely things like that. But I'll bet you say it to all the girls."

"I have never said it to anybody before," Malone said flatly. "And I never will again."

The girl sighed. "I'll treasure it," she said. "My one great moment. Goodbye, Mr.—Malone, isn't it?"

"Ken," Malone said. "Just call me Ken."

"And I'm Lou," the girl said. "Goodbye."

An elevator arrived and Malone ducked into it. Louie? he thought. Louise? Luke? Of course, there was Sir Lewis Carter, who might be called Lou. Was he related to the girl?

No, Malone thought wildly. Relations went by last names. There was no reason for Lou to be related to Sir Lewis. They didn't even look alike. For instance, he had no desire whatever to make a date with Sir Lewis Carter, or to take him to a glittering nightclub, or to make him any whispered propositions. And the very idea of Sir Lewis Carter sitting on the Malone lap was enough to give him indigestion and spots before the eyes.

Sternly, he told himself to get back to business. The elevator stopped at the lobby and he got out and started down the street, feeling that consideration of the lady known as Lou was much more pleasant. After all, what did he have to work with, as far as his job was concerned?

So far, two experts had told him that his theory was full of lovely little holes. Worse than that, they had told him that mass control of human beings was impossible, as far as they knew.

And maybe it was impossible, he told himself sadly. Maybe he should just junk his whole theory and think up a new one. Maybe there was no psionics involved in the thing at all, and Boyd and O'Connor were right.

Of course, he had a deep-seated conviction that psionics was somewhere at the root of everything, but that didn't necessarily mean anything. A lot of people had deep-seated convictions that they were beetles, or that the world was flat And then again, murderers often suffered as a result of deep-seated convictions of one sort or another.

On the other hand, maybe he had invented a whole new psionic theory or, at least, observed some new psionic facts. Maybe they would call the results Malonizing, instead of O'Connorizing. He tried to picture a man opening a door and saying: "Come out quick, Mr. Frembits is Malonizing again."

It didn't sound very plausible. But, after all, he did have a deep-seated conviction. He tried to think of a shallow-seated conviction, and failed. Didn't convictions ever stand up, anyhow, or lie down?

He shook his head, discovered that he was on 69th Street, and headed for the FBI Headquarters. His convictions, he had found, were sometimes an expression of his precognitive powers; he determined to ride with them, at least for awhile.

By the time he came to the office of the agent-in-charge, he had figured out the beginnings of a new line of attack.

"How about the ghosts?" the agent-in-charge asked as he passed.

"They'll be along," Malone said. "In a big bundle, addressed to me personally. And don't open the bundle."

"Why not?" the agent-in-charge asked.

"Because I don't want the things to get loose and run around saying boo to everybody," Malone said brightly, and went on.

He opened the door of his private office, went inside and sat down at the desk there. He took his time about framing a thought, a single, clear, deliberate thought:

Your Majesty, I'd like to speak to you.

He hardly had time to finish it. A flash of color appeared in the room, just a few feet from his desk. The flash resolved itself into a tiny, grandmotherly-looking woman with a coronal of white hair and a kindly, twinkling expression. She was dressed in the full court costume of the First Elizabethan period, and this was hardly surprising to Malone. The little old lady believed, quite firmly, that she was Queen Elizabeth I, miraculously preserved over all these centuries. Malone, himself, had practically forgotten that the woman's real name was Rose Thompson, and that she had only been alive for sixty-five years or so. For most of that time, she had been insane.

For all of that time, however, she had been a genuine telepath. She had been discovered during the course of Malone's first psionic case, and by now she had even learned to teleport by "reading" the process in Malone's mind.

"Good afternoon, Sir Kenneth," she said in a regal, kindly voice. She was mad, he knew, but her delusion was nicely kept within bounds. All of her bright world hinged on the single fact that she was unshakably certain of her royalty. As long as the FBI catered to that notion— which included a Royal dwelling for her in Yucca Flats, and the privilege of occasionally knighting FBI agents who had pleased her unpredictable fancy—she was perfectly rational on all other points. She co-operated with Dr. O'Connor and with the FBI in the investigation of her psionic powers, and she had given her Royal word not to teleport except at Malone's personal request.

"I'd like to talk to you," Malone said, "Your Majesty."

There was an odd note in the Queen's voice, and an odd, haunted expression on her face. "I've been hoping you'd ask me to come," she said.

"I had a hunch you were following me telepathically," Malone said. "Can you give me any help?"

"I—I really don't know," she said. "It's something new, and something disturbing. I've never come across anything like it before."

"Like what?" Malone asked.

"It's the—" She made a gesture that conveyed nothing at all to Malone. "The—the static," she said at last.

Malone blinked. "Static?" he said.

"Yes," she said. "You're not telepathic, so I can't tell you what it's really like. But—well, Sir Kenneth, have you ever seen disturbance on a TV screen, when there's some powerful electric output nearby? The bright, senseless snowstorms, the meaningless hash?"

"Sure," Malone said.

"It's like that," she said. "It's a sudden, meaningless, disturbing blare of telepathic energy."

The telephone rang once. Malone ignored it.

"What's causing these disturbances?" he asked.

She shook her head. "I don't know, Sir Kenneth. I don't know," she said. "I can't pick up a person's mind over a distance unless I know him, and I can't see what's causing this at all. It's—frankly, Sir Kenneth, it's rather terrifying."

The phone rang again.

"How long have you been experiencing this disturbance?" Malone asked. He looked at the phone.

"The telephone isn't important," Her Majesty said. "It's only Sir Thomas, calling to tell you he's arrested three spies, and that doesn't matter at all."

"It doesn't?"

"Not at all," Her Majesty said. "What does matter is that I've only been picking up these flashes since you were assigned to this new case, Sir Kenneth. And..." She paused.

"Well?" Malone said.

"And they only appear," Her Majesty said, "when I'm tuned to *your* mind!"

5

Malone stared. He tried to say something but he couldn't find any words. The telephone rang again and he pushed the switch with a sense of relief. The beard-fringed face of Thomas Boyd appeared on the screen.

"You're getting hard to find," Boyd said. "I think you're letting fame and fortune go to your head."

"I left word at the office that I was coming here," Malone said aggrievedly.

"Sure you did," Boyd said. "How do you think I found you? Am I telepathic? Do I have strange powers?"

"Wouldn't surprise me in the least," Malone said. "Now, about those spies—"

"See what I mean?" Boyd said. "How did you know?"

"Just lucky, I guess," Malone murmured. "But what about them?"

"Well," Boyd said, "we picked up two men working in the Senate Office Building, and another one working for the State Department."

"And they are spies?" Malone said. "Real spies?"

"Oh, they're real enough," Boyd said. "We've known about 'em for years, and I finally decided to pick them up for questioning. God knows, but maybe they have something to do with all this mess that's bothering everybody."

"You haven't the faintest idea what you mean," Malone said. "Mess is hardly the word."

Boyd snorted. "You go on getting yourself confused," he said, "while some of us do the real work. After all—"

"Never mind the insults," Malone said. "How about the spies?"

"Well," Boyd said, a trifle reluctantly, "they've been working as janitors and maintenance men, and of course we've made sure they haven't been able to get their hands on any really valuable information."

"So they've suddenly turned into criminal masterminds," Malone said. "After being under careful surveillance for years."

"Well, it's possible," Boyd said defensively.

"Almost anything is possible," Malone said.

"Some things," Boyd said carefully, "are more possible than others."

"Thank you, Charles W. Aristotle," Malone said. "I hope you realize what you've done, picking up those three men. We might have been able to get some good lines on them, if you'd left them where they were."

There is an old story about a general who went on an inspection tour of the front during World War I, and, putting his head incautiously up out of a trench, was narrowly missed by a sniper's bullet. He turned to a nearby sergeant and bellowed: "Get that sniper!"

"Oh, we've got him spotted, sir," the sergeant said. "He's been there for six days now."

"Well, then," the general said, "why don't you blast him out of there?"

"Well, sir, it's this way," the sergeant explained. "He's fired about sixty rounds since he's been out there, and he hasn't hit anything yet. We're afraid if we get rid of him they'll put up somebody who *can* shoot."

This was standard FBI policy when dealing with minor spies. A great many had been spotted, including four in the Department of Fisheries. But known spies are easier to keep track of than unknown ones. And, as long as they're allowed to think they haven't been spotted, they may lead the way to other spies or spy networks.

"I thought it was worth the risk," Boyd said. "After all, if they have something to do with the case—"

"But they don't," Malone said.

"Damn it," Boyd exploded, "let me find out for myself, will you? You're spoiling all the fun."

"Well, anyhow," Malone said, "they don't."

"You can't afford to take any chances," Boyd said. "After all, when I think about William Logan, I tell myself we'd better take care of every lead."

"Well," Malone said finally, "you may be right. And then again, you may be normally wrong."

"What is that supposed to mean?" Boyd said.

"How should I know?" Malone said. "I'm too busy to go around and around like this. But since you've picked the spies up, I suppose it won't do any harm to find out if they know anything."

Boyd snorted again. "Thank you," he said, "for your kind permission."

"I'll be right down," Malone said.

"I'll be waiting," Boyd said. "In Interrogation Room 7. You'll recognize me by the bullet hole in my forehead and the strange South American poison, hitherto unknown to science, in my esophagus."

"Very funny," Malone said. "Don't give up the ship."

Boyd switched off without a word. Malone shrugged at the blank screen and pushed his own switch. Then he turned slowly back to Her Majesty, who was standing, waiting patiently, at the opposite side of the desk. Interference, he thought, located around him...

"Why yes," she said. "That's exactly what I did say."

Malone blinked. "Your Majesty," he said, "would you mind terribly if I asked you questions before you answered them? I know you can see them in my mind, but it's simpler for me to do things the normal way, just now."

"I'm sorry," she said sincerely. "I do agree that matters are confused enough already. Please go on."

"Thank you, Your Majesty," Malone said. "Well, then. Do you mean that *I'm* the one causing all this mental static?"

"Oh, no," she said. "Not at all. It's definitely coming from somewhere else, and it's beamed at you, or beamed around you."

"But—"

"It's just that I can only pick it up when I'm tuned to your mind," she said.

"Like now?" Malone said.

She shook her head. "Right now," she said, "there isn't any. It only happens every once in awhile, every so often, and not continuously."

"Does it happen at regular intervals?" Malone asked.

"Not as far as I've been able to tell," Her Majesty said. "It just happens, that's all. There doesn't seem to be any rhyme or reason to it. Except that it did start when you were assigned to this case."

"Lovely," Malone said. "Perfectly lovely. And what is it supposed to mean?"

"Interference," she said. "Static. Jumble. That's all it means. I just don't know any more than that, Sir Kenneth; I've never experienced anything like it in my life. It really does disturb me."

That, Malone told himself, he could believe. It must be an experience, he told himself, like having someone you were looking at suddenly dissolve into a jumble of meaningless shapes and lights.

"That's a very good analogy," Her Majesty said. "If you'll pardon me speaking before you've voiced your thought."

"Not at all," Malone said. "Go right ahead."

"Well, then," Her Majesty said. "The analogy you use is a good one. It's just as disturbing and as meaningless as that."

"And you don't know what's causing it?" Malone said.

"I don't know," she said.

"Nor what the purpose of it is?" he said.

Her Majesty shook her head slowly. "Sir Kenneth," she said, "I don't even know whether or not there *is* any purpose."

Malone sighed deeply. Nothing in the case seemed to make any sense. It wasn't that there were no clues, or no information for him to work with. There were a lot of clues, and there was a lot of information. But nothing seemed to link up with anything else. Every new fact was a bright, shiny arrow pointing nowhere in particular.

"Well, then—" he started.

The intercom buzzed. Malone jabbed ferociously at the button. "Yes?" he said.

"The ghosts are here," the agent-in-charge's voice said.

Malone blinked. "What?" he said.

"You said you were going to get some ghosts," the agent-in-charge said. "From the Psychical Research Society, in a couple of large bundles. And they're here now. Want me to exorcise 'em for you?"

"No," Malone said wearily. "Just send them in to join the crowd. Got a messenger?"

"I'll send them down," the agent-in-charge said. "About one minute."

Malone nodded, realized the man couldn't see him, said: "Fine," and switched off. He looked at his watch. A little over half an hour had passed since he had left the Psychical Research Society offices. That, he told himself, was efficiency.

Not that the books would mean anything, he thought. They would just take their places at the end of the long row of meaningless, disturbing, vicious facts that cluttered up his mind. He wasn't an FBI agent any more; he was a clown and a failure, and he was through. He was going to resign and go to South Dakota and live the life of a hermit. He would drink goat's milk and eat old shoes or something, and whenever another human being came near he would run away and hide. They would call him Old Kenneth, and people would write articles for magazines about The Twentieth Century Hermit.

And that would make him famous, he thought wearily, and the whole circle would start all over again.

"Now, now, Sir Kenneth," Queen Elizabeth said. "Things aren't quite that bad."

"Oh, yes, they are," Malone said. "They're even worse."

"I'm sure we can find an answer to all your questions," Her Majesty said.

"Sure," Malone said. "Even I can find an answer. But it isn't the right one."

"You can?" Her Majesty said.

"That's right," Malone said. "My answer is: to hell with everything."

* * * * *

Malone's Washington offices didn't look any different. He sighed and put the two big packages from the Psychical Research Society down on his desk, and then turned to Her Majesty.

"I wanted you to teleport along with me," he said, "because I need your help."

"Yes," she said. "I know."

He blinked. "Oh. Sure you do. But let me go over the details."

Her Majesty waved a gracious hand. "If you like, Sir Kenneth," she said.

Malone nodded. "We're going on down to Interrogation Room 7 now," he said. "Next door to it, there's an observation room, with a one-way panel in the wall. You'll be able to see us, but we won't be able to see you."

"I really don't require an observation panel," Her Majesty said. "If I enter your mind, I can see through your eyes."

"Oh, sure," Malone said. "But the observation room was built for more normal people—saving your presence, Your Majesty."

"Of course," she said.

"Now," Malone went on, "I want you to watch all three of the men we're going to bring in, and dig everything you can out of their minds."

"Everything?" she said.

"We don't know what might be useful," Malone said. "Anything you can find. And if you want any questions asked—if there's anything you think I ought to ask the men, or say to them—there's a non-vision phone in the observation room. Just lift the receiver. That automatically rings the one in the interrogation room and I'll pick it up. Understand?"

"Perfectly, Sir Kenneth," she said.

"Okay, then," Malone said. "Let's go." They headed for the door. Malone stopped as he opened it. "And by the way," he said.

"Yes?"

"If you get any more of those disturbances, let me know."

"At once," Her Majesty promised.

They went on down the hall and took the elevator down to Interrogation Room 7, on the lowest level. There was no particular reason for putting the interrogation section down there, except that it tended to make prisoners more nervous. And a nervous prisoner, Malone knew, was very possibly a confessing prisoner.

Malone ushered Her Majesty through the unmarked door of the observation chamber, made sure that the panel and phone were in working order, and went out. He stepped into Interrogation Room 7 trying hard to look bored, businesslike and unbeatable. Boyd and four other agents were already there, all standing around and talking desultorily in low tones. None of them looked as if they had a moment's worry in their lives. It was all part of the same technique, of course, Malone thought. Make the prisoner feel resistance is useless, and you've practically got him working for you.

The prisoner was a hulking, flabby fat man in work coveralls. He had black hair that spilled all over his forehead, and tiny button eyes. He was the only man in the room who was sitting down, and that was meant to make him feel even more inferior and insecure. His hands were clasped fatly in his lap, and he was staring down at them in a regretful manner. None of the agents paid the slightest attention to him. The general impression was that something really tough was coming up, but that they were in no hurry for it. They were willing to wait for the third degree, it seemed, until the blacksmith had done a really good job with the new spikes for the Iron Maiden.

The prisoner looked up apprehensively as Malone shut the door. Malone paid no attention to him, and the prisoner unclasped his hands, rubbed them on his coveralls and then reclasped them in his lap. His eyes fell again.

Boyd looked up too. "Hello, Ken," he said. He tapped a sheaf of papers on the single table in the room. Malone went over and picked them up.

They were the abbreviated condensations of three dossiers. All three of the men covered in the dossiers were naturalized citizens, but all had come in as "political refugees" from Hungary, from Czechoslovakia, and from East Germany. Further checking had turned up the fact that all three were actually Russians. They had been using false names during their stay in the United States, but their real ones were appended to the dossiers.

The fat one in the interrogation room was named Alexis Brubitsch. The other two, who were presumably waiting separately in other rooms, were Ivan Borbitsch and Vasili Garbitsch. The collection sounded, to Malone, like a seedy musical-comedy firm of lawyers: Brubitsch, Borbitsch and Garbitsch. He could picture them dancing gaily across a stage while the strains of music followed them, waving legal forms and telephones and singing away.

Brubitsch did not, however, look very gay. Malone went over to him now, walking slowly, and looked down. Boyd came and stood next to him.

"This is the one who won't talk, eh?" Malone said, wondering if he sounded as much like Dick Tracy as he thought he did. It was a standard opening, meant to make the prisoner think his fellows had already confessed.

"That's him," Boyd said.

"Mmm," Malone said, trying to look as if he were deciding between the rack and the boiling oil. Brubitsch fidgeted slightly, but he didn't say anything.

"We didn't know whether we had to get this one to talk, too," Boyd said. "What with the others, and all. But we did think you ought to have a look at him." He sounded very bored. It was obvious from his tone that the FBI didn't care in the least if Alexis Brubitsch never opened his mouth again, in what was likely to be a very short lifetime.

"Well," Malone said, equally bored, "we might be able to get a few corroborative details."

Brubitsch swallowed hard. Malone ignored him.

"Now, just look at him," Boyd said. "He certainly doesn't *look* like the head of a spy ring, does he?"

"Of course he doesn't," Malone said. "That's probably why the Russians used him. They figured nobody would ever look twice at a fat slob like this. Nobody would ever suspect him of being the head man."

"I guess you're right," Boyd said. He yawned, which Malone thought was overacting a trifle. Brubitsch saw the yawn, and one hand came up to jerk at his collar.

"Who'd ever think," Malone said, "that he plotted those killings in Redstone—all three of them?"

"It is surprising," Boyd said.

"But, then," Malone said, "we know he did. There isn't any doubt of that."

Brubitsch seemed to be turning a pale green. It was a fascinating color, unlike any other Malone had ever seen. He watched it with interest.

"Oh, sure," Boyd said. "We've got enough evidence from the other two to send this one to the chair tomorrow, if we want to."

"More than enough," Malone agreed.

Brubitsch opened his mouth, shut it again and closed his eyes. His lips moved silently.

"Tell me," Boyd said conversationally, leaning down to the fat man. "Did your orders on that job come from Moscow, or did you mastermind it all by yourself?"

Brubitsch's eyes stirred, then snapped open as if they'd been pulled by a string. "Me?" he said in a hoarse bass voice. "I know nothing about this murder. What murder? I know nothing about it."

There were no such murders, of course. But Malone was not ready to let Brubitsch know anything about that. "Oh, the ones you shot in Redstone," he said in an offhand way.

"The what?" Brubitsch said. "I shot people? Never."

"Oh, sure you did," Boyd said. "The others say you did."

Brubitsch's head seemed to sink into his neck. "Borbitsch and Garbitsch, they tell you about a murder? It is not true. Is a lie."

"Really?" Malone said. "We think it's true."

"Is a lie," Brubitsch said, his little eyes peering anxiously from side to side. "Is not true," he went on hopefully. "I have alibi."

"You do?" Boyd said. "For what time?"

"For time when murder happened," Brubitsch said. "I was someplace else."

"Well, then," Malone said, "how do you know when the murders were done? They were kept out of the newspapers." That, he reflected, was quite true, since the murders had never happened. But he watched Brubitsch with a wary eye.

"I know nothing about time," Brubitsch said, jerking at his collar. "I don't know when they happened."

"Then how can you have an alibi?" Boyd snapped.

"Because I didn't do them!" Brubitsch said tearfully. "If I didn't, then I *must* have alibi!"

"You'd be surprised," Malone said. "Now, about these murders—"

"Was no murder, not by me," Brubitsch said firmly. "Was never any killing of anybody, not even by accident."

"But your two friends say—" Boyd began.

"My two friends are not my friends," Brubitsch said firmly. "If they tell you about murder and say it was me, they are no friends. I did not murder anybody, I have alibi. I did not even murder anybody a little bit. They are no friends. This is terrible."

"There," Malone said reflectively, "I agree with you. It's positively awful. And I think we might as well give it up. After all, we don't need your testimony. The other two are enough; they'll get maybe ten years apiece, but you're going to get the chair."

"I will not sit down," Brubitsch said firmly. "I am innocent. I am innocent like a small child. Does a small child commit a murder? It is ridiculous."

Boyd picked up his cue with ease. "You might as well give us your side of the story, then," he said easily. "If you didn't commit any murders—"

"I am a small child," Brubitsch announced.

"Okay," Boyd said. "But if you didn't commit any murders, just what *have* you been doing since you've been in this country as a Soviet agent?"

"I will say nothing," Brubitsch announced. "I am a small child. It is enough." He paused, blinked, and went on, "I will only tell you this: no murders were done by our group in any of our activities."

"And what were your activities?" Malone asked.

"Oh, many things," Brubitsch said. "Many, many things. We—"

The telephone rang loudly, and Malone scooped it up with a practiced hand. "Malone here," he said.

Her Majesty's voice was excited. "Sir Kenneth!" she said. "I just got a tremendous burst of static!"

Malone blinked. *Is my mind acting up again?* he thought, knowing she would pick it up. *Am I being interfered with?*

He didn't feel any different. But then, how was he supposed to feel?

"It's not *your* mind, Sir Kenneth," Her Majesty said. "Not this time. It's *his* mind. That sneaky-thinking Brubitsch fellow."

Brubitsch? Malone thought. *Now what is that supposed to mean?*

"I don't know, Sir Kenneth," Her Majesty said. "But get on back to your questioning. He's ready to talk now."

"Okay," Malone said aloud. "Fine." He hung up and looked back to the Russian sitting on his chair. Brubitsch was ready to talk, and that was one good thing, anyhow. But what was all the static about?

What was going on?

"Now, then," Malone said. "You were telling us about your group activities."

"True," Brubitsch said. "I did not commit any murders. It is possible that Borbitsch committed murders. It is maybe even possible that Garbitsch committed murders. But I do not think so."

"Why not?" Boyd said.

"They are my friends," Brubitsch said. "Even if they tell lies. They are also small children. Besides, I am not even the head of the group."

"Who is?" Malone said.

"Garbitsch," Brubitsch said instantly. "He worked in the State Department, and he told us what to look for in the Senate Office Building."

"What were you supposed to look for?" Boyd said.

"For information," Brubitsch said. "For scraps of paper, or things we overheard. But it was very bad, very bad."

"What do you mean, bad?" Malone said.

"Everything was terrible," Brubitsch said mournfully. "Sometimes Borbitsch heard something and forgot to tell Garbitsch about it. Garbitsch did not like this. He is a very inflamed person. Once he threatened to send Borbitsch to the island of Yap as a spy. That is a very bad place to go to. There are no enjoyments on the island of Yap, and no ones likes strangers there. Borbitsch was very sad."

"What did you do with your information?" Boyd said.

"We remembered it," Brubitsch said. "Or, if we had a scrap of paper, we saved it for Garbitsch and gave it to him. But I remember once that I had some paper. It had a formula on it. I do not know what the formula said."

"What was it about?" Malone said.

Brubitsch gave a massive shrug. "It was about an X and some numbers," he said. "It was not very interesting, but it was a formula, and Garbitsch would have liked it. Unfortunately, I did not give it to him."

"Why not?" Boyd said.

"I am ashamed," Brubitsch said, looking ashamed. "I was lighting a cigarette in the afternoon, when I had the formula. It is a very relaxing thing to smoke a cigarette in the afternoon. It is soothing to the soul." He looked very sad. "I was holding the piece of paper in one hand," he said. "Unfortunately, the match and the paper came into contact. I burned my finger. Here." He stuck out a finger toward Malone and Boyd, who looked at it without much interest for a second. "The paper is gone," he said. "Don't tell Garbitsch. He is very inflamed."

Malone sighed. "But you remember the formula," he said. "Don't you?"

Brubitsch shook his massive head very slowly. "It was not very interesting," he said. "And I do not have a mathematical mind."

"We know," Malone said. "You are a small child."

"It was terrible," Brubitsch said. "Garbitsch was not happy about our activities."

"What did Garbitsch do with the information?" Boyd said.

"He passed it on," Brubitsch said. "Every week he would send a short-wave message to the homeland, in code. Some weeks he did not send the message."

"Why not?" Malone said.

"The radio did not work," Brubitsch said simply. "We received orders by short-wave, but sometimes we did not receive the orders. The radio was of very poor quality, and some weeks it refused to send any messages. On other weeks, it refused to receive any messages."

"Who was your contact in Russia?" Boyd said.

"A man named X," Brubitsch said. "Like in the formula."

"But what was his real name?" Malone said.

"Who knows?" Brubitsch said. "Does it matter?"

"What else did you do?" Boyd said.

"We met twice a week," Brubitsch said. "Sometimes in Garbitsch's home, sometimes in other places. Sometimes we had information. At other times, we were friends, having a social gathering."

"Friends?" Malone said.

Brubitsch nodded. "We drank together, talked, played chess. Garbitsch is the best chess player in the group. I am not very good. But once we had some trouble." He paused. "We had been drinking Russian liquors. They are very strong. We decided to uphold the honor of our country."

"I think," Malone murmured sadly, "I know what's coming."

"Ah?" Brubitsch said, interested. "At any rate, we decided to honor our country in song. And a policeman came and talked to us. He took us down to the police station."

"Why?" Boyd said.

"He was suspicious," Brubitsch said. "We were singing the *Internationale*, and he was suspicious. It is unreasonable."

"Oh, I don't know," Boyd said. "What happened then?"

"He took us to the police station," Brubitsch said, "and then after a little while he let us go. I do not understand this."

"It's all right," Malone said. "I do." He drew Boyd aside for a second, and whispered to him: "The cops were ready to charge these three clowns with everything in the book. We had a hell of a time springing them so we could go on watching them. I remember the stir-up, though I never did know their names until now."

Boyd nodded, and they returned to Brubitsch, who was staring up at them with surly eyes.

"It is a secret you are telling him," Brubitsch said. "That is not right."

"What do you mean, it's not right?" Malone said.

"It is wrong," Brubitsch went on. "It is not the American way."

He went on, with some prodding, to tell about the activities of the spy ring. It did not seem to be a very efficient spy ring; Brubitsch's long sad tale of forgotten messages, mixed orders, misplaced documents and strange mishaps was a marvel and a revelation to the listening officers. "I've never heard anything like it," one of them whispered in a tone of absolute wonder. "They're almost working on our side."

Over an hour later, Malone turned wearily away from the prisoner. "All right, Brubitsch," he said. "I guess that pretty much covers things for the moment. If we want any more information, though—"

"Call on me," Brubitsch said sadly. "I am not going anyplace. And I will give you all the information you desire. But I did not commit any murders."

"Goodbye, small child," Malone said, as two agents led the fat man away. The other two left soon afterward, and Malone and Boyd were alone.

"Think he was telling the truth?" Boyd said.

Malone nodded. "Nobody," he said, "could make up a story like that."

"I suppose so," Boyd said, and the phone rang. Malone picked it up.

"Well?" he asked.

"He was telling the truth, all right," Her Majesty said. "There are a few more details, of course, like the girl Brubitsch was involved with, Sir Kenneth. But she doesn't seem to have anything to do with the spy ring, and besides, she isn't a very nice person. She always wants money."

"Sounds perfectly lovely," Malone said. "As a matter of fact, I think I know her. I know a lot of girls who always want money. It seems to be in fashion."

"You don't know this one, Sir Kenneth," Her Majesty said, "and besides, she wouldn't be a good influence on you."

Malone sighed. "How about the static explosions?" he said. "Pick up any more?"

"No," she said. "Just that one."

Malone nodded at the receiver. "All right," he said. "We're going to bring in the second one now. Keep up the good work."

He hung up.

"Who've you got in the observation room?" Boyd asked.

"Queen Elizabeth I," Malone said. "Her Royal Majesty."

"Oh," Boyd said without surprise. "Well, was Brubitsch telling the truth?"

"He wasn't holding back anything important," Malone said, thinking about the girl. It would be nice to meet a bad influence, he thought mournfully. It would be nice to go somewhere with a bad influence (a bad influence, he amended, with a good figure) and forget all about his job, about the spies, about telepathy, teleportation, psionics and everything else. It might be restful.

Unfortunately, it was impossible.

"What's this business about a static explosion?" Boyd said.

"Don't ask silly questions," Malone said. "A static explosion is a contradiction in terms. If something is static, it doesn't move— whoever heard of a motionless explosion?"

"If it is a contradiction in terms," Boyd said, "they're your terms."

"Sure," Malone said. "But I don't know what they mean. I don't even know what I mean."

"You're in a bad way," Boyd said, looking sympathetic.

"I'm in a perfectly terrible way," Malone said, "and it's going to get worse. You wait and see."

"Of course I'll wait and see," Boyd said. "I wouldn't miss the end of the world for anything. It ought to be a great spectacle." He paused. "Want them to bring in the next one?"

"Sure," Malone said. "What have we got to lose but our minds? And who is the next one?"

"Borbitsch," Boyd said. "They're saving Garbitsch for a big finish."

Malone nodded wearily. "Onward," he said, and picked up the phone. He punched a number, spoke a few words and hung up.

A minute later, the four FBI agents came back, leading a man. This one was tall and thin, with the expression of a gloomy, degenerate and slightly nauseated bloodhound. He was led to the chair and he sat down in it as if he expected the worst to start happening at once.

"Well," Malone said in a bored, tired voice. "So this is the one who won't talk."

6

Midnight.

Kenneth J. Malone sat at his desk, in his Washington office, surrounded by piles of papers covering the desk, spilling off onto the floor and decorating his lap. He was staring at the papers as if he expected them to leap up, dance round him and shout the solution to all his problems at him in trained choral voices. They did nothing at all.

Seated cross-legged on the rug in the center of the room, and looking like an impossible combination of the last Henry Tudor and Gautama Buddha, Thomas Boyd did nothing either. He was staring downward, his hands folded on his ample lap, wearing an expression of utter, burning frustration. And on a nearby chair sat the third member of the company, wearing the calm and patient expression of the gently-born under all vicissitudes: Queen Elizabeth I.

"All right," Malone said into the silence. "Now let's see what we've got."

"I think we've got cerebral paresis," Boyd said. "It's been coming on for years."

"Don't be funny," Malone said.

Boyd gave a short, mirthless bark. "Funny?" he said. "I'm absolutely hysterical with joy and good humor. I'm out of my mind with happiness." He paused. "Anyway," he finished, "I'm out of my mind. Which puts me in good company. The entire FBI, Brubitsch, Borbitsch, Garbitsch, Dr. Thomas O'Connor and Sir Lewis Carter—we're all out of our minds. If we weren't, we'd all move away to the moon."

"And drink to forget," Malone added. "Sure. But let's try and get some work done."

"By all means, Sir Kenneth," Her Majesty said. Boyd had not included her in his list of insane people, and she looked slightly miffed. It was hard for Malone to tell whether she was miffed by the mention of insanity, or at being left out.

"Let's review the facts," Malone said. "This whole thing started with some inefficiency in Congress."

"And some upheavals elsewhere," Boyd said. "Labor unions, gangster organizations."

"Just about all over," Malone said. "And though we've found three spies, it seems pretty obvious that they aren't causing this."

"They aren't causing much of anything," Boyd said. "Except a lot of unbelieving laughter further up the FBI line. I don't think anybody is going to believe our reports of those interviews."

"But they're true," Her Majesty said.

"Sure they're true," Boyd said. "That's the unbelievable part. They read like farce, and not very good farce at that."

"Oh, I don't know," Malone said. "I think they're pretty funny."

"Shall we get back to the business at hand?" Her Majesty said gently.

"Ah," Malone said. "Anyhow, it isn't the spies. And what we now have is confusion even worse compounded."

"Confounded," Boyd said. "John Milton. *Paradise Lost*, I heard it somewhere."

"I don't mean confounded," Malone said. "I mean confusion. Anyhow, the Russian espionage rings in this country seem to be in as bad a state as the Congress, the labor unions, the syndicates, and all the rest. And all of them seem to have some sort of weird tie-in to these flashes of telepathic interference. Right, Your Majesty?"

"I believe so, Sir Kenneth," she said. The old woman looked tired and confused. Somehow, a lot of the brightness seemed to have gone out of her life. "That's right," she said. "I didn't realize there was so much of it going on. You see, Sir Kenneth, you're the only one I can pick up at a distance who has been having these flashes. But now that I'm here in Washington, I can feel it going on all around me."

"It may not have anything to do with everything else," Boyd said.

Malone shook his head. "If it doesn't," he said, "it's the weirdest coincidence I've ever even dreamed about, and my dreams can be pretty strange. No, it's got to be tied in. There's some kind of mental static that is somehow making all these people goof up."

"But why?" Boyd said. "What is it being done for? Just fun?"

"God only knows," Malone said. "But we're going to have to find out."

"In that case," Boyd said, "I suggest lots and lots of prayers."

Her Majesty looked up. "That's a fine idea," she said.

"But God helps those," Malone said, "who help themselves. And we're going to help ourselves. Mostly with facts."

"All right," Boyd said. "So far, all the facts have been a great help."

"Well, here's one," Malone said. "We got one flash each from Brubitsch, Borbitsch and Garbitsch while we were questioning them. And in each case, that flash occurred just before they started to blab everything they knew. Before the flash, they weren't talking. They were behaving just like good spies and keeping their mouths shut. After the flash, they couldn't talk fast enough."

"That's true," Boyd said reflectively. "They did seem to give up pretty fast, even for amateurs."

Malone nodded. "So the question is this," he said. "Just what happens during those crazy bursts of static?"

He looked expectantly at Her Majesty, but she shook her head sadly. "I don't know," she said. "I simply don't know. It's just noise to me, meaningless noise." She put her hands slowly over her face. "People shouldn't do things like that to their Sovereign," she said in a muffled voice.

Malone got up and went over to her. She wasn't crying, but she wasn't far from it. He put an arm around her thin shoulders. "Now, look, Your Majesty," he said in gentle tones, "this will all clear up. We'll find out what's going on, and we'll find a way to put a stop to it."

"Sure we will," Boyd said. "After all, Your Majesty, Sir Kenneth and I will work hard on this."

"And the Queen's own FBI," Malone said, "won't stop until we've finished with this whole affair, once and for all."

Her Majesty brought her hands down from her face, very slowly. She was forcing a smile, but it didn't look too well. "I know you won't fail your Queen," she said. "You two have always been the most loyal of my subjects."

"We'll work hard," Malone said. "No matter how long it takes."

"Because, after all," Boyd said in a musing, thoughtful tone, "it is a serious crime, you know."

The words seemed to have an effect on Her Majesty, like a tonic. For a second her face wore an expression of Royal anger and indignance, and the accustomed strength flowed back into her aged voice. "You're quite correct, Sir Thomas!" she said. "The security of the Throne and the Crown are at stake!"

Malone blinked. "What?" he said. "Are you two talking about something? What crime is this?"

"An extremely serious one," Boyd said in a grave voice. He rose unsteadily to his feet, planted them firmly on the carpet, and frowned.

"Go on," Malone said, fascinated. Her Majesty was watching Boyd with an intent expression.

"The crime," Boyd said, "the very serious crime involved, is that of Threatening the Welfare of the Queen. The criminal has committed the crime of Causing the Said Sovereign, Baselessly, Reasonlessly and Without

Consent or Let, to Be in a State of Apprehension for Her
Life or Her Well-Being. And this crime—"

"Aha," Malone said. "I've got it. The crime is—"

"High treason," Boyd intoned.

"High treason," Her Majesty said with satisfaction
and fire in her voice.

"Very high treason," Malone said. "Extremely high."

"Stratospheric," Boyd agreed. "That is, of course," he
added, "if the perpetrators of this dastardly crime are Her
Majesty's subjects."

"My goodness," the Queen said. "I never thought of
that. Suppose they're not?"

"Then," Malone said in his most vibrant voice, "it is an
Act of War."

"Steps," Boyd said, "must be taken."

"We must do our utmost," Malone said. "Sir Thomas—
"

"Yes, Sir Kenneth?" Boyd said.

"This task requires our most fervent dedication,"
Malone said. "Please come with me."

He went to the desk. Boyd followed him, walking
straight-backed and tall. Malone bent and removed from
a drawer of the desk a bottle of bourbon. He closed the
drawer, poured some bourbon into two handy water-
glasses from the desk, and capped the bottle. He handed
one of the water-glasses to Boyd, and raised the other one
aloft.

"Sir Thomas," Malone said, "I give you Her Majesty,
the Queen!"

"To the Queen!" Boyd echoed.

They downed their drinks and turned, as one man, to
hurl the glasses into the wastebasket.

In thinking it over later, Malone realized that he
hadn't considered anything about that moment silly at
all. Of course, an outsider might have been slightly
surprised at the sequence of events, but Malone was no

outsider. And, after all, it was the proper way to treat a Queen, wasn't it?

And...

When Malone had first met Her Majesty, he had wondered why, although she could obviously read minds, and so knew perfectly well that neither Malone nor Boyd believed she was Queen Elizabeth I, she insisted on an outward show of respect and dedication. He'd asked her about it at last, and her reply had been simple, reasonable and to the point.

According to her—and Malone didn't doubt it for an instant—most people simply didn't think their superiors were all they claimed to be. But they acted as if they did, at least while in the presence of those superiors. It was a common fiction, a sort of handy oil on the wheels of social intercourse.

And all Her Majesty had ever insisted on was the same sort of treatment.

"Bless you," she'd said, "I can't help the way you *think*, but, as Queen, I do have some control over the way you *act*."

The funny thing, as far as Malone was concerned, was that the two parts of his personality were becoming more and more alike. He didn't actually believe that Her Majesty was Queen Elizabeth I, and he hoped fervently that he never would. But he did have a great deal of respect for her, and more affection than he had believed possible at first. She was the grandmother Malone had never known; she was good, and kind, and he wanted to keep her happy and contented. There had been nothing at all phony in the solemn toast he had proposed, nor in the righteous indignation he had felt against anyone who was giving Her Majesty even a minute's worth of discomfort.

And Boyd, surprisingly enough, seemed to feel the same way. Malone felt good about that; Her Majesty needed all the loyal supporters she could get.

But all of this was later. At the time, Malone was doing nothing except what came naturally. Nor, apparently, was Boyd. After the glasses had been thrown, with a terrifying crash, into the metal wastebasket, and the reverberations of that second had stopped ringing in their ears, a moment of silence had followed.

Then Boyd turned, briskly rubbing his hands. "All right," he said. "Let's get back to work."

Malone looked at the proud, happy look on Her Majesty's face; he saw the glimmer of a tear in the corner of each eye. But he gave no indication that he had noticed anything at all out of the ordinary.

"Fine," he said. "Now, getting on back to the facts, we've established something, anyhow. Some agency is causing flashes of telepathic static all over the place. And those flashes are somehow connected with the confusion that's going on all around us. Somehow, these flashes have an effect on the minds of people."

"And we know at least one manifestation of that effect," Boyd said. "It makes spies blab all their secrets when they're exposed to it."

"These three spies, anyhow," Malone said.

"If spies is the right word," Boyd said.

"Okay," Malone said. "And now we've got another obvious question."

"It seems to me we've got about twelve," Boyd said.

"I mean, who's doing it?" Malone said. "Who is causing these telepathic flashes?"

"Maybe it's just happening," Boyd said. "Out of thin air."

"Maybe," Malone said. "But let's go on the assumption that there's a human cause. The other way, we can't do a thing except sit back and watch the world go to hell."

Boyd nodded. "It doesn't seem to be the Russians," he said. "Although, of course, it might be a Red herring."

"What do you mean?" Malone said.

"Well," Boyd said, "they might have known we were on to Brubitsch, Borbitsch and Garbitsch—" He stopped. "You know," he said, "every time I say that name I have to reassure myself that we're not all walking around in the world of Florenz Ziegfeld."

"Likewise," Malone said. "But go on."

"Sure," Boyd said. "Anyhow, they might have set the three of them up as patsies, just in case we stumbled on to this mess. We can't overlook this possibility."

"Right," Malone said. "It's faint, but it is a possibility. In other words, the agency behind the flashes might be Russian, and it might not be Russian."

"That clears that up nicely," Boyd said. "Next question?"

"The next one," Malone said grimly, "is, what's behind the flashes? Some sort of psionic power is causing them, that much is obvious."

"I'll go along with that," Boyd said. "I have to go along with it. But don't think I like it."

"Nobody likes it," Malone said. "But let's go on. O'Connor isn't any help; he washes his hands of the whole business."

"Lucky man," Boyd said.

"He says that it can't be happening," Malone said, "and if it is we're all screwy. Now, right or wrong, that isn't an opinion that gives us any handle to work with."

"No," Boyd said reflectively. "A certain amount of comfort, to be sure, but no handles."

"Sir Lewis Carter, on the other hand—" Malone said. He fumbled through some of the piles of paper until he had located the ones the president of the Psychical Research Society had sent. "Sir Lewis Carter," he went on, "does seem to be doing some pretty good work. At least, some of the more modern stuff he sent over looks pretty solid. They've been doing quite a bit of research into the subject, and their theories seem to be all right, or nearly all right, to me. Of course, I'm not an expert."

"Who is?" Boyd said. "Except for O'Connor, of course."

"Well, somebody is," Malone said. "Whoever's doing all this, for instance. And the theories do seem okay. In most cases, for instance, they agree with O'Connor's work, though they're not in complete agreement."

"I should think so," Boyd said. "O'Connor wouldn't recognize an astral plane if TWA were putting them into service."

"I don't mean that sort of thing," Malone said. "There's lots about astral bodies and ghosts, ectoplasm, Transcendental Yoga, theosophy, deros, the Great Pyramid, Atlantis, Mu, norns, and other such ridiculous pets. That's just silly, as far as I can see. But what they have to say about parapsychology and psionics as such does seem to be reasonably accurate."

"I suppose so," Boyd said tiredly.

"Okay, then," Malone said. "Did anybody notice anything in that pile of stuff that might conceivably have any bearing whatever on our problems?"

"I did," Boyd said. "Or I think I did."

"You both did," Her Majesty said. "And so did I, when I looked through it. But I didn't bother with it. I dismissed it."

"Why?" Malone said.

"Because I don't think it's true," she said. "However, my opinion is really only an opinion." She smiled around at the others.

Malone picked up a thick sheaf of papers from one of the piles of his desk. "Let's get straight what it is we're talking about," he said. "All right?"

"Anything's all right with me," Boyd said. "I'm easy to please."

Malone nodded. "Now, this writer—what's his name?" he said. He glanced at the copy of the cover page. *"Minds and Morons,"* he read. "By Cartier Taylor."

"Great title," Boyd said. "Does he say which is which?"

"Let's get back to serious business," Malone said, giving Boyd a single look. There was silence for a second, and then Malone said, "He mentions something, in the book, that he calls 'telepathic projection.' As far as I understand what he's talking about, that's some method of forcing your thoughts on another person." He glanced over at the Queen. "Now, Your Majesty," he said, "you don't think it's true—and that may only be an opinion, but it's a pretty informed one. It seems to me as if Taylor makes a good case for this 'telepathic projection' of his. Why don't you think so?"

"Because," Her Majesty said flatly, "it doesn't work."

"You've tried it?" Boyd put in.

"I have," she said. "And I have had no success with it at all. It's a complete failure."

"Now, wait a minute," Boyd said. "Just a minute."

"What's the matter?" Malone said. "Have you tried it, and made it work?"

Boyd snorted. "Fat chance," he said. "I just want to look at the thing, that's all." He held out his hand, and Malone gave him the sheaf of papers. Boyd leafed through them slowly, stopping every now and again to consult a page, until he found what he was looking for. "There," he said.

"There what?" Malone said.

"Listen to this," Boyd said. "'For those who draw the line at demonic possession, I suggest trying telepathic projection. Apparently, it is possible to project one's own thoughts directly into the mind of another—even to the point of taking control of the other's mind. Hypnotism? You tell me, and we'll both know. Ever since the orthodox scientists have come around to accepting hypnotism, I'm been chary of it. Maybe there really is an astral body or a soul that a person has stashed about him somewhere— something that he can send out to take control of another human being. But I, personally, prefer the telepathic projection theory. All you have to do is squirt your thoughts across space and spray them all over the other fellow's brain. Presto-bingo, he does pretty much what you want him to do.'"

"That's the quote I was thinking of," Malone said.

"Of course it is," Her Majesty said. "But it really doesn't work. I've tried it."

"How have you tried it?" Malone said.

"There were many times, Sir Kenneth," Her Majesty said, "when I wanted someone to do something particular for me or for some other person. After all, you must remember that I was in a hospital for a long time. Of course, that represents only a short segment of my lifespan, but it seemed long to me."

Malone, who was trying to view the years from age fifteen to age sixty-odd as a short segment of anybody's lifetime, remembered with a shock that this was not Rose Thompson speaking. It was Queen Elizabeth I, who had never died.

"That's right, Sir Kenneth," she said kindly. "And in that hospital, there were a number of times when I wanted one of the doctors or nurses to do what I wanted them to. I tried many times, but I never succeeded."

Boyd nodded his head. "Well—" he began.

"Oh, yes, Sir Thomas," Her Majesty said. "What you're thinking is certainly possible. It may even be true."

"What *is* he thinking?" Malone said.

"He thinks," Her Majesty said, "that I may not have the talent for this particular effect—and perhaps I don't. But, talent or not, I know what's possible and what isn't. And the way Mr. Taylor describes it is simply silly, that's all. And unladylike. Imagine any self-respecting lady 'squirting' her thoughts about in space!"

"Well," Malone said carefully, "aside from its being unladylike—"

"Sir Kenneth," Her Majesty said, "you are not telepathic. Neither is Sir Thomas."

"I'm nothing," Boyd said. "I don't even exist."

"And it is very difficult to explain to the non-telepath just what Mr. Taylor is implying," Her Majesty went on imperturbably. "Before you could inject any thoughts into anyone else's mind, you'd have to be able to see into that mind. Is that correct?"

"I guess so," Malone said.

"And in order to do that, you'd have to be telepathic," Her Majesty said. "Am I correct?"

"Correct," Malone said.

"Well, then," Her Majesty said with satisfaction, and beamed at him.

A second passed.

"Well, then, what?" Malone said in confusion.

"Telepathy," Her Majesty said patiently, "is an extremely complex affair. It involves a sort of meshing with the mind of this other person. It has nothing, absolutely nothing, in common with this simple 'squirting' of thoughts across space, as if they were orange pips you were trying to put into a wastebasket. No, Sir Kenneth, I cannot believe in what Mr. Taylor says."

"But it's still possible," Malone said.

"Oh," Her Majesty said, "it's certainly possible. But I should think that if any telepaths were around, and if they were changing people's minds by 'squirting' at them, I would know it."

Malone frowned. "Maybe you would at that," he said. "I guess you would."

"Not to mention," Boyd put in, "that if you were going to control everything we've come across like that you'd need an awful lot of telepathic operators."

"That's true," Malone admitted. "And the objections seem to make some sense. But what else is there to go on?"

"I don't know," Boyd said. "I haven't the faintest idea. And I'm rapidly approaching the stage where I don't care."

"Well," Malone said, heaving a sigh, "let's keep looking."

He bent down and picked up another sheaf of copies from the Psychical Research Society.

"After all," he said, without much hope, "you never know."

* * * * *

Malone looked around the office of Andrew J. Burris as if he'd never seen it before. He felt tired, and worn out, and depressed; it had been a long night, and here it was morning and the head of the FBI was giving him instructions. It was, Malone told himself, a hell of a life.

"Now, Malone," Burris said, "this is a very ticklish situation. You've got to handle it with great care."

"I can see that," Malone said apprehensively. "It certainly looks ticklish. And unusual."

"Well, we don't want any trouble," Burris said. "We have enough trouble now."

"Sometimes I think we have too much," Malone said.

"That's our job," Burris said, looking grim.

Malone blinked. "What is?" he said.

"Having trouble," Burris said.

There was a short silence. Malone broke it. "Anyhow," he said, "you feel we have enough trouble, so we're trying to make things easy for everybody."

Burris nodded. "I've talked with the president," he said, "and he feels this is the best way to handle matters."

Malone tried to imagine Burris explaining the incredible complexities of the situation to the president, and was torn between relief that he hadn't been there and a curious wish to have heard the scrambled conversation that must have taken place. "The way it seems to me," he said cautiously, "shipping those spies back to Russia is a worse punishment than sending them to the federal pen."

"Maybe it is," Burris said. "Maybe it is. How would you feel if you were being sent to jail?"

"Innocent," Malone said instantly.

"But that isn't the point," Burris went on. "You see, Malone, we don't really have much damaging evidence against those spies, except for their confessions. During all the time we were watching them, we took care that they never did come up with anything dangerous; we weren't fishing for them but for their superiors, for the rest of the network."

"There doesn't seem to be any more network," Malone said. "Not in this country, anyhow."

"Sure," Burris said. "We know that now, thanks to the confessions, and to Her Majesty. But we can't prosecute on that sort of evidence. You know what a good defense attorney could do with unsupported confessions—and even if we wanted to take the lid off telepathy for the general public, it would be absolute hell bringing it into court."

"So," Malone said, "we can't put them in prison, even if we want to."

"Oh, I didn't say that," Burris said hastily. "We could probably win, even against a good defense. But they wouldn't get much time in prison, and we'd only end up deporting them in any case."

Malone fished for a cigarette, lit it and blew out smoke. "So we're going to save the taxpayers some money," he said. "That'll be nice for a change."

"That's right," Burris said, beaming. "We're going to save Federal funds by shipping them back to their motherland now. After all, they did take out their naturalization papers under false names, and their declarations are chockfull of false information. So all it takes is a court order to declare their citizenships null and void, and hand all three of them back to the Soviets."

"A nice, simple housecleaning," Malone said. "All open and above-board. And the confessions will certainly stand up in a deportation hearing."

"No question of it," Burris said. "But the reason I called you here, Malone, is that there's still one thing bothering me."

Malone blew out some more smoke, thought wistfully about cigars, and said: "What? Everything seems simple enough to me."

Burris frowned and leaned back in his chair. "It's this notion of yours, Malone," he said.

"Notion?"

"About going over there," Burris said. "Now, I can understand your wanting some facts on Moscow, current background and all that sort of thing. So far, everything makes sense."

"Fine," Malone said warily.

"But, after all, Malone," Burris said, "we do have such a thing as the Central Intelligence Agency. They send us reports. That's what they're for. And why you want to ignore the reports and make a trip over there to walk around and see for yourself—"

"It's because of everything that's happening," Malone said.

Burris looked puzzled. "What?" he said.

"Because of all the confusion," Malone said. "Frankly, I can't trust the CIA, or any other branch of the government. I've got to see for myself."

Burris considered this for a second. "It's going to look very peculiar," he said.

Malone shrugged. "Everything looks peculiar," he said. "A little more won't hurt anything. And if I do turn up anything we can use, the whole trip will be worth it."

"But sending an FBI man along with Brubitsch, Borbitsch and Garbitsch is a little strange," Burris said. "Not to mention Her Majesty."

"There is that," Malone said. "I wonder what our Red friends are going to think of the Queen."

"God knows," Burris said. "If they take her seriously, they're liable to call her some sort of capitalist deviationist."

"And if they don't take her seriously?" Malone said.

"Then they're going to wonder why she's *pretending* to be a capitalist deviationist," Burris said.

Malone flicked his cigarette at an ashtray. "You can't win," he said.

"Frankly," Burris said, "I wouldn't allow Her Majesty to go along under any circumstances—except that there is an excuse for having an older woman around."

"There is?" Malone said.

Burris nodded. "As a chaperone," he said.

"Now, wait a minute," Malone said. "Brubitsch, Borbitsch and what's-his-name don't need a chaperone."

"I didn't say it was for them," Burris said.

"Me?" Malone asked in a tone of absolute wonder. "Now, Chief, I don't need a chaperone. I'm a grown man. I know my way around. And the idea of having Her Majesty along to chaperone me is going to make everything look even stranger. After all, Chief—"

"Malone," Burris said, in a voice of steel.

"Sorry," Malone mumbled. "But, really, I'm not some young, innocent girl in a Victorian novel."

"No," Burris said, a trifle sadly, "you're not. But there is one going along on the trip with the rest of you."

"There is?" Malone said. "Who is she? Rebecca?"

"Her name's Luba," Burris said. "Luba Garbitsch."

"Garbitsch's wife?" Malone said.

Burris shook his head. "His daughter," he said. "And don't tell me there isn't any such name as Luba. I know there isn't. But what would you pick to go with Garbitsch?"

"Wastepaper basket," Malone said instantly. "Grapefruit rinds. Lemon peels. Coffee grounds."

"Damn it, Malone," Burris said, "this is serious."

"Well," Malone said, "it doesn't sound serious. What are we doing, deporting the entire family?"

"I suppose we could," Burris said, "if we really wanted to get complicated about it. What with Garbitsch's false declaration, I haven't the faintest idea what his daughter's status would be—but she *was* born here,

Malone, and as far as we can tell she's perfectly loyal to the United States."

"Fine," Malone said. "So you're sending her to Russia. This is making less and less sense, you know."

Burris rubbed a hand over his face. "Malone," he said in a quiet, patient voice, "why don't you wait for me to finish? Then everything will make sense. I promise."

"Well, all right," Malone said doubtfully. "Luba Garbitsch is going along to Russia, in spite of the fact that she's perfectly loyal."

"True," Burris said. "You see, Malone, she loves her traitorous old daddy just the same. Family affection. Very touching."

"And if he's going to Moscow—"

"She wants to go along," Burris said. "That's right."

"And you're going to send her along," Malone said, "out of the goodness of your kindly old heart. Just like Santa Claus. Or the Easter bunny."

Burris looked acutely uncomfortable. "Now, Malone," he said. "It's not exactly that, and you know it."

"It isn't?" Malone said, trying to look surprised.

Burris shook his head. "If we send Luba Garbitsch along," he said, "that gives us a good excuse for Her Majesty. As a chaperone."

"Are you sure," Malone asked slowly, "that anybody with a name like Luba Garbitsch could plausibly need a chaperone? Even in a den of vice? Because somehow it doesn't sound right: Luba Garbitsch, chaperoned by Her Majesty Queen Elizabeth I."

"Well," Burris said, "it won't be the Queen. I mean, she won't be known as the Queen."

"Incognito?" Malone said.

Burris shrugged. "In away," he said. "What do you think would be a good name for her to travel under?"

Malone considered. "I don't know," he said at last. "But no more Lubas."

"I was thinking," Burris said carefully. "How about Rose Thompson?"

There was a long silence.

"I don't know whether she'll go for the idea," Malone said. "But I'll try it."

"You can do it, Malone," Burris said instantly. "I know you can. I just know it."

"Your faith," Malone said with a sigh, "is going to be too much for me one of these days."

Burris shrugged. "Just take it easy, Malone," he said. "You said you wanted to have Her Majesty over there to read a few minds, and you've got her. But remember, don't get involved in anything complicated. Don't start any fireworks."

"I hope not," Malone said.

"Stay out of political arguments," Burris said.

Malone blinked. "What do you think I'm going to do?" he said. "Bring along a soapbox?"

"You never know," Burris said. "Just keep quiet, and don't go prowling around where you're not wanted."

"That," Malone said decisively, "would keep me out of Russia entirely."

"Damn it," Burris said, "you know what I mean. We don't want any international incidents, understand?"

"Yes, sir," Malone said.

Burris nodded. "All right, then," he said. "Your plane leaves from the airport in an hour. You'd better go and talk to Her Majesty first."

"Right," Malone said.

"And I hope you know what you're doing," Burris said.

So do I, Malone thought privately. Aloud, he said, "I just want to get the feel of things over there, that's all, sir. I won't cause any more trouble than an ordinary tourist."

"Malone," Burris said, "don't be an ordinary tourist. They're empty-headed morons and they do make trouble. Be an invisible tourist. Be nice to everybody. Be polite and kind. Don't step on any toes, no matter whose and no matter why."

"Yes, sir," Malone said.

"Remember, they're going to know who you are," Burris said.

"It's not as if we could keep it a secret."

"Yes, sir," Malone said. "I'll remember."

"All right." Burris extended his hand. "Good luck, Malone," he said, with a deeper feeling of sincerity than Malone had experienced from him in months.

Malone shook the hand. "Thank you, sir," he said.

*   *   *   *   *

A little less than an hour later, Malone sat on the steps of the landing ramp that led up to the open door of the big Air Force transport plane on the runway. The plane was waiting, and so was Malone. He didn't feel confident, or even excited. He felt just a little bit frightened. Burris' complicated warnings had had some effect, and Malone was fighting down a minor case of the shakes.

Next to him, her face wreathed in happy smiles, sat a smartly-dressed grey-haired woman in her sixties. She wore an unobtrusive tailored suit and a light jacket, and she looked as if she might be one of the elder matrons of the society set, very definitely an upper-crust type. In spite of the normality of her clothing, Her Majesty looked every inch a Queen, Malone thought.

"And that, Sir Kenneth, is only natural," she said sweetly. "Even when traveling incognito, one must retain one's dignity. And I don't object at all to using the name of Rose Thompson in a good cause; it was used for so many years it almost feels like part of me."

"I shouldn't be at all surprised," Malone said mildly.

A voice from above and behind him interrupted his worried thoughts. "Mr. Malone!" it said. "Mr. Malone?"

Malone screwed his head around and looked up. An Air Force colonel was standing in the doorway of the plane, looking down with a stern, worried expression. "Yes?" Malone said. "What is it?"

"Takeoff, Mr. Malone," the colonel said. "We're due to go in fifteen minutes, and our clearance has been established."

"Fine," Malone said.

"But your passengers," the colonel said. "Where are they?"

Malone tried to look calm, cool and collected. "They'll be here," he said. "Don't worry about a thing." Privately, he hoped he was right. Boyd hadn't shown up yet, and Boyd was bringing the musical-comedy spy trio. It wasn't, Malone thought, that Boyd was usually late. But with Brubitsch, Borbitsch and Garbitsch in tow, almost anything could happen, he thought. He hoped fervently that it wouldn't.

"It won't," Her Majesty said. "At least, it hasn't so far. They're all in a car, and they're driving right here. Boyd is thinking that he ought to be here within five minutes."

Malone nodded, wiping his forehead. "Five minutes, Colonel," he called back to the figure at the door. The colonel nodded efficiently at him, turned and disappeared inside the plane. Malone looked at his watch. The second hand was going around awfully fast, he thought. He wondered if it were possible for time to speed up while he waited, so that by the time Boyd arrived he would be an old, old man. He felt about eight years older already, he told himself, and a minute hadn't even passed.

He forced his eyes away from the moving second hand. Looking at it, he knew, would only make him more nervous. Maybe there was some scenery around that he could stare at. He raised his eyes and looked out toward the gates that led to the interior of the air terminal.

Scenery, he told himself in sudden wonder, was no word for it.

He stared. He wanted to blink, but at the same time he felt that it would be a shame to close his eyes for even a tenth of a second. He held his eyelids apart by main force and went right on staring.

The girl walking toward him across the field was absolutely beautiful. She seemed to make everything light up and start singing. Malone was sure that, somewhere, he could hear birds plugging their favorite numbers, and the soft rustle of the wind through pine branches. He could feel the soft caress of the wind on his face, and he could smell the odor of lilacs and honeysuckles and violets and whatever all those other flowers were. They had all different colors and shapes, and he couldn't remember many of their names, but he could tell they were all around him. They had to be all around him. Especially all the red ones.

The girl had red hair that tossed gently in the wind. The bottom two-thirds of her figure, Malone was happy to note, was not only as good as the top third but a good deal better. It took him several seconds to reach this conclusion, because at first he was willing to swear that he had never seen such a beautiful girl before.

But, he told himself with a shade of apprehension, he had.

As she approached, he stood up. "Well, well," he said brightly. "If it isn't the Lady That's Known as Lou. Did the Psychical Research Society give you the day off, or are you here to see about a misplaced broom?"

The girl beamed at him. "My, my," she said. "How are you?"

"Fine," Malone said. "And—"

"And how are the others?" she said.

Malone blinked. "Others?" he said.

She nodded. "Grumpy, Sleepy, Happy, Dopey, Bashful and Doc," she said.

Malone opened his mouth, shut it again, and thought for a second. "Now, wait a minute," he said at last. "That's not fair. I—"

"Oh," she said. "And I nearly forgot. I owe you one from last time: *gesundheit.*"

"And many happy returns," Malone said. "Seriously, what are you doing out here?"

"Talking," the girl said. "To you. Or hadn't you noticed?"

"I mean in general," Malone said desperately.

"In general," she said agreeably, "I'm here to take a little trip."

"Oh," Malone said. "By plane?"

She smiled sweetly and shook her head. "Not at all," she said. "I'm waiting for the next scheduled broomstick."

Malone took a deep breath. "When does your plane leave?" he said doggedly.

"In ten minutes or so," she said.

"Then you'd better hurry and get on," he said.

She nodded. "That's what I thought," she said.

A second passed.

"Did you want to say something?" Malone said uncomfortably.

She shook her head. "Not particularly," she said.

"Well, then—"

"The time *is* growing short," she said.

"Isn't it, though?" Malone said, feeling a little mystified. "Well, now. Goodbye. I'll see you soon."

"Goodbye," she said.

Another second passed.

"Your plane—" Malone started.

"How about yours?" she said.

"I'm all right," Malone said nervously. "But if your plane's leaving in ten minutes you'd better get on it."

"I intend to," she said, without moving.

"Well—" Malone started.

"As soon as you quit blocking the ramp," she said. "Would you mind terribly if I climbed over your head? Because I do have to get on board."

"Now wait a minute," Malone said. "This isn't your plane."

"How do you know?" she said. "Do you own it? Are you flying it away?"

"Well," Malone said helplessly, "it's my plane, and there's nobody going on it but—"

He paused. A great light seemed to burst in his mind, shedding a perfectly horrible glow over the wreck of his mental processes. "You know," he said in a tentative tone, "we never have been properly introduced. I only know your name is Lou."

"That's what people call me," the girl said. "For short. I'm Luba Garbitsch."

"And I'm Kenneth Malone," Malone said. "Kenneth J. Malone. Of the FBI."

She nodded. "Yes," she said. "I know."

"Your father—"

"My father is going to Russia," she said, "and I am going along with him."

"Oh," Malone said. "Sure. Sure. Oh."

There was a longer silence.

"Can I get on board now?" Luba said.

"There isn't any hurry," Malone said. "We're still waiting for—for passengers. And this is one of them." He turned and indicated the Queen. "This is Her—Rose Thompson. She'll be traveling along with us."

Her Majesty was wearing a broad, broad grin, Malone noticed nervously as he turned. Undoubtedly she had been tuned in to the whole conversation, and knew just what had gone on in both minds. But she only said, "I'm very pleased to meet you, my dear."

Lou blinked, smiled and stretched out her hand. "Well, then," she said. "Hello. And let's all have a happy trip."

"By all means," Malone said. "And the trip seems to be about to start."

He could hear the tramping of a lot of feet coming across the field toward them. He looked and saw that the feet were all neatly attached to bodies, two to a body. There were Thomas Boyd's feet, the assorted twelve feet of six FBI agents, and three pairs that belonged to Alexis Brubitsch, Ivan Borbitsch and Vasili Garbitsch. Brubitsch looked even fatter than ever, Borbitsch even thinner. Garbitsch was of an indeterminate middling shape; he had grey hair and a pair of pince-nez, and he walked a trifle unevenly, like a duck, with his hands clasped low in front of him. He was looking down at the ground as the crowd shoved him along.

When the crowd neared the steps, Luba went over to him. Garbitsch looked up, with a pleasant, somehow wistful smile on his face. "Hello, Luba, my child," he said.

Luba smiled, too. "Hello, Dad," she said. "All ready to go?"

"Certainly I am ready," he said. "I am all packed. We take off in a few minutes. And you, Luba, my child?"

"Fine, Dad," she said.

She looked down. "They've got handcuffs on you," she said. "Why, that's—"

Garbitsch shrugged. He looked even more wistful. "A formality," he said. "It makes no difference."

"Okay," Boyd said suddenly. "We've got to get out of here pretty soon, and you'll be taking off. Let's break it up. Miss Thompson, you and Luba go aboard. Malone, you follow with the others."

Malone rounded up Brubitsch, Borbitsch and Garbitsch and followed the ladies aboard.

He came back to the door then, and stuck his head out. "The keys," he said.

Boyd stared. "What?"

"The keys to the handcuffs," Malone said. "I'll need 'em."

"You're going to take them off when they get to Russia?" Boyd said.

Malone shook his head. "No," he said. "Now."

"But—"

"I think we'll have plenty of warning if they decide to try anything, Tom," Malone said quietly. "Her Majesty, after all, is keeping them under surveillance."

Without another word, Boyd tossed up the keys. Malone caught and pocketed them. "I'll be back as soon as possible," he said. "Meanwhile, you can keep digging on other stuff—what we've discussed and anything it seems to lead into."

"Right," Boyd said. "Stay out of trouble, Ken. So long."

Malone nodded and ducked back into the plane. He unlocked the handcuffs, and Brubitsch and Borbitsch immediately went and sat down mournfully together at the back of the plane. Malone looked for Lou, but she was already seated—with Her Majesty, naturally. He sighed briefly and sat down, at last, next to the wistful Garbitsch.

"It will be nice to see Russia again," Garbitsch said. "I hardly hoped to do so."

The plane shuddered, roared and took off. Then it settled down to its normal state of unnatural quiet. Malone sat back and tried to relax.

It was impossible.

7

Red Square was, somehow, disappointing. It was crowded with men and women, all looking very Russian in an undefined sort of way, and the big glass windows sparkled from every side. "I know it's silly," Luba said in a baffled voice, "but, somehow, I always expected Red Square to be red."

"And why should that be?" the MVD man next to her said. He was a burly man with a sour expression, as if he had eaten too many onions the day before.

"Well," Malone said, "it is Red Square, after all."

"But red is symbolic only," the MVD man said surlily. "Is not color. Only symbol of glorious Russia."

"I suppose so," Luba said. "But it's still disappointing."

"You expect, perhaps, that we recruit our glorious Red Army from American Indian tribes?" the MVD man said sourly. "You are literal-minded bourgeois intellectual. This is not good thing to be."

"Somehow," Malone mused, "I didn't think it was."

"But this is different," Luba said. "The Red Army is made up of Russians. But this is just a square. You could paint it."

"After all," Malone offered, "the White House is white, isn't it?"

"White is cowardly color," the MVD man pointed out with satisfaction.

"Never mind that," Malone said. "We call it a white house, and it is a white house. You call this a red square, and it isn't even pink. Not even a little bit pink. It's just—just—"

"Just building-colored," Luba put in. Malone turned to her and executed a small bow.

"Thank you," he said.

"Think nothing of it," Luba said.

"Oh, don't worry," Malone said. "I will."

The MVD man hissed like a teakettle and both heads swung round to look at him again. Her Majesty, who had been admiring some dresses in a shop window, also turned. "My goodness," she said. "That's a terrible wheeze. Do you take something for it?"

"Is not wheeze," the MVD man said. "Is noise representing impatience with arrogance and stupidity of capitalist warmonger conversation."

"Arrogance?" Luba said.

"Stupidity?" Malone said.

Her Majesty drew herself to her full height. "We do not monger war," she said. "Not in the least. We are not mongers."

The MVD man looked at her, blinked, sighed and looked away. "This color discussion," he said, "it is very silly. Look at the Blue Ridge Mountains, in your country. Are they blue?"

"Well—" Malone said.

"What color, for example, is the Golden Gate Bridge?" the MVD man continued, with heavy sarcasm. "Is not even a gate. Is a bridge. Is not golden. But you say we disappoint. No. You disappoint."

There seemed to be no immediate answer to that, so Malone didn't try for one. Instead, he went back to looking at the Square, and beyond it to where the inverted turnips of the Kremlin gleamed in the moonlight. The turnips were very pretty, if a little odd for building-tops. But Red Square, in spite of all its historic associations, seemed to be a little dull. The buildings were just buildings, and the streets were filled with Russians. They were not bomb-throwing Russians, bearded Russians or even "Volga Boatman"-singing Russians. They were just ordinary, dull Russians of every sort, shade, race, color and previous condition of servitude.

It was just about what he'd expected after the trip. That hadn't been exciting either, he told himself. There had been no incident of any kind. None of the three spies seemed to be exactly overjoyed about being sent back to good old Mother Russia, but none seemed inclined to make much fuss about the matter, either. Malone had blandly told them that they were being deported, instead of tried, because there was no evidence that was worth the expense of a trial. And, besides that, he had particularly emphasized that the FBI did not believe any of the stories the three men had told.

"They just don't match up," he said. "You all told different stories, and there's too much disagreement between them. Frankly, we don't believe any of them— not yet, we don't. But mark my words. We'll find out the truth some day."

He'd thought it was a good speech, and Her Majesty had agreed with him. It had its desired effect, since the plane was the first place the three had had a chance to meet since their arrest. "Each one knows that he told the truth," Her Majesty said, "but nobody knows what the other two said."

"That's what I figured," Malone said. "They didn't have a chance to talk to each other."

"And so each one is lying his head off to the others," Her Majesty said, "and telling them all about how he, too, lied gloriously and bravely in defense of the Motherland. It's really very funny."

"Well," Malone said, "it makes them happy. And why not?"

Luba, too, had chatted with her father quite a lot of the time. Her Majesty reported that none of this conversation could possibly be understood as dangerous or harmful. It was just simple conversation.

Of course, Luba and her father hadn't talked all the time, and Malone did have a chance to get a few words in edgewise. Her Majesty made no report on those conversations, but Malone was comfortably aware that they did not belong in the harmless class. His relationship with the girl seemed, he told himself happily, to be improving slightly. Now and again, he even won a round from her.

As the American plane crossed the border, it was picked up by an escort of Russian fighter craft, which stuck with them all the way into Moscow. The fighters didn't do anything; they were just there, Malone figured, for insurance. But they made him nervous when he looked out the window. The trip from the border to Moscow seemed to take a long time.

Then, at the airfield, a group of MVD men had almost elbowed the American Embassy delegation out of the way in greeting the disembarking little band. There was a lot of palaver, in Russian, English and various scrambled mixtures which nobody understood. The American delegation greeted Malone, Luba and Her Majesty formally, and the MVD concentrated on Brubitsch, Borbitsch and Garbitsch. The three spies were hustled away, apparently to MVD Headquarters, without much fuss. Luba said goodbye to her father calmly enough, and Vasili Garbitsch seemed almost entirely unaffected by his surroundings. As the plane touched ground, he had said: "Ah, the soil of Mother Russia," but, outside of a goodbye or two, those were his last words before leaving.

One MVD man stayed behind, even after the American delegation had left. His name, he explained, was Vladimir Josefovitch Petkoff. "It will be my pleasure to show your group the many historic and interesting sights of Moskva," he announced to Malone.

"Pleasure?" Malone said. Petkoff was tall and heavy, and wore a row of medals that strung out across his chest like a newspaper headline.

"My duty," Petkoff said flatly, "is my pleasure. That is how we arrange matters in Russia."

And so the tour had started, with Red Square. Malone told himself he didn't really mind if it weren't red, but he did think it could at least look sinister. Unfortunately, the Square did not seem particularly willing to oblige.

"So this is Red Square," Malone said, after a long silence.

"You do not sound interested," Petkoff said in what sounded like a vaguely ominous voice. "Because it is not painted in capitalistic and obvious colors, it bores you?"

"Not exactly," Malone said. "But when you've seen one Square, you've seen them all, is how I feel about it. There must be somewhere else to sight-see."

"Somewhere?" Petkoff said. "There is everywhere. This is Moskva, the capital and the greatest city in Mother Russia. That is what we are told to say." He lowered his voice. "Personally," he added, "I come from Leningrad. I prefer it. But in Moskva one talks only of Moskva."

"I know just how you feel," Malone assured him. "I've been to San Francisco."

"Well, then," Petkoff said, almost smiling at him. "What is there you would like to see?"

Malone fished in his pocket for an American cigarette. He'd brought a carton with him, having once tried Russian makes. They seemed to be mostly cardboard, both the long filter and the tobacco. He lit the cigarette and thought for a second. "I don't suppose," he said cautiously, "that we could take a look around inside the Kremlin, could we?"

"Aha," Petkoff said. "I see what is in your mind."

"You do?" Malone said, startled.

"Naturally," Petkoff said. "You wish to see the tomb of Lenin. It is famous throughout the world."

Malone considered that for a minute. "Somehow," he said cautiously, "the coffin of Lenin doesn't exactly sound like a gay start for sight-seeing."

Petkoff looked pleased instantly. "I understand," he said. "Truly I understand. You, too, feel sad over the death of the great Lenin. How beautiful! How cultured!"

Malone wondered whether or not to disillusion the man, and decided against it. "Well, something like that," he said vaguely.

"I'll tell you what: is there a restaurant around here where we could get something to eat?"

"To eat?" Petkoff said, still looking pleased. "You wish to eat?"

"Well," Malone said, "I'm rather hungry, and I guess the ladies must be, too."

"What?" Luba said, returning to the group. She had joined Her Majesty in viewing the display of dresses. The Queen came scurrying over, too, through the silent and jostling Russian crowds.

"I was suggesting a restaurant," Malone said.

"Best idea anybody's had all day," Lou said. Her Majesty graciously consented to agree, and Petkoff beamed like the rising sun.

"My friends," he said. "My very fine friends—although you are capitalistic bourgeois intellectuals, thrown aside by the path of progress—in Moskva we have the finest restaurants in all the world."

"How about ... oh, Leningrad?" Malone said in a low voice.

"In Leningrad," Petkoff admitted, "the restaurants are better. But in Moskva, the restaurants are very good indeed. Much better than one might expect, if one knows Leningrad."

"Well," Malone said, "I suppose we've just got to put up with Moscow."

They went back to the corner, and hailed the long, black, sleek-looking limousine that had brought them in from the airport. The two silent men in the front seat of the gleaming Volga sedan were waiting patiently. Malone, Her Majesty and Lou got into the back, Petkoff in front. The two men were as still as statues—and rather unpleasant-looking statues, Malone thought—until Petkoff snapped something in Russian. Then one of them, at the wheel, said: *"Da, Tovarishch."*

The car started down the Moscow streets.

Her Majesty was silent and somewhat abstracted during the ride, just as she had been during the entire trip so far. She was, Malone knew, prying into every mind she could touch. He smiled inwardly when he thought about that.

The MVD, all unbeknownst to itself, was busily carrying around and protecting the single most dangerous spy in Moscow.

Nobody else spoke, either, until the car was moving along at a good clip. Petkoff began some small talk then, but it wasn't very interesting until he finally managed to edge it around to the subject he really wanted to talk about.

"By the way, Mr. Malone," he said, in a voice that sounded as if Petkoff were trying to establish an offhand manner, and not succeeding in the least. "It was thoughtful, very thoughtful, of American government, to return to us those men. Very kind."

Malone's expression conveyed nothing but the sheerest good will. "Well, you know how it is," he said. "Anything we can do to preserve peace and amity between our countries—we'll do it. You know that. Getting along, coexistence, that sort of thing. Oh, we're glad to oblige."

"I am sure," Petkoff said darkly. "You realize, of course, that they are criminals? Deserters from Red Army, embezzlers. Embezzlers of money."

Wondering vaguely what else you could be an embezzler of, Malone nodded. "That's what your ambassador in Washington said, when we told him about the deportation order."

"But Dad's not an embezzler," Luba broke in. "Or a deserter, either. He—"

"We have the records," Petkoff said.

"But—"

"Ordinarily, Mr. Malone," Petkoff said pointedly, "we do not find it the policy of the American government to send back political refugees."

"Now, listen," Lou said. "If you think you can shut me up—"

"That is exactly what I think," Petkoff said. "Let me assure you that no offense has been intended."

Lou opened her mouth and started to say something. Then she shut it again. "Well," she said, "I guess this isn't the time to argue about it. I'm sorry, Mr. Petkoff."

The MVD man beamed back at her. "Call me Vladimir," he said.

Malone broke in hastily. "You see, Major," he said, "these men are all embezzlers, as you've said yourself. We have the word of your government on that."

Petkoff took his eyes off Lou with what seemed real reluctance. "Oh," he said. "Yes. Of course you do."

"Therefore," Malone said smoothly, "the three are criminals and not political refugees."

"Indeed," Petkoff said blandly. "Very interesting. Your government has done a good deal of thinking in this matter."

"Sure we have," Malone said. "After all, we don't want to cause any trouble."

"No," Petkoff said, and frowned. "Of course not."

"Naturally," Malone said.

After that, there was silence for almost a full minute. Then Major Petkoff turned to Malone again with a frown. "Wait," he said.

"Wait?" Malone said.

"The Union of Soviet Socialist Republics," Petkoff said, "has no extradition treaty with your capitalist warmongering country."

"We're not warmongers," Her Majesty put in. Both men ignored her.

"True," Malone admitted.

"Then there was no reason to send these men back to us," Petkoff said.

"Oh, no," Malone said. "There was a very good reason. You see, we didn't want them in our country, either."

"But—"

"And when we found that they'd lied on their naturalization papers, why, naturally, we took immediate steps. The only steps we could take, as a matter of fact."

"The only steps?" Petkoff said. "You could have preferred charges. This was not done. Why was it not done?"

"That," Malone said, sidestepping neatly, "is a matter of governmental policy, Major Petkoff. And I can't provide any final answer."

"Ah?" Petkoff said.

"But, after all, a trial would not make sense," Malone said, now busily attacking from the side. "You see, at first we thought they were espionage agents."

"A foolish conclusion," Petkoff said uneasily.

Malone nodded. "That's what we finally realized," he said. "We questioned them, but their stories were nonsense, absolute nonsense. Of course, we had no idea of what foreign government might have employed them."

"Of course not," Petkoff said, shifting slightly in his seat. The car took a wide curve and swayed slightly, and Malone found himself nearly in Lou's lap. The sensation was so pleasant that all conversation was delayed for a couple of seconds, until the car had righted itself.

"So," Malone went on when he had straightened out, "we decided to save ourselves the expense of a trial."

"Very natural," Petkoff said. The slight delay apparently allowed him to recover his own mental balance. "The capitalist countries think only of money."

"Sure," Malone said agreeably. "Well, anyhow, that's the way it was. There was no point, really, in putting them in prison—what for? What good could it do us?"

"Who knows?" Petkoff said.

"Exactly," Malone said. "So, since all we wanted to do was get rid of them, and since we had an easy way to do that, why, we took it, that's all, and shipped them here."

"I see," Petkoff said. "And the Union of Soviet Socialist Republics is properly grateful."

"My goodness," Her Majesty put in, apparently out of an irrepressible sense of fun. "Maybe we'll get medals."

"Medals," Petkoff said sternly, "are not given to capitalist agitators."

"We are not agitated," Her Majesty said, and folded her hands in her lap, looking quite satisfied with herself.

Petkoff thought for a second. "And why," he said, "did you feel that such elaborate precautions were necessary in returning these men to us?"

Malone shrugged. "Well, we couldn't have them just running around all over the world, could we?" he said. "We felt that here they'd be properly housed and fed, in their own homeland, even if they didn't get a job."

"They will be properly taken care of," Petkoff prophesied darkly.

"Now, wait a minute—" Lou began, and then stopped. "Sorry," she said.

Malone felt sorry for her, but there was nothing he could say to make things any better. "Exactly," he told Petkoff with what he hoped was a smile.

"Ah, well," Petkoff said. "My friend and colleague, we should cease this shoptalk. Shoptalk?"

"Quite correct," Malone said.

"I have studied English a long time," Petkoff said. "It is not a logical language."

"You're doing very well," Malone said. Petkoff gave him a military duck of the head.

"I appreciate your compliments," he said. "But I fear we are boring the ladies."

The major had timed his speech well. At that moment, the ornate Volga pulled up to a smooth stop before a large, richly decorated building that glowed brightly under the electric lights of a large sign. The sign said something incomprehensible in Cyrillic script. Under it, the building entrance was gilded and carved into fantastic rococo shapes. Malone stared at the sign, and was about to ask a question about it when Petkoff spoke.

"Trotkin's," he said. "The finest restaurant in all the world—in Moskva, this is what they say of it."

"I understand," Malone said.

"Come," Petkoff said grandly, and got out of the car. One of the two silent men leaped out and opened the back door, and Her Majesty, Lou and Malone climbed out and stood blinking on the sidewalk under the sign.

Petkoff leaned over and said something to the driver. The second silent man got back into the car, and it drove away down the street, turned a corner and disappeared. The party of four started toward the entrance of the restaurant.

The door swung open before Major Petkoff reached it. A doorman was holding it, and bowing to each of the four as they passed. He was dressed in Victorian livery, complete to knee-breeches and lace, and Malone thought this was rather odd for the classless Russian society. But the doorman was only the opening note of a great symphony.

Inside, there were tables and chairs—or at least, Malone told himself, that's what he thought they were. They were massive wood affairs, carved into tortuous shapes and gilded or painted in all sorts of colors that glittered madly under the barrage of several electric chandeliers.

The chandeliers hung from a frescoed ceiling, and looked much too heavy. They swayed and tinkled in time to the music that filled the room, but for a second Malone looked past them at the ceiling. It appeared to represent some sort of Russian heaven, at the end of the Five-Year Plan. There were officers and ladies eating grapes, waltzing, strolling on white puffy clouds, singing, drinking, making love. There was an awful lot of activity going on up on the ceiling, and it wasn't until Malone lowered his gaze that he realized that none of this activity had been exaggerated.

True, there were no white puffy clouds, and he couldn't immediately locate a bunch of grapes anywhere. But there were the musicians, in the same Victorian outfits as the doorman: three fiddlers, a cellist, and a man who played piano. "Just like in night-clubs in bourgeois Paris," Petkoff said, following Malone's gaze with every evidence of pride.

Between the musicians and Malone were a lot of tables and chairs and ancient, proud-looking waiters who appeared to have been hired when Trotkin's had opened—and that, Malone thought, had been a long, long time ago. He felt like those two ladies, whose names he couldn't remember, who said they'd slipped back in time. Officers and their ladies, the men in glittering uniforms, the ladies in ball dresses of every imaginable shade, cut, material and degree of exposure, were waltzing around the room looking very polite and old-world. Others were sitting at the tables, where candles fluttered, completely useless in the electric glare. The noise was something terrific, but, somehow, it was all very well-bred.

The headwaiter was suddenly next to them. He hadn't walked there, at least not noticeably; he appeared to have perfected the old-world manner of the silent servant. Or, of course, Malone thought, the man might be a teleport.

"Ah, Major Petkoff," he said, in a silken voice. "It is so good to see you again. And your friends?"

"Americans," Petkoff said. "They have come to see the glorious Soviet Union."

"Ah," the headwaiter said. "Your usual table, Major?"

Petkoff nodded. The headwaiter led the party through the dancers, snaking slowly along until they reached a large table near the musicians and at the edge of the dance floor. Her Majesty automatically took the seat nearest the musicians, which she imagined to be the head of the table. Lou sat at her left hand, and Malone at her right, his back against a wall. Petkoff took the foot of the table, called a waiter over, and ordered for the party. He did a massive job of it, with two waiters, at last, taking down what seemed to be his entire memoirs, plus the list of all soldiers in the Red Army below the rank of Grand Exalted Elk, or whatever it might have been. Malone had no idea what the major was ordering, except that it sounded extensive and very, very Russian.

Finally the waiter went on his way. Major Petkoff turned to Malone and smiled. "Naturally," he said, "we will begin with vodka, *nyet?*"

Malone considered saying *nyet,* but he didn't feel that this was the time or the place. Besides, he told himself grimly, it would be a sad day when a Petkoff could drink a Malone under the table. His proudest heritage from his father was an immense capacity, he told himself. Now was his chance to test it.

"And, naturally, a little caviar to go with it," Petkoff added.

"Certainly," Malone said, as if caviar were the most common thing in the world in his usual Washington saloons.

It wasn't long before the waiter reappeared, bringing four glasses and three bottles of vodka chilled in an ice-bucket, like a bouquet of champagne. Petkoff bowed him out after one bottle had been opened, set the glasses up and began to pour.

"Oh, goodness," Her Majesty started to say.

"None for me, thanks," Lou chimed in.

"Oh, yes," Her Majesty said. "I don't think I'll have any either. An old lady has to be very careful of her system, you know."

"You do not look like an old lady," Petkoff said gallantly. "Middle-aged, perhaps, to be cruel. But certainly not old. Not over ... oh, perhaps forty."

Her Majesty smiled politely at him. Malone began to wonder if it had been gallantry, after all. From what he'd seen of the Russian women, it was likely, after all, that Petkoff really thought Her Majesty wasn't much over forty at that.

"You're very flattering, Major," Her Majesty said. "But I assure you that I'm a good deal older than I look."

Malone tried to tell himself that no one else had noticed the stifled gulp that had followed that remark. It had been his own stifled gulp. And his face, he felt sure, had aged one hundred and twelve years within a second or so. He waited for Her Majesty to tell Major Petkoff just how old she really was...

But she said nothing else. After a second she turned and smiled at Malone.

"Thanks," he said.

"Oh, you're quite welcome," she said.

Petkoff frowned at both of them, shrugged, and readied the bottle. "Well, then," he said. "It seems as if the drinking will be done by men—and that is right. Vodka is the drink for men."

He had filled his own glass full of the cold, clear liquid. Now he filled Malone's. He stood, glass in hand. Malone also climbed to his feet.

"To the continued friendship of our two countries!" Petkoff said. He raised his glass for a second, then downed the contents. Malone followed suit. The vodka burned its merry way into his stomach. They sat.

A waiter arrived with a large platter. "Ah," Petkoff said, turning. "Try some of this caviar, Mr. Malone. You will find it the finest in the world."

Malone, somehow, had never managed to develop a taste for caviar. He was willing to admit, if pressed, that this made him an uncultured slob, but caviar always made him think of the joke about the country bumpkin who thought it was marvelous that you could soften up buckshot just by soaking it in fish oil.

Now, though, he felt he had to be polite, and he tried some of the stuff. All things considered, it wasn't quite as bad as he'd thought it was going to be. And it did make a pretty good chaser for the vodka.

Her Majesty also helped herself to some caviar. "My goodness," she said. "This reminds me of the old days."

Malone waited, once again, with bated breath. But, though Her Majesty may have been crazy, she wasn't stupid. She said nothing more.

Petkoff, meanwhile, refilled the glasses and looked expectantly at Malone. This time it was his turn to propose the toast. He thought for a second, then stood up and raised his glass.

"To the most beautiful woman in all the world," he said, feeling just a little like a character in *War and Peace*. "Luba Vasilovna Garbitsch."

"Ah," Petkoff said, smiling approvingly. Malone executed a little bow in Lou's direction and followed Petkoff in downing the drink. Two more glasses of vodka wended their tortuous ways into the interior.

"Tell me, colleague," Petkoff said as be spooned up some more caviar, "how are things in the United States?"

Malone shot a glance at Her Majesty, but she was concentrating on something else, and her eyes seemed far away. "Oh, all right," he said at last.

"Of course, you must say so," Petkoff murmured. "But, as one colleague to another, tell me: how much longer do you think it will be before the proletarian uprising in your country?"

There were a lot of answers to that, Malone told himself. But he chose one without too much difficulty. "Well, that's hard to judge," he said. "I'd hate to make any prediction. I don't have enough information."

"Not enough information?" Petkoff said. "I don't understand."

Malone shrugged. "Since our proletariat," he said, "have shown no sign of wanting any rebellion at all, how can I predict when they're going to rebel?"

Petkoff gave him an unbelieving smile. "Well," he said. "We must have patience, eh, colleague?"

"I guess so," Malone said, watching Petkoff pour more vodka.

By the time the meal came, Malone was feeling a warm glow in his interior, but no real fogginess. The dance floor had been cleared by this time, and a group of six costumed professionals glided out and took places. The musicians broke out into a thunderous and bumpy piece, and the dancers began some sort of Slavic folk dance that looked like a combination of a *kazotska* and a shivaree. Malone watched them with interest. They looked like good dancers, but they seemed to be plagued with clumsiness; they were always crashing into one another. On the other hand, Malone thought, maybe it was part of the dance. It was hard to tell.

The dinner was as extensive as anything Malone had ever dreamed of: *borshcht*, beef Stroganoff, smoked fish, vegetables in gigantic tureens, ices and cheeses and fruits. And always, between the courses, during the courses and at every available moment, there was vodka.

The drinking didn't bother him too much. But the food was too much. Unbelieving, he watched Petkoff polish off a large red apple, a pear and a small wedge of white, creamy-looking cheese at the end of the towering meal. Her Majesty was staring, too, in a very polite manner. Lou simply looked glassy-eyed and overstuffed. Malone felt a good deal of sympathy for her.

Petkoff finished the wedge of cheese and ripped off a belch of incredible magnitude and splendor. Malone felt he should applaud, but managed to restrain himself. Her Majesty looked startled for a second, and then regained her composure. Only Lou seemed to take the event as a matter of course, which set Malone to wondering about her home-life. Somehow he couldn't picture her wistful little father ever producing a sound of such awesome magnitude.

"My dear colleague," Petkoff was saying. Malone turned to him and tried to look interested. "There is one thing I have wondered for many years."

"Really?" Malone said politely.

"That is right," Petkoff said. "For years, there has never been a change of name in your organization of secret police."

"We're not secret police," Malone said.

Petkoff gave a massive shrug. "Naturally," he said, "one must say this. But surely, one tires of being called FBI all the time."

"One does?" Malone said. "I don't know. It gives a person a sort of sense of security."

"Ah," Petkoff said. "But take us, for instance. We pride ourselves on our ability to camouflage ourselves. GPU, and then OGPU—which were, I understand, subject for many capitalist jokes."

Malone tried to look as if he couldn't imagine such a thing. "I suppose they might have been," he said.

"Then we were NKVD," Petkoff said, "and now MVD. And I understand, quite between us, Mr. Malone, that there is talk of further change."

There was a sudden burst of applause. Malone wondered what for, looked at the dance floor and realized that the six Slavic dancers were taking bows. As he watched, one of them slipped and nearly fell. The musicians obliged with a final series of chords and the dancers trotted away. A waltz began, and couples from the tables began crowding the floor.

"How can you manage the proletariat," Petkoff asked, "if you do not keep them confused?"

"We don't, exactly," Malone said. "They more or less manage us."

"Ha," Petkoff said, dismissing this with a wave of his hand. "Propaganda." And then he, too, turned to watch the dancers. The waltz was finishing, and a fox-trot had begun. "With your permission, Mr. Malone," he said, rising, "I should like to ask so-lovely Miss Garbitsch to dance with me."

Malone glanced at the girl. She gave him a quick smile, with just a hint of nervousness or strain in it, and turned to Petkoff. "I'd be delighted, Major," she said. Malone shut his own mouth. As the girl rose, he got to his feet and gave the couple a small, Victorian bow. Petkoff and Lou walked to the floor, and Malone, sitting down again, watched enviously as he took her in his arms and began to guide her expertly across the floor in time to the music.

Malone sighed. Some men, he told himself, had all the luck. But, of course, Lou had to be polite, too. She didn't really like Petkoff, he told himself; she was just being diplomatic. And he had made some progress with her on the plane, he thought.

He looked over at Her Majesty, but the Queen was staring abstractedly at a crystal chandelier. Malone sighed again, took a little caviar and washed it down with vodka. The vodka felt nice and warm, he thought vaguely. Vodka was good. It was too bad that the people who made such good vodka had to be enemies. But that was the way things were, he told himself philosophically.

Terrible. That's how things were.

The fox-trot went to its conclusion. Malone saw Petkoff, chatting animatedly with Lou, lead her off to a small bar at the opposite side of the room. "Some people," he muttered, "have too much luck. Or too much diplomacy."

Her Majesty was tugging at his arm. That, Malone thought, was going to be more bad news.

It was.

"Sir Kenneth," she said softly, "do you realize that this place is full of MVD men? Of course you don't; I haven't told you yet."

Malone opened his mouth, shut it again, and thought in a hurry. If the place were full of MVD men, that meant they probably had it bugged. And that meant several things, all of them unpleasant. Her Majesty shouldn't have said anything—she shouldn't have shown any nervousness or anxiety in the first place, she shouldn't have known there were so many MVD men in the second place—because there was no way for her to know, except through her telepathy, a little secret Malone did not want the Russians to find out about. And she should definitely, most definitely, not have called him "Sir Kenneth."

"Oh," Her Majesty said. "I am sorry, Sir—er—Mr. Malone. You're quite right, you know."

"Sure," Malone said. "Well. My goodness." He thought of something to say, and said it at once. "Of course there are MVD men here. This is just the place for good old MVD men to come when they go off duty. A nice, relaxing place full of fun and dancing and food and vodka..." And he was thinking, at the same time: *Are they doing anything odd?*

"Russian, you know," Her Majesty said, almost conversationally, "is an extremely difficult language. It takes a great deal of practice to learn to think in it really fluently."

"Yes, I should think it would," Malone said absently. *You mean you haven't been able to pick up what these people are thinking?*

"Oh, one can get the main outlines," Her Majesty went on, "but a really full knowledge is nearly impossible. Though, of course, it isn't quite as bad as all that. A man who speaks both languages, like our dear Major Petkoff, for instance—so charming, so full of *joie de vivre*—could be an invaluable assistant to anyone interested in learning exactly how Russians really think." She smiled nervously. Her face was suddenly set and strained. "I find that—"

She stopped then, very suddenly. Her eyes widened, and her right hand reached out to grasp Malone's arm more strongly than he had thought she ever could. "Sir Kenneth!" Her voice, all restraint gone, was a hissing whisper. Malone started to say something, but Her Majesty went on, her eyes wide. "Do something quickly!" she said.

"What?" Malone said.

"They've put something in Lou's drink!" Her Majesty hissed.

Malone was on his feet before she'd finished, and he took a step across the room.

"She's already swallowed it!" the Queen said. "Do something! Quickly!"

The dancers on the floor were no concern of his, Malone told himself grimly. He didn't decide to move; he was on his way before any thought filtered through into his mind. Officers and their ladies looked after him with shocked stupor as he plowed his way across the dance floor, using legs, elbows, shoulders and anything else that allowed him free passage. Sometimes the dancers managed to get out of his way. Sometimes they didn't. It was all the same to Kenneth J. Malone.

Her Majesty followed in his wake, silent and stricken, scurrying after him like a small destroyer following a battleship, or like a ball-carrying grandmother following up her interference.

Malone caught sight of Lou, standing at the bar. In that second, she seemed to realize for the first time that something was wrong. She pushed herself violently away from the bar, and looked frantically around, her mouth opening to call. Petkoff was a blur next to her; Malone didn't look at him clearly. Lou took a step...

And two men with broken, lumpy faces came through a door somewhere in the rear of the restaurant, closer to her than Malone. Petkoff suddenly swam into sight; he was standing very still and looking entirely baffled.

Malone pushed through a pair of dancers, ignored their glares and the man's hissed insult, which he didn't understand anyhow, and found his view suddenly blocked by a large expanse of dark grey.

It was somebody's chest, in a uniform. Malone shifted his gaze half an inch and saw a row of gold buttons. He looked upward.

There, towering above him, was a face. It stared down, looking heavy and cruel and stupid. Malone, his legs still carrying him forward, bounced off the chest and staggered back a step or two. He heard a hissed curse behind him, and realized without thinking about it that he had managed to collide with the same pair of dancers again. He didn't look around to see them. Instead, he looked ahead, at the giant who blocked his path.

The man was about six feet six inches tall, a great Mongol who weighed about a sixth of a ton. But he didn't look fat; he looked strong instead, and enormously massive. Malone sidestepped, and the Mongol moved slightly to block him. To one side, Malone saw Her Majesty scurrying by. The Mongol was apparently more interested in Malone than in trying to stop sweet little old ladies. Malone saw Her Majesty heading for the bar, and forgot about her for the second.

The Mongol shifted again to block Malone's forward progress.

"What seems to be such great hurry, *Tovarishch?*" he said in a voice that sounded like an earthquake warning. "Have you no culture? Why you run across floor in such impolite manner?"

The man might have been blocking his way because of Lou, or might simply want to teach an uncultured *Amerikanski* a lesson. Malone couldn't tell which, and it didn't seem to matter. He whirled and reached for a glass of vodka standing momentarily unattended on a nearby table.

He tossed the vodka at the giant's eyes, and scooted around the mountain of flesh before it erupted with a volcanic succession of Russian curses that shook the room with their volume and sincerity.

But Lou and Her Majesty were nowhere in sight. Major Petkoff was staring, and Malone followed his line of sight.

A door in the rear of the restaurant was just closing. Behind it Malone saw Her Majesty and Lou, disappearing from sight.

Malone knocked over a waiter and headed for Petkoff. "What's going on here?" he bellowed over the crash of dishes and the rising wave of Russian profanity.

Petkoff shrugged magnificently. "I have no ideas, colleague," he said. "I have no ideas."

"But she—"

"Miss Garbitsch was taken suddenly ill," Petkoff said.

"Damn sudden," Malone growled.

"Her friend, Miss Thompson, has taken her to the ladies' room," Petkoff said. He gestured, narrowly missing a broken, lumpy face Malone had seen before.

"You are under arrest," the face said. Its partner peered over Petkoff's shoulder.

"I?" Petkoff said.

"Not you," the face said. "Him." He started for Malone and Petkoff threw out both arms.

"Hold!" he said. "My orders are to see that this man is not molested."

The guests had suddenly and silently melted away. Malone backed off a step, looking for something to stage a fight with.

"On the other hand, Comrade," one of the lumpy-faced men said, "we have orders also."

"My orders—" Petkoff began.

"Your orders do not exist," the other lumpy man said. "We are to arrest this man. Our orders say so."

"You are fools," Petkoff said. He spread his arms wider, blocking both of them. Malone edged back against the bar, feeling behind him for a bottle or maybe a bungstarter. Instead, his hand touched a sleeve.

A voice behind him bellowed: "Cease!"

The two lumpy-faced men goggled. Petkoff did not move.

Malone turned, and saw a tall, thin civilian with dark glasses. "Cease," the civilian repeated. "It is the girl we are to arrest! The girl!"

"This is not a girl," one of the lumpy men said. "Sir. We are to arrest this man. Our orders say distinctly—"

"Never mind your orders!" Petkoff said. "Go and reduce your orders to shreds and stuff them up your nostrils and die of suffocation! My orders say—"

"The girl!" the civilian said. "Where is the girl?"

Malone darted forward. Petkoff caught him neatly with one arm as he went by. "Until we decide what to do," the MVD man said, "you stay here." Malone bucked against him, but could get nowhere. "Meanwhile," Petkoff said, "I am for letting you go."

"I appreciate it," Malone said through his teeth. "How about proving it?"

"If you let him go," a lumpy man said, "you will answer to our group head."

Petkoff tightened his hold protectively. Meanwhile, the civilian was climbing up into a stratospheric rage.

"You are dolts, imbeciles, worms without brains and walking bellies filled with carrion!" he said magnificently. "I have orders which I am sworn to carry out!"

"You are not alone," Petkoff said.

Malone took another try at a getaway, and failed.

"We take precedence," a lumpy man said. "We can talk later. Arrest comes first."

"But who?" the civilian snapped. "I insist—"

"There shall be no arrest!" Petkoff screamed. "No one is to be arrested at all!"

"I swear by the bones of Stalin that my orders state—" the tall man began.

"The bones of Stalin are with us!" a lumpy man said. "Go and die in a kennel filled with fleas and old newspaper! Go and freeze to the likeness of an obscene statue of a bourgeois deity! Go and hang by the ears from a monument four thousand feet high in the center of the great desert!"

Inspired, the other lumpy man screamed "Charge!" and came for Petkoff and the civilian. Petkoff whirled, letting go of Malone in order to beat back this wave of maddened attackers, and Malone took the advantage. He ducked free under Petkoff's left arm and started around the gesticulating, screaming, fighting group for the door at the back of the restaurant. He took exactly four steps.

Then he stopped. The Mongol, his eyes red with a combination of vodka and bull-roaring rage, was charging toward him, his hands outflung and his fingers grasping at the air. "Warmonger!" he was shouting. "Capitalist slave-owner! Leprous and ancient cannibal without culture! You have begun a war you can not finish!"

"Ha!" Malone said, feeling inadequate to the occasion. As the Mongol charged, he felt a wave of intense pragmatism come over him. He reached back toward the bar, grabbed a bottle of vodka and tossed several glassfuls into the giant's face. The Mongol, deluged and screaming, clawed wildly at his eyes and spun round several times, cursing Malone and all his kin for the next twenty-seven generations, and grabbing thin air in his attempt to reach the *Amerikanski*.

All of the customers appeared to have discovered urgent engagements elsewhere. There was little for the Mongol to collide with except empty tables and chairs. But he did manage to swipe one of the lumpy-faced men on the side of the head with one flail of his arms. The lumpy-faced man said "Yoop!" and went staggering away into Petkoff, who spun him around and threw him away in the general direction of the bandstand. The diversion provided Malone with just enough time to start moving again.

Four uniformed men were making their way toward the ladies' room from the opposite side of the restaurant.

They were carrying a stretcher, which seemed pitifully inadequate for the carnage Malone had just left.

He blocked their path. "Where are you going?" he said.

"You are American?" one of them said. "I speak English good, no?"

Behind him, Malone heard a yowl and a crunch, as of a body striking wood. It sounded as if somebody had fetched up against the bar. "You speak English fine," he said, feeling wildly out of place. "Have you been taking lessons?"

"Me?" the man said. "It is no time for talk. We got to get lady for hospital."

"Lady?" Malone said. "For hospital?"

"Miss Garbitsch her name is," the stretcher-man said, trying to get past Malone. The FBI agent shifted slightly, blocking the path. "We wait outside one revolution—"

"One what?"

"When hands revolve once," the man said. "One hour. Now we get call so we take her to hospital."

It sounded suspicious to Malone. He heard more yells behind him, and they sounded a little closer. The sound of running men came to his ears. "Well," he said happily, "goodbye all."

The stretcher-bearer said, "Vot?" Malone shoved him backward into the approaching mob, grabbed the stretcher away from the other three men, who were acting a little dazed, and swung it in a wide arc. He caught an MVD man in the stomach, and the man doubled up with a weird whistling groan, turned slightly in agony, and hit another MVD man with his bowed head. The second man fell; Malone heard more crashes and screaming, but he didn't find out any details. Instead, he threw the stretcher at the milling mob and turned, already in motion, racing for the ladies' room.

He had no notion of what he was going to do when he got there, or what he was going to find. Her Majesty and Lou were in there, all right, but how were they going to get out without being arrested, clubbed, disemboweled or taken to a Russian hospital for God alone knew what novel purposes?

His mind was still a little foggy from the vast amounts of vodka he had poured down, and he wasn't in the least sure that teleportation would even work. He tried to figure out whether Her Majesty had already carried Lou off that way—but he doubted it. Lou was quite a burden for the old woman. And besides, he wasn't at all sure whether it was possible to teleport a human being. A lump of inanimate matter is one thing; an intelligent woman with a mind of her own is definitely something else.

It seemed to take forever for him to reach the door, and he was panting heavily when he reached for it. Suddenly, another hand shot in front of his, turning the doorknob. Malone looked up.

It was impossible to figure out where she had come from, or what she thought she was doing, but a bulging, slightly intoxicated Russian matron with bluish hair piled high on her head, a rusty orange dress and altogether too many jewels scattered here and there about her ample person, stood regarding him with a mixture of scorn, surprise and shock.

Malone crowded her aside without a thought and jerked the door open. Behind her he could see the melee still continuing, though it looked by now as if the Russians weren't very sure who they were supposed to be fighting. The Mongol's great head rose for a second above the storm, shouting something unintelligible, and dropped again into the crowd.

Malone focused on the matron, who was standing with her mouth open staring at him.

"Madam," he said with stern dignity, "wait your turn!"

He ducked inside and slammed the door behind him. There was a small knob to bolt the door with, and he used it. But it wasn't going to hold long, he knew. If the mob outside ever got straightened out, the door would go down like a piece of cardboard, bolt or no bolt. Undoubtedly the gigantic Mongol could do the job with one hand tied behind his back.

Malone turned around and put his own back to the door. Women were looking up and making up their minds whether or not to scream. Time stood absolutely still, and nobody seemed to be moving—not even the two directly before him: a frightened-looking little old lady, who was trying to hold up a semiconscious redhead.

And, somewhere behind him, he knew, was a howling mob of thoroughly maddened Russians.

8

The door rattled against Malone's back as a hand twisted the knob and shook it. He braced himself for the next assault, and it came: the shudder of a heavy body slamming up against it. Miraculously, the door held, at least for the moment. But the roars outside were growing louder and louder as the second team came up.

Where was the Mongol? he wondered. But there was no time for idle contemplation. The scene inside the room demanded his immediate attention.

He was in the anteroom, a gilded and decorated parlor filled with overstuffed chairs and couches. There was a door at the far side of the room, and a woman suddenly came out of it holding a pocketbook in one hand and a large powder-puff in the other. She saw Malone and reacted instantly.

Her scream seemed to be a signal. The two other women sitting on couches screamed, too, and jumped up with their hands to their faces. Malone shouted something unintelligible but very loud at them and brandished a fist menacingly. They shrieked again and ran for the interior room.

Malone heard the roaring outside, and pressed his back tighter against the door. Then, suddenly, he broke away from it and ran over to Her Majesty and Lou. He looked down. Lou was apparently completely unconscious by this time, and there was a peaceful look on her face. The Queen looked down at her, then up at Malone.

"I'm sorry, Sir Kenneth," she said, "but we really haven't time for romantic thoughts just now."

Malone passed a hand over his brow. "We haven't got time for anything," he said. "You can see what's going on outside."

"My goodness," Her Majesty said. "Oh, yes. My goodness, yes."

"Okay," Malone said. "We've got to teleport out, if we can—and if we can take Lou with us."

"I don't know, Sir Kenneth," the Queen said.

"We've got to try," Malone said grimly, looking down. There was a crash as something hit the door. It shuddered, creaked, and held. Malone took a breath. Lou was too beautiful to leave behind, no matter what.

"I'll mesh my mind with yours," Her Majesty said, "so we'll be synchronized."

"Right," Malone said. "The plane. Let's go."

There was another crash, but he hardly heard it. He closed his eyes and tried to visualize the interior of the plane that was waiting for them at the airfield. He wasn't sure he could do it; the vodka might have clouded his mental processes just enough to make teleporting impossible. He concentrated. The crash came again, and a shout. He almost had it ... he almost had it...

The last sound he heard was the splintering of the door, and a great shout that was cut off in the middle.

Malone opened his eyes.

"We made it," he said softly. "And I wonder what the MVD is going to think."

Her Majesty took a deep breath. "My goodness," she said. "That *was* exciting, wasn't it?"

"Not half as exciting as it's going to be if we don't hurry now," Malone said. "If you know what I mean."

"I do," Her Majesty said.

"That's good," Malone said at random. "I don't." He helped the Queen ease the unconscious body of Luba Garbitsch into one of the padded seats, and Malone pushed a switch. The seat gave a tiny squeak of protest, and then folded back into a flat bedlike arrangement. Lou was arranged on this comfortable surface, and Malone took a deep breath. "Take care of her for a minute, Your Majesty," he said.

"Of course," the Queen said.

Malone nodded. "I'm going to see who's up front," he said. He walked through the corridors of the plane and rapped authoritatively on the door of the pilot's cabin. A second passed, and he raised his hand to knock again.

It never reached the door, which opened very suddenly. Malone found himself facing a small black hole.

It was the muzzle and the bore of the barrel of an M-2 .45 revolver, and it was pointing somewhere in the space between Malone's eyes. Behind the gun was a hard-eyed air force colonel with a grim expression.

"You know," Malone said pleasantly, "they're good guns, but they really can't compare to the .44 Magnum."

The pilot blinked, and his gun wavered just a little. "What?" he said.

"Well," Malone said, "if you'd only join the FBI, like me, you'd have a .44 Magnum, and you could compare the guns."

The pilot blinked again. "You're—"

"Malone," Malone said. "Kenneth J. Malone, FBI. My friends call me Snookums, but don't try it. Why not let's put the gun away and be friends?"

"Oh," the colonel said weakly. "Mr.—sure. I'm sorry, Mr. Malone. Didn't recognize you for a second there."

"Perfectly all right," Malone said. The gun was still pointing at him, and in spite of the fact that he felt pleasantly like Philip Marlowe, or maybe the Saint, he was beginning to get a little nervous. "The gun," he said.

The colonel stared at it for a second, then reholstered it in a hurry. "I am sorry," he said. "But we've been worried about Russians coming aboard. I've got my copilot and navigator outside, guarding the plane, and they were supposed to let me know if anybody came in. When they didn't let me know, and you knocked, I assumed you were Russians. But, of course, you—"

Conversation came to a sudden dead stop.

"About these Russians—" Malone said desperately. But the pilot's eyes got a little glazed. He wasn't listening.

"Now, wait a minute," he said. "Why *didn't* they notify me?"

"Maybe they didn't see me," Malone said. "I mean us."

"But—"

"I'm not very noticeable," Malone said hopefully, trying to look small and undistinguished. "They could just have ... not noticed me. Okay?" He gave the pilot his most friendly smile.

"They'd have noticed you," the pilot said. "If they're still out there. If nothing's happened to them." He leaned forward. "Did you see them, Malone?"

Malone shrugged. "How would I know?" he said.

"How would you—" The pilot seemed at a loss for words. Malone waited patiently, trying to look as if everything were completely and perfectly normal. "Mr. Malone," the pilot said at last, "how *did* you get aboard this aircraft?"

He didn't wait for an answer, and Malone was grateful for that. Instead, he stepped over to a viewport and looked out. On the field, two air force officers were making lonely rounds about the plane. Fifty yards farther away, a squad of Russian guards also patrolled the brightly-lit area. There was nothing else in sight.

"There isn't any way you could have done it," the pilot said without turning.

"That's the FBI for you," Malone said. "We've got our little trade secrets, you know." Somehow, the pilot's back looked unconvinced. "Disguise," Malone added. "We're masters of disguise."

The pilot turned very slowly. "Now what the hell would you disguise yourself as?" he said. "A Piper Cub?"

"It's a military secret," Malone said hurriedly.

The pilot didn't say anything for what seemed a long time. "A military secret?" he asked at last, in a hushed voice. "And you can't tell me? You're a civilian, and I'm a colonel in the United States Air Force, and you can't tell me a military secret?"

Malone didn't hesitate a second. "Well, Colonel," he said cheerfully, "that's the way things are."

The pilot threw up his hands. "It's none of my business," he said loudly. "I'm not even going to think about it. Because if I do, you'll have a mad pilot on your hands, and you wouldn't like that, would you?"

"I would hate it," Malone said sincerely, "like hell. Particularly since I've got a sick woman aboard."

"Disguised," the pilot offered, "as Lenin, I suppose."

Malone shook his head. "I'm not kidding now," he said. "She is sick, and I want a doctor for her."

"Why didn't you bring one with you?" the pilot said. "Or wasn't the disguise big enough for three?"

"Four," Malone said. "We've got three now; me and Miss Garbitsch and Miss Thompson. Lou—Miss Garbitsch is the one who's sick. But I want a doctor from the American Embassy."

"I think we could all use one," the pilot said judiciously. "But you'd better tell me what's the matter with the girl."

Malone gave him a brief and highly censored version of the melee at Trotkin's, particularly omitting the details of the final escape from the MVD men.

When he had finished, the pilot gave a long, low whistle. "You have been having fun," he said. "Can I go on your next adventure, or is it only for accredited Rover Boys?"

"You have to buy a pin and a special compass that works in the dark," Malone said. "I don't think you'd like it. How about that doctor?"

The pilot nodded wearily. "I'll send my navigator over to the airfield phone," he said. "As a matter of fact, I'll tell him to tell the doctor I'm the one who's sick, so the Russians don't get suspicious. It may even be true."

"Just so he gets here," Malone said. The pilot was flagging his navigator through the viewport as Malone went out, closing the door gently behind him. He went back down the plane corridor to Her Majesty and Lou.

Lou was still lying on the makeshift bed, her eyes closed. She looked more beautiful and defenseless than ever, and Malone wanted to do something big and terrible to all the Russians who had tried to take her away or dope her. With difficulty, he restrained himself. "How is she?" he asked.

"She seems to be all right," the Queen said. "The substance they put in her drink doesn't appear to have had any other effect than putting her to sleep and making her a little sick—and that was a good thing."

"Oh, sure," Malone said. "That was fine."

"Well," Her Majesty said, "she did get rid of quite a bit of the drug in the ladies' room." She smiled, just a trifle primly. "I think she'll be all right," she said.

"There's a doctor on the way, anyhow," Malone said, staring down at her. He tried to think of something he could do for her—fan her, or bring her water, or cool her fevered brow. But she didn't look very fevered. She just looked helpless and beautiful. He felt sorry for all the nasty things he had said to her, and all the nasty things she had said to him. If she got well—and of course she was going to get well, he told himself firmly—things would be different. They'd be sweet and kind to each other all the time, and do nice things for each other.

And she was definitely going to get well. He wouldn't even think about anything else. She was going to be fine again, and very soon. Why, she was hardly hurt at all, he told himself, hardly hurt at all.

"Sir Kenneth," Her Majesty said. "I've been thinking: while we were about it, why didn't we just teleport all the way back home?"

Malone turned. "Because," he said, "we'd have had the devil of a time explaining just how we managed to do it."

"Oh," she said. "I see. Of course."

"This teleportation gimmick is supposed to be a secret," Malone went on. "We don't want to let out anything more about it than we have to. As it is, there's going to be some fierce wondering among the Russians about how we got out of that restaurant."

"Obviously," the Queen said, entirely unexpectedly, "a bourgeois capitalistic trick."

"Obviously," Malone agreed. "But we don't want to start up any more questions than we have to."

"And how about the plane itself?" Her Majesty went on. "Do you think they'll let us take off?"

"I don't know how they can stop us," Malone said.

"You don't?"

"Well, they don't want to cause any incidents now," Malone said. "At least, I don't think they do. If they could have captured us—me, or Lou, or both of us, depending on which side of the argument you want to take— anyhow, if they could have grabbed us on their own home grounds, they'd have had an excuse. Lou got sick, they'd say, and they just took her to the hospital. They wouldn't have to call it an arrest at all."

"Oh, I see," Her Majesty said. "But now we're not on their home grounds."

"Not so long as we stay in this plane, we're not," Malone said. "And we're going to stay here until we take off."

Her Majesty nodded.

"I wish I knew what they thought they were doing, though," Malone mused. "They certainly couldn't have held us for very long, no matter how they worked things."

"I know what was on their minds," Her Majesty said. "At least partly. It was all so confused it was difficult to get anything really detailed or complete."

"There," Malone said fervently, "I agree with you."

"The whole trouble was," the Queen said, "that nobody knew about anybody else."

"I'd gathered something like that," Malone said. "But what exactly was it all about?"

"Well," the Queen said, "Major Petkoff was supposed to tell Lou, in effect, that if she didn't agree to do espionage work for the Soviet Union, things would go hard with her father."

"Nice," Malone said. "Very friendly gentleman."

"Well," the Queen continued, "he was supposed to tell her about that at the bar, when he had her alone. But she got that drugged drink before he could begin to say anything."

"Then who drugged it?" Malone said. "Lou?"

The Queen shrugged. "Someone else," she said. "Major Petkoff didn't know anything about the drugged drink."

"A nice surprise for him, anyhow," Malone said.

"It was a surprise for everybody," the Queen said. "You see, the drugged drink was meant to get her to the hospital, where they'd have her alone for a long time and could really put some pressure on her."

"And then," Malone said, "there were the men who wanted to arrest me. And the ones who wanted to take Lou to jail. And the mad Mongol who just wanted to fight, I guess."

"There were so many different things, all going on at once," the Queen said.

Malone nodded. "There seems to be quite a lot of confusion in the Soviet Union, too," he said. "That does not sound to me like an efficient operation."

"It wasn't, very," the Queen said. "You see, they have Garbitsch now, but they can't do anything to him because they can't get to Lou. And it doesn't do them any good to do anything to her father, unless she knows about it first."

"It sounds," Malone said, "as if the USSR is going along the same confused road as the good old United States."

The Queen nodded agreement. "It's terrible," she said. "I get those same flashes of telepathic static, too."

"You do?" Malone said, leaning forward.

"Just the same," the Queen said. "Whatever is operating in the United States is operating over here, too."

Malone sat down in a seat on the aisle. "Everything," he announced, "is now perfectly lovely. The United States is being confused and mixed up by somebody, and the Somebody looked like a Russian spy. But now Russia is being confused, too."

"Do you think there are some American spies working here?" the Queen said.

"If they're using psionics," Malone said, "as they obviously are—and I don't know about them, Burris doesn't know about them, O'Connor doesn't know about them and nobody else I can find knows about them— then they don't exist. That's flat."

"How about outer space?" the Queen said. "I mean, spies from outer space trying to take over the Earth."

"It's a nice idea," Malone said sourly. "I wish they'd hurry up and do it."

"Then you don't think—"

"I don't know what to think," Malone said. "There's some perfectly simple explanation for all this. And somewhere, in all the running around and looking here and there I've been doing, I've got all the facts I need to come up with that answer."

"Oh, my," the Queen said. "That's wonderful."

"Sure it is," Malone said. "There's only one trouble, as a matter of fact. I don't know what the explanation is, and I don't know which facts are important and which ones aren't."

There was a short silence.

"I wish Tom Boyd were here," Malone said wistfully.

"Really?" the Queen said. "Why?"

"Because," Malone said, "I feel like hearing some really professional cursing."

*   *   *   *   *

Three-quarters of an hour passed, each and every minute draped in some black and gloomy material. Malone sat in his seat, his head supported by both hands, and stared at the back of the seat ahead of him. No great messages were written on it. The Queen, respecting his need for silent contemplation, sat and watched Lou and said nothing at all.

It was always possible, of course, Malone thought, that he would fall asleep and dream of an answer. That kind of thing kept happening to detectives in books. Or else a strange man in a black trenchcoat would sidle up to him and hand him a slip of paper. The words: "Five o'clock, watch out, the red snake, doom," would be written on the paper and these words would provide him with just the clues he needed to solve the whole case. Or else he would go and beat somebody up, and the exercise would stimulate his brain and he would suddenly arrive at the answer in a blinding flash.

Wondering vaguely if a blinding flash were anything like a dungeon, because people kept being in them and never seemed to come out, Malone sighed. Detectives in books were great, wonderful people who never had any doubts or worries. Particularly if they were with the FBI. Only Kenneth J. Malone was different.

Maybe someday, he thought, he would be a real detective, instead of just having a few special gifts that he hadn't really worked for, anyhow. Maybe someday, in the distant future, he would be the equal of Nick Carter.

Right now, though, he had a case to solve. Nick Carter wasn't around to help.

And Kenneth J. Malone, FBI, was getting absolutely nowhere.

Finally, his reverie was broken by the sounds of argument outside the plane door. There were voices speaking both English and Russian, very loudly. Malone went to the door and opened it. A short, round, grey-haired man who looked just a little like an over-tired bear who had forgotten to sleep all winter almost fell into his arms. The man was wearing a grey overcoat that went nicely with his hair, and carrying a small black bag.

Malone said: "Oog," replaced the man on his own feet and looked past him at the group on the landing ramp outside. The navigator was there, arguing earnestly with two men in the uniform of the MVD.

"Damn it," the navigator said, "you can't come in here. Nobody comes in but the doctor. This is United States territory."

The MVD men said something in Russian.

"No," the navigator said. "Definitely no."

One of the MVD men spat something that sounded like an insult.

The navigator shrugged. "I don't understand Russian," he told them. "All I know is one word. No. *Nyet* Definitely, absolutely irrevocably *nyet*."

"Sikin sin Amerikanyets!"

The MVD men turned, as if they'd been a sister act, and went down the steps. The navigator followed them, wiping his forehead and breathing deeply. Malone shut the door.

"Well, well, well," the doctor said, in a burbling sort of voice. "Somehow, we thought it might be you. Anyhow, the ambassador did."

"Really?" Malone said, trying to sound surprised.

"Oh, yes," the doctor assured him. "You have raised something of a stench in and around good old Moscow, you know."

"I'm innocent," Malone said.

The doctor nodded. "Undoubtedly," he said judiciously. "Who isn't? And where, by the way, is the girl?"

"Over there." Malone pointed. News apparently traveled with great speed in Moscow, MVD and censorship notwithstanding. At any rate, he thought, it traveled with great speed to the ears of the Embassy staff.

The doctor lifted Lou's limp wrist to time her pulse, his lips pursed and his eyes focused on a far wall.

"What have you heard?" Malone said.

"The MVD boys are extremely worried," the doctor said. "Extremely." He didn't let go of the wrist, a marvel of which Malone had never grown tired. Doctors always seemed to be able, somehow, to examine a patient and carry on a conversation about totally different things, without even showing the strain. This one was no exception. Malone watched in awe.

"According to the reports we got from them," the doctor said, "you wandered off from *Trotkin's* without your escort."

"Well," Malone said at random, "I didn't think to leave them a farewell note. I hope they don't think I disliked their company."

"Officially," the doctor said, lifting Lou's left eyelid and gazing thoughtfully into the blue iris thus exposed, "they're afraid you're lost, and they were apologetic as all hell about it to the ambassador." The iris appeared to lose its fascination; the doctor dropped the eyelid and fished in his black bag, which he had put on the seat next to Lou.

"And unofficially?" Malone asked.

"Unofficially," the doctor said, "we've got news of a riot at *Trotkin's* tonight, in which you seem to have been involved. Mr. Malone, you must be quite a barroom brawler when you're at home."

"Frankly," Malone said, "I'm a little out of practice. And I hope I never have the chance to get back *into* practice."

The doctor nodded, removing a stethoscope from the bag and applying it to Lou's chest. He waited a second, frowned and then took the plugs out of his ears. "I know just what you mean," he said. "You might be interested to know the first unofficial score of that little match."

"Score?" Malone said.

The doctor nodded again. "Three concussions," he said, "one possible skull fracture, a broken arm, two bitten hands, and a large and varied assortment of dental difficulties and plain hysteria. No dead, however. I really don't understand why not."

"Well," Malone said, "nobody wanted to create an international incident."

"Hmf," the doctor said. "I see. Or I think I do, which is as far as I care to go in the matter. The Russians suspect, by the way, that you've managed to get aboard the plane. They do know, of course, about the girl, and when the pilot called for me they put two and two together. In spite of his story about being sick. What they can't figure out is how you managed to *get* aboard the plane."

"Neither can I," Malone said at random. The doctor gave him a single bright stare.

"Well," he said at last, "I suppose you know your own business best. By the way, my examination accords pretty well with our unofficial information about the girl—that she was given some sort of drug in a drink. Is that what happened?"

Malone nodded. "As far as we know," he said. "She did get rid of a lot of it within a few minutes, though."

"Good," the doctor said. "Very sensible."

"Sense had nothing to do with it," Malone said.

"In any case," the doctor went on doggedly, "there can't be too much left in her system. Her pulse is good, she's breathing easily and there don't seem to be any complications, so I should doubt strongly that there's been much damage done. Besides all which, of course, the Russians would hardly have wanted to hurt her; what they gave her would probably have done little more harm even if she'd ingested it all, and kept it down."

"Good," Malone said sincerely.

"I'll give you some pills," the doctor said, fishing in his bag again, "and you can give them to her when she wakes up."

"Is that all?" Malone said, vaguely disappointed.

The doctor eyed him keenly. "Well," he said, "I could give her an injection, but I'd be a little afraid to. If it had a synergistic action with the drug, she might be worse off than before."

"Oh," Malone said. "By all means. Just the pills."

"I'm glad you agree," the doctor said. "Oh, and about leaving—"

"Yes?" Malone said. "We want to get out of here in a hurry, if we can."

"I think you can," the doctor said. "The ambassador mentioned that he'd try to arrange it with the Russians. I don't know what he'll tell them—but then, that's why he's an ambassador, and I'm a doctor." He straightened up and handed Malone an envelope containing three green capsules. "Give her these if she wakes up with a headache," he said. "If she feels all right, just forget all about them."

"Sure," Malone said. "And thanks, Doctor. Tell the ambassador we'd appreciate it if he got us out of here as soon as possible."

"Certainly," the doctor said. "After all, I might as well take on the job of a diplomatic courier."

Malone nodded. "Well," he said, "goodbye, Mr. Courier."

The doctor went to the door, opened it and turned.

"Absolutely," he said, "Mr. Ives."

9

Lou didn't wake up until the plane was dropping toward the Washington airfield, and when she did awaken it was as if she had merely come out of an especially deep sleep. Malone was standing over her, which was far from a coincidence; he had been waiting and watching virtually every minute since takeoff.

During his brief periods of rest, Her Majesty had taken over, and she was now peacefully asleep at the back of the plane, looking a little more careworn, but just as regal as ever. She looked to Malone as if she had weathered a small revolution against her rule, but had managed to persuade the populace (by passing out cookies to the children, probably) that all was, in the last analysis, for the best in this best of all possible worlds. She looked, he thought, absolutely wonderful.

So did Lou. She blinked her eyes open and moved one hand at her side, and then she came fully awake. "Well," she said. "And a bright hello to you, Sleuth. If it's not being too banal, where am I?"

"It is," Malone said, "but you're in an airplane, coming into Washington. We ought to be there in a few minutes."

Lou shook her head slowly from side to side. "I have never heard any news that sounded better in my entire life," she said. "How long ago did we leave Moscow?"

"Our trip to Beautiful Moskva," Malone said, "ended right after they tried to get you to the hospital, by giving you a drugged drink. Do you remember that?"

"I remember it, all right," she said. "I'm never going to forget that moment."

"How do you feel?" Malone said.

"Fine," Lou said. "And how are *you*?"

"Me?" Malone said. "I'm all right. I've *been* all right. Don't worry about *me.*"

"Well, one never knows," Lou said. "With your cold and all."

"I think that's better," Malone said hastily. "But you're sure you feel fine?"

Lou nodded. "A little tired, maybe, but that's all." She paused. "I remember Miss Thompson taking me to the ladies' room. I got pretty sick. But from there on, I'm not sure what happened."

"I came in," Malone said, "and got you out."

"How brave!" Lou said.

"Not very," Malone said casually. "After all, what could happen to me in a ladies' room?"

"You'd be surprised," Lou murmured. "And you came and got me, and took me to the plane and all. And I—" She hesitated, and for a second she looked very small and wistful. "Do you—do you think they'll do anything to Dad?" she said.

"I don't see why," Malone said confidently. "After all, the only thing he did wrong was to get caught, and that's an occupational risk if you're in the spy business. Lots of people get caught. Happens all the time. Don't worry about it."

"I—all right," she said. "I won't, then."

"Good," Malone said. He fished in his pocket. "I've got some pills here," he said, "in case you have a headache. The doctor said I could give them to you if you had a headache, but otherwise I should just forget about them."

Lou smiled. "I think you'd better just forget about them," she said.

Malone's hand came out of his pocket empty. "I just want to make sure you're okay," he said. "Probably very silly. Of course you're okay."

"Of course I am," she said. "But I don't think you're silly." She smiled again, a very warm smile. Malone took a deep breath and discovered that he hadn't been breathing at all regularly for several minutes. Lou's smile increased a trifle in intensity and he stopped breathing all over again. "All things considered," she said, "I think you're pretty wonderful, Ken."

Malone's voice sounded to him as if it were coming from a great distance. He wondered if the strange feeling in his stomach were the pangs of love, or the descent of the plane. Then he realized that he didn't care. "Well, well," he said airily. "Well, well, well. Frankly, Lou, I'm inclined to agree with you. Though I'm not sure about the qualification."

"Fine thing," she said. "Tell a man he's wonderful and he just nods his head as if he knew it all along."

Malone swallowed hard. "Maybe I did," he said. "And how did you come to this startling conclusion?"

It was Lou who broke the light mood of their speech first. "Look, Ken," she said seriously, "I'm the daughter of an enemy spy. You know that. You're an FBI agent."

"So what?" he said.

"So," she said, "you don't treat me like the daughter of a spy. You treat me just like anybody else."

"I do not," Malone said instantly.

"All right," she said, and shrugged. "But I'm sure none of this is in the FBI manual for daughters of convicted spies."

"Now, you look," Malone said. "Just what do you think this is? The McCarthy era? Any way I treat you, it has nothing to do with your father. He's a spy, and we caught him and we sent him back to Moscow. That's our job. But all this about the sins of the fathers being visited on the heads of the children, even unto the seventh generation— this is just plain silly. You're you; you're not your father. You haven't done anything—why should I treat you as if you have?"

"How do you know I'm not a spy, too?" she said.

"Because," Malone said flatly, "I know."

"Really?" she said softly. "Do you really?"

Malone opened his mouth, shut it and then started again. "Strictly speaking," he said carefully, "I don't know. But we're in the United States now, where a person is considered innocent until proven guilty."

"And that," Lou said, "is all you're going on, I suppose."

"Not all," Malone said.

"I didn't think so," Lou said, still smiling.

"Don't ask me how," Malone said, "but we're pretty sure you knew nothing about your father's activities. Forget it."

Lou looked suddenly slightly disappointed. Malone wondered why. Of course, there was one more reason, and maybe she'd thought of that. "It does make it easier," he said, "that you happen to be a beautiful girl."

She smiled again, and started to say something, but she never got the chance. The landing gear of the aircraft bumped gently against the runway, and the ship rolled slowly in to a stop.

A second passed. From the back of the plane a voice said: "Are we back in Washington, S—Mr. Malone?"

"That's right, Miss Thompson," Malone told the Queen.

"And Miss Garbitsch—"

"I'm fine, Miss Thompson," Luba said. She swung her feet around to the deck.

"Wait a minute," Malone said. "Do you think you ought to get up?"

Lou's smile seemed to reduce him to small, very hot ashes. "Ken," she said, "the doctor said I was fine, so what are you worrying about? I can get up. I'll be all right."

"Oh, okay," he said, and stepped back. Her Majesty had already left the plane. Lou got up, and wavered just a little. Malone held out his arms, and found her in them before he had thought about it.

A long time seemed to pass. Malone wasn't sure whether he was standing still because he wanted to, or because he was absolutely incapable of motion. Lou didn't seem in any hurry to break away, either.

Then she put her arms around his neck.

"Sleuth," she said, "don't you ever follow up a hint?"

"Hint?" Malone said.

"Damn it," Lou said in a soft, sweet voice, "kiss me, Ken."

Malone had no answer to that—at least, no verbal answer.

One didn't seem to be needed.

When he finally came up for air, he said: "Lou..."

"Yes, Ken?"

"Lou, where are you going from here?"

Lou stepped back a pace. "What?" she said.

"I mean, back to New York?" Malone said. "Or someplace else? I mean— well, what are you going to do?"

"Oh," Lou said. "Oh, yes. I'll be going back to New York. After all, Ken, I do have a living to make, such as it is, and Sir Lewis is expecting me."

"I don't know," Malone said, "but it still sounds funny. A girl like you working for—well, for the Psychical Research people. Ghosts and ectoplasm and all that."

Lou stepped back another pace. "Now, wait a minute," she said. "You seemed to need their information, all right."

"But that was—oh, well," Malone said. "Never mind. Maybe I'm silly. It really doesn't matter."

"I guess it doesn't, now," she said. "Except that it does mean I've got to leave for New York almost at once."

"Can you cut out that 'almost'?" Malone said. "Because I've got to be there myself, and right away. If you hurry, we can get the same plane."

"That would be great," she said.

"Okay, then," Malone said. "Don't you worry about a thing, I'll take care of reservations and everything."

"My, my," Lou said. "What it must be like to have all that pull and influence."

"What?" Malone said.

Lou grinned. "Nothing," she said. "Nothing."

"Then it's all settled. I'll take care of the reservations, and we'll go in together," Malone said.

"Fair enough," Lou said, "my fine feathered Fed."

* * * * *

Actually, it took Malone nearly three hours to get everything set in Washington for his New York departure. He had to make a verbal report to Andrew J. Burris first, and that consumed quite a lot of time, since Burris was alternately shocked, horrified, gleeful and confused about the whole trip, and spent most of his time interrupting Malone and crying out for God's vengeance, mercy, justice or understanding.

Then Malone had to dictate a longer report for the written record. This didn't take quite as long, since there were no interruptions, but by the time it was over he felt as if he were going out to become a Carthusian monk. He felt, as he rubbed his raw throat, that it wouldn't be a bad idea at all to take a nice vow of silence for awhile. He could write people little notes, and they would all treat him kindly and gently. He would be pointed out to strangers, and people would try to do him favors.

Unfortunately, he couldn't take the vow at once. During his absence, his desk log showed, several calls had come in, all of which had to be taken care of at once. Some of them dealt with evidence or statements from old cases, some were just nuisances. The most urgent was from Dr. O'Connor at Yucca Flats.

"If you're not too busy," O'Connor said in his icily polite tone, "I would like to have Miss Thompson back as soon as possible." He sounded as if Malone had borrowed his scalpel.

"I'll see what I can do," Malone said carefully.

"There is a new series of tests," O'Connor said, "on which I am now at work; the assistance of Miss Thompson would be invaluable to me at this time."

After he'd hung up, Malone called Her Majesty at her Washington hotel. She was very glad of the chance to return to Yucca Flats, she said. There, Malone knew, she would be able to return to her accustomed dignity as Queen of the Greater English Commonwealth, a district which, in her mind, seemed to include the greater part of the Western world. On her present mission, she was plain Miss Thompson and, though the idea of going about incognito had its charms, it became a little dull after awhile. The adventuring was fine, although a little rougher than she'd thought it would be; the sight of the Queen's Own FBI in action was still a powerful attraction for Her Majesty. But the peace and quiet and dignity of Her Own Royal Palace won out without too much trouble.

"Of course," Malone said, "you'll be on call in case I need you."

"I am always in touch with my subjects," Her Majesty said with dignity, "and most especially with you, Sir Kenneth. I shall so remain."

And then there was a little paperwork to take care of. By the time Malone had finished, he would have been glad to teleport to New York on his own. But on reflection he decided that he would much rather travel with Lou, and hurried down to the airport.

By the time the plane landed at La Guardia, and they'd taken a 'copter to the East Side Terminal and a taxi to the big blue-aluminum-and-glass Ravell Building, Malone had reached a new decision. It would be nothing short of wonderful, he felt, if he could spend the rest of his life traveling around with Luba Garbitsch.

Of course, that name was something of a handicap. It was hardly a romantic one. He wondered, very briefly, whether or not "Luba Malone" were an improvement. But he buried the thought before it got any further. Enough, he told himself firmly, was enough.

"It's been a nice trip," Lou said. She, too, sounded subdued, as if she were thinking about something terribly serious.

"Great," Malone said happily. "A wonderful trip."

"I enjoyed being with you," Lou said.

"Me, too," Malone said. He paid off the taxi-driver and they got out at the corner. Malone went to the newsstand there and picked up a copy of the *Post*.

"That," Lou said over his shoulder, "is one whole hell of a headline."

It filled the entire page, four lines of thick black capitals:

JUDGE   DROPS   UNION   SUIT!

"Well, well," Malone said. "Let's see what this is all about." He flipped to page three. Lou craned her neck over his shoulder and they read the start of the story together.

DISTRICT COURT RULES UNION HAS NO CASE

New York [AP], August 23. Judge James Lefkowitz of the New York Supreme Court ruled today that the International Truckers' Brotherhood had no grounds for their suit against the United Transport Corp. and its officers. The action, a bitterly fought contest, involved a complaint by the Brotherhood that UTC had violated their contract with the Brotherhood by hiring "unqualified drivers" to work for the corporation.

In a statement made immediately after the ruling, Judge Lefkowitz said: "It is obvious that a man with a state-certified chauffeur's license is not an 'unqualified driver.'"

Effects of this ruling are thought to be far-reaching. Comment from the international Truckers' Brotherhood...

There was more to it, a lot more, but Malone didn't feel like reading it. It sounded just as confused as he expected news to sound these days, but it also sounded a little dull. He could feel Lou's breathing against his ear as he read, and he lost interest in the paper almost at once.

"My, my," she said. "And I expected a real expose of a story, after that headline."

"This is an expose," Malone said. "But I'm not sure what of."

"It sounds pretty confused," Lou said.

"Everything seems to, these days," Malone said. "Including any story of what's been happening during the last little while."

"Agreed," Lou said. "Without argument."

"Listen," Malone said suddenly. "Would it help if I went up and told Sir Lewis that there's no mark against your record?"

"Mark?" Lou said. "Against my record?"

"Well," Malone said, "I mean—well, he isn't the sort of man who'd fire somebody, because of—because of something like this?"

"You mean because I know an FBI man?" Lou said.

"I—"

"Never mind," she said. "I know what you mean. And he won't. He'll understand." She came round to face him, and patted his cheek. "Thanks," she said. "Thanks a lot, anyway."

"If there's anything I can do—"

"There won't be," Lou said. "You'll call me, though, about tonight?"

"Sure I will," Malone said. He hoped that the tentative date he'd made with her for that evening wouldn't be broken up because of a sudden onslaught of work. "I'll let you know before five, for sure."

"Fine," Lou said. "I'll wait to hear from you."

She turned to walk away.

"Hey," Malone said. "Wait a minute."

"What?" she said, turning again.

Malone looked judicious. "I think," he said weightily, "that, considering all the fun we've had, and all the adventuring and everything else, the least you could do would be to kiss me goodbye."

"On Fifth Avenue?"

"No," Malone said. He tapped his lips. "Here."

She laughed, bent closer and pecked him on the cheek. Then, before he could say anything else, she was gone.

10

On the way to FBI Headquarters on 69th Street, he read the *Post* a little more carefully. The judge and his union suit weren't the only things that were fouled up, he saw. Things were getting pretty bad all over.

One story dealt with the recent factional fights inside the American Association for the Advancement of Medicine. A new group, the United States Medical-Professional Society, appeared to be forming as a competitor to the AAAM, and Malone wasn't quite so sure, when he thought about it, that this news was as bad as it appeared on the surface. Fights between doctors, of course, were reasonably rare, at least on the high hysterical level the story appeared to pinpoint. But the AAAM had held a monopoly in the medical field for a long time; maybe it was about time some competition showed itself. From what he could find out in the story, the USMPS seemed like a group of fairly sensible people.

But that was one of the few rays of light Malone could discern amid the encircling bloom of the news. The gang wars had reached a new high; the *Post* was now publishing what it called a Daily Scoreboard, which consisted in this particular paper of six deaths, two disappearances and ten hospitalizations. The six deaths were evenly scattered throughout the country: two in New York, one each in Chicago and Detroit, and two more in San Francisco. The disappearances were in Los Angeles and in Miami, and the hospitalizations were pretty much all over.

The unions had been having trouble, too. Traditional forms of controversy appeared to have gone out the window, in favor of startling disclosures, beatings, wild cries of foul and great masses of puzzling evidence. How, for instance, Malone wondered, had the president of Local 7574 of the Fishermen's Fraternal Brotherhood managed to mislay a pile of secret records, showing exactly how the membership was being bilked of dues, on a Boston subway train? But, somehow, he had, and the records were now causing shakeups, denials and trouble among the fishermen.

Of course, the news was not all bad. There were always the comic strips. Pogo was busily staving off an approaching wedding between Albert Alligator and a new character named Tranquil Portly, who appeared to be a brown bear. He was running into some resistance, though, from a wolflike character who planned to abscond with Albert's cigars while Albert was honeymooning. This character, Don Coyote by name, looked like a trouble-maker, and Malone vowed to keep a careful eye on him.

And then there were other headlines:

FUSION POWER SOON COMMERCIALLY AVAILABLE SAYS AEC HEAD

Sees Drastic Cut in Power Rates

UN POLICE CONTINGENT OKAYED: MILLION MEN TO FORM 1ST GROUP Member Countries Pledge $20 Billion in Support Moneys

OFFICIAL STATES: "WE'RE AHEAD AFTER 17 YEARS!"

US Space Program Tops Russian Achievements

ARMED FORCES TO TOUGHEN TRAINING PROGRAM IN 1974

Gen. Foote: "Our aim is to train fighting men, not to run a country club."

GOVERNMENT TO SAVE $1 BILLION ANNUALLY? Senator Hits Duplication of Effort in Government, Vows Immediate Reform

Malone read that one a little more carefully, because it looked, at first sight, like one of the bad-news items. There had been government-spending reforms before, almost all of which had resulted in confusion, panic, loss of essential services—and twice as many men on the payroll, since the government now had to hire useless efficiency experts, accountants and other such supernumerary workers.

But this time, the reform looked as if it might do some good. Of course, he told himself sadly, it was still too early to tell.

The senator involved was Deeks, of Massachusetts, who was also in the news because of a peculiar battle he had had with Senator Furbisher of Vermont. Congress, Malone noted, was still acting up. Furbisher claimed that the moneys appropriated for a new Vermont dam were really being used for the dam. But Deeks had somehow come into possession of several letters written by a cousin of Furbisher's, detailing some of the graft that was going on in the senator's home state. Furbisher was busily denying everything, but his cousin was just as busy confessing all to anybody who would listen. It was building up into an extremely interesting fracas, and, Malone thought, it would have been even funnier than Pogo except that it was happening in the Congress of the United States.

He heaved a sigh, folded up the paper and entered the building that housed the New York contingent of the FBI.

Boyd was waiting in his office when he arrived.

"Well, there, Kenneth," he said. "And how are all our little Slavic brothers?"

"Unreasonable," Malone said, "and highly unpleasant."

"You refer, no doubt," Boyd said, "to the *Meeneestyerstvoh Vnootrenikh Dyehl?*"

"Gesundheit," Malone said kindly.

"The MVD," Boyd said. "I've been studying for days to pull it on you when you got back."

Malone nodded. "Very well, then," he said in a stately, orotund tone. "Say it again."

"Damn it," Boyd said, "I *can't* say it again."

"Cheer up," Malone said. "Maybe some day you'll learn. Meantime, Thomas, did you get the stuff we talked about?"

Boyd nodded. "I think I got enough of it," he said. "Anyhow, there is a definite trend developing. Come on into the private office, and I'll show you."

There, on Boyd's massive desk, were several neat piles of paper.

"It looks like enough," Malone said. "As a matter of fact, it looks like too much. Haven't we been through all this before?"

"Not like this, we haven't," Boyd said. "Information from all over, out of the everywhere, into the here." He picked up a stack of papers and handed them to Malone.

"What's this?" Malone said.

"That," Boyd said, "is a report on the Pacific Merchant Sailors' Brotherhood."

"Goody," Malone said doubtfully.

Boyd came over, pulling at his beard thoughtfully, and took the top few sheets out of Malone's hands. "The report," he said, looking down at the sheets, "includes the checks we made on the office of the president of the Brotherhood, as well as the Los Angeles local and the San Francisco local."

"Only two?" Malone said. "That seems as if you've been lying down on the job."

"They're the top two in membership," Boyd said. "But listen to this: the president and three of his underlings resigned day before yesterday, and not quite in time. The law—by which I mean us, and a good many other people—is hot on their tails. It seems somebody accidentally mixed up a couple of envelopes."

"Sounds like a case for the Post Office," Malone said brightly.

"Not these envelopes," Boyd said. "There was a letter that was supposed to go to the head of the San Francisco local, dealing with a second set of books—not the ones used for tax purposes, but the real McCoy. The letter didn't get to the San Francisco man. Instead, it went to the attorney general of the state of California."

"Lovely," Malone said. "Meanwhile, what was San Francisco doing?"

Boyd smiled. "San Francisco was getting confused," he said. "Like everybody else. The San Francisco man got a copy of an affidavit dealing with merchant-ship tonnage. That was supposed to go to the attorney general."

"Good work," Malone said. "So when the Frisco boys woke up to what was happening—"

"They called the head man, and he put two and two together, resigned and went into hiding. Right now, he's probably living an undercover life as a shoe salesman in Paris, Kentucky."

"And, after all," Malone added, "why not? It's a peaceful life."

"The attorney general, of course, impounded the second set of books," Boyd went on. "A grand jury is hearing charges now."

"You know," Malone said reflectively, "I almost feel sorry for the man. Almost, but not quite."

"I see what you mean," Boyd said. "It is a hell of a thing to happen."

"On the other hand—" Malone leafed through the papers in a hurry, then put them back on Boyd's desk with a sigh of relief. "I've got the main details now," he said. "I can go through the thing more thoroughly later. Anything else?"

"Oh, lots," Boyd said. "And all in the same pattern. The FPM, for instance, literally dropped one in our laps."

"Literally?" Malone said. "What was the Federation of Professional Musicians doing in your lap?"

"Not mine," Boyd said hastily. "Not mine. But it seems that some secretary put a bunch of file folders on the windowsill of their second-floor offices, and they fell off. At the same time, an agent was passing underneath, slipped on a banana peel and sat down on the sidewalk. Bingo, folders in lap."

"Wonderful," Malone said. "The hand of God."

"The hand of something, for sure," Boyd said. "Those folders contain all the ammunition we've ever needed to get after the FPM. Kickbacks, illegal arrangements with nightclubs, the whole works. We're putting it together now, but it looks like a long, long term ahead for our friends from the FPM."

And Boyd went to his desk, picked up a particularly large stack of papers. "This," he said, "is really hot stuff."

"What do you call the others?" Malone said. "Crime on ice?"

"The new show at the Winter Garden," Boyd said blithely. "Don't miss it if you can."

"Sure," Malone said. "So what's so hot?"

Boyd smiled. "The police departments of seven major cities," he said. "They're all under attack either by the local prosecuting attorney or the state's attorney general. It seems there's a little graft and corruption going on."

"This," Malone said, "is not news."

"It is to the people concerned," Boyd said. "Four police chiefs have resigned, along with great handfuls of inspectors, captains and lieutenants. It's making a lovely winging all over the country, Ken."

"I'll bet," Malone said.

"And I checked back on every one," Boyd went on. "Your hunch was absolutely right, Ken. The prosecuting attorneys and the attorneys general are all new men—all the ones involved in this stuff. Each one replaced a previous incumbent in a recent election. In two cases, the governor was new, too—elected last year."

"That figures," Malone said. "What about the rest?"

Boyd's grandiose wave of a hand took in all the papers on the desk. "It's all the same," he said. "They all follow a pattern, Ken, *the* pattern. The one you were looking for."

Malone blinked. "I'll be damned," he said. "I'll be doubly damned."

"And how about the Russians?" Boyd said.

"You mean the *Meeneestyerstvoh Vnootrenikh Dyehl?*" Malone said.

"Now," Boyd said, "I'll be damned. And after I practiced for days."

"Ah," Malone said. "But I was *there.* The Russians are about as mixed up as a group of Transylvanian villagers with two vampires to track down and not enough flambeaux for all. Here, for instance, is just one example: the conflicting sets of orders that were given about me and Her Majesty and L—Miss Garbitsch."

Briefly, he outlined what had happened.

"Sounds like fun," Boyd said.

"They were so busy arguing with each other," Malone finished, "that I have a feeling we hardly needed the teleportation to escape. It would just have taken longer, that's all." He paused. "By the way, Tom, about the stakeout—"

"Luba Garbitsch is being protected as if she were Fort Knox," Boyd said. "If any Soviet agent tries to approach her with a threat of any kind, we'll have him nabbed before he can say Ivan Robinovitch."

"Or," Malone suggested, "*Meeneestyerstvoh*—"

"If we waited for that one," Boyd said, "we might have to wait all day." He paused. "But who's doing it?" he went on. "That's still the question. Martians? Venerians? Or is that last one Venusians?"

"Aphrodisiacs," Malone suggested diplomatically.

"Thank you, no," Boyd said politely. "I never indulge while on duty."

"Thomas," Malone said, "you are a Rover Boy First-Class."

"Good," Boyd said. "But, meanwhile, who is doing all this? Would you prefer Evil Beings from the Planet Ploor?"

"I would not," Malone said firmly.

"But I have a strange feeling," Boyd said, "that, in spite of all the evidence to the contrary, you do not hold with the Interplanetary Alien Theory."

"Frankly," Malone said, "I'm not sure of anything. Not really. But I do want to know why, if it's interplanetary aliens doing this stuff, they're picking such a strange way of going about it."

"Strange?" Boyd said. "What's strange about it? You wouldn't expect Things from Ploor to come right out and *tell* us what they want, would you? It's against custom. It may even be against the law."

"Well, maybe," Malone said. "But it is pretty strange. The difference between what's happening in Russia and what's happening here—"

"What difference?" Boyd said. "Everybody's confused. Here, and over there. It all looks the same to me."

"Well, it isn't," Malone said. "Take a look at the paper, for instance." He tossed the *Post* at Boyd, who caught it with a spasmodic clutching motion and reassembled it slowly.

"Why throw things?" Boyd said. "You sore or something?"

"I guess I am," Malone said. "But not at you. It's— somebody or something. Person or persons unknown."

"Or Ploorians," Boyd said.

"Whatever," Malone said. "But take a look at the paper and see if you see what I see." He paused. "Does that mean anything?" he said.

"Probably," Boyd said. "We'll figure it out later." He leafed through the newspaper slowly, pulling thoughtfully at his beard from time to time. Malone watched him in breathless silence.

"See it?" he said at last.

Boyd looked up and, very slowly, nodded. "You're right, Ken," he said in a quiet voice. "You're absolutely right. It's as plain as the nose on your face."

"And that," Malone said, "sounds like an insult. It's much plainer than that. Suppose you tell me."

Boyd considered. "Over here," he said at last, "there are a lot of confused jerks and idiots. Right?"

"Correct," Malone said.

"And in Russia," Boyd went on, "there's a lot of confusion. Right?"

"Sure," Boyd said. "It's perfectly clear. I wonder why I didn't see it before."

"That's it!" Malone cried. "That's the difference!"

"Sure," Boyd said. "It's perfectly clear. I wonder why I didn't see it before."

"Because you weren't looking for it," Malone said. "Because nobody was. But there's one more check I want to make. There's one area I'm not sure of, simply because I don't have enough to go on."

"What area is that?" Boyd said. "It seems to me we did a pretty good job—"

"The Mafia," Malone said. "We know they're having trouble, but—"

"But we don't know what kind of trouble," Boyd finished. "Right you are."

Malone nodded. "I want to talk to Manelli," he said. "Can we set it up?"

"I don't see why not," Boyd said. "The A-in-C can give us the latest on him. You want me with you?"

"No," Malone said after some thought. "No. You go and see Mike Sand, heading up the International Truckers' Union. We know he's tied up with the Syndicate, and maybe you can get some information from him. You know what to dig for?"

"I do now," Boyd said. He reached for the intercom phone.

* * * * *

Cesare Antonio Manelli was a second-generation Prohibition mobster, whose history can most easily be described by reference to the various affairs of State which coincided with his development. Thus:

When Cesare was a small toddler of uncertain gait and chubby visage, the Twenty-First Amendment to the Constitution of the United States canceled out not only the Eighteenth Amendment, but the thriving enterprises conducted by Manelli, Sr., and many of his friends.

When Cesare was a young schoolboy, poring over the multiplication tables, his father and his father's friends were busy dividing. They were dividing, to put it more fully, husbands from families as a means of requesting ransom, and money from banks as a means of getting the same cash without use of the middleman, or victim. This was the period of the Great Readjustment, and the frenzied search among gangland's higher echelons for a substitute for bootlegging.

And when Cesare was an innocent high-schooler, sporting a Paleolithic switchblade knife and black leather jacket, his father and his father's friends had reached a new plateau. They consolidated into a Syndicate, and began to concentrate on gambling and the whole, complex, profitable network of unions.

And then World War II had come along, and it was time for Cesare to do his part. Bidding a fond farewell to his father and such of his father's friends as had survived the disagreements of Prohibition, the painful legal processes of the early Thirties and the even more painful consolidations of the years immediately before the war, young Cesare went off to foreign lands, where he distinguished himself by creating and running the largest single black-market ring in all of Southern Europe.

Cesare had followed in his father's footsteps. And, before his sudden death during a disagreement in Miami, Giacomo "Jack the Ripper" Manelli was proud of his son.

"Geez," he often said. "Whattakid, huh? Whattakid!"

At the war's end, young Cesare, having proven himself a man, took unto himself a nickname and a shotgun. He did not have to use the shotgun very much, after the first few lessons; soon he was on his way to the top.

There was nowhere for Cesare "Big Cheese" Antonio Manelli to go, except up.

Straight up.

Now, in 1973, he occupied a modestly opulent office on Madison Avenue, where he did his modest best to pretend to the world at large that he was only a small cog— indeed, an almost invisible cog—in a large advertising machine. His best was, for all practical purposes, good enough.

Though it was common knowledge among the spoil-sport law enforcement officers who cared to look into the matter that Manelli was the real owner of the agency, there was no way to prove this. He didn't even have a phone under his own name. The only way to reach him was by going through his front man in the agency, a blank-faced, truculent Arab named Atif Abdullah Aoud.

According to the agent-in-charge of the New York office, Malone had his choice of two separate methods of getting to Manelli. One, more direct, was to walk in, announce that he was an agent of the FBI, and insist on seeing Manelli. If he had a search warrant, the A-in-C told him, he might even get in. But, even if he did, he would probably not get anything out of Manelli.

The second and more diplomatic way was to call up Atif Abdullah Aoud and arrange for an appointment.

Malone made his decision in a flash. He flipped on the phone and punched for a PLaza exchange.

The face that appeared on the screen was that of a fairly pretty, if somewhat vapid, brunette. "Rodger, Willcoe, O'Vurr and Aoud, good afternoon," she said.

Malone blinked.

"Who is calling, please?" the girl said. She snapped gum at the screen and Malone winced and drew away.

"This is Kenneth J. Malone," he said from what he considered a safe distance. "I want to talk to Mr. Aoud."

"Mr. Aoud?" she said in a high, unhelpful whine.

"That's right," Malone said patiently. "You can tell him that there may be some government business coming his way."

"Oh," she said. "But Mr. Aoud isn't in."

Mr. Aoud wasn't in. Mr. Aoud was out. Malone turned that over in his mind a few times, and decided to try and forget it just as quickly as possible. "Then," he said, "let me talk to one of the other partners."

"Partners?" the girl said. She popped her gum again. Malone moved back another inch.

"You know," he said. "The other people he works with. Rodger, or Willcoe, or O'Vurr."

"Oh," the girl said. "Them."

"That's right," Malone said patiently.

"How about Mr. Willcoe?" the girl said after a second of deep and earnest thought. "Would he do?"

"Why not let's try him and see?" Malone said.

"Okay," the girl said brightly. "Let's." She flashed Malone a dazzling smile, only slightly impeded by the gum, and flipped off. Malone stared at the blank screen for a few seconds, and then the girl's voice said, invisibly: "Mr. Willcoe will speak to you now, Mr. Melon. Thank you for waiting."

"I'm not—" Malone started to say, and then the face of Frederick Willcoe appeared on the screen.

Willcoe was a thin, wrinkle-faced man with very pale skin. He seemed to be in his sixties, and he looked as if he had just lost an all-night bout with Count Dracula. Malone looked interestedly for puncture marks, but failed to find any.

"Ah," Willcoe said, in a voice that sounded like crinkled paper. "Mr. Melon. Good afternoon."

"I'm not Mr. Melon," Malone said testily.

Willcoe looked gently surprised, like a man who has discovered that his evening sherry contains cholesterol. "Really?" he said. "Then I must be on the wrong line. I beg your pardon."

"You're not on the wrong line," Malone said. "I am Mr. Melon in a way." That didn't sound very clear when he got it out, so he added: "Your secretary got my name wrong. She thinks I'm Mr. Melon—Kenneth J. Melon."

"But you're not," Willcoe said.

Malone resisted an impulse to announce that he was really Lamont Cranston. "I'm Kenneth J. Malone," he said.

"Ah," Willcoe said. "Quite amusing. Imagine my mistaking you for a Mr. Melon, when you're really Mr. Malone." He paused, and his face got even more wrinkled. "But I don't know you under either name," he said. "What do you want?"

"I want to talk to Mr. Manelli," Malone said.

"But Mr. Aoud—"

"Mr. Aoud," Malone said, wondering if it sounded as silly to Willcoe as it did to him, "isn't in. So I thought you might be able to arrange an appointment for this afternoon."

Willcoe bit his lip. "Mr. Manelli isn't in just now," he said.

"Yes," Malone said. "I didn't think he would be. That's why I want to arrange an appointment for later, when he *will* be in."

"Does Mr. Manelli know you?" Willcoe said suspiciously, the wrinkles deepening again.

"He knows my boss," Malone said carefully. "You just tell him that this is something that ought to be worth time and money to him. His time, and his money."

"Hmm," Willcoe said. "I see. Would you wait a moment, Mr. Mel—Mr. Malone?"

The screen blanked out immediately. The wait this time was slightly longer.

And the next face that appeared on the screen was that of Cesare "Big Cheese" Antonio Manelli, the nearly invisible cog.

For a cog, the face was not a bad one. It was strong and well-muscled, and it had dark, wavy hair running along the top. At the sides of the face, the hair was greying slightly, and behind the grey two large ears stuck out. Manelli's nose was a long, faintly aquiline affair and his eyes were very pleasant and candid. They were light grey.

"Aha," Manelli said. "You are Mr. Malone, right?" His voice was guttural, but it was obvious that he was trying for control. "I regret announcing that I was out, Mr. Malone," he said. "But a man in my position—I like privacy, Mr. Malone, and I try to keep privacy for myself. Let me request you to answer a question, Mr. Malone: do I know you, Mr. Malone?"

"Not personally," Malone said. "I—"

"But I'm supposed to know your boss," Manelli said. "I don't know him, either, so far."

Malone shrugged. "I'm sure you do," he said, and dropped the name almost casually: "Andrew J. Burris."

Manelli raised his eyebrows. "So that's who you are," he said. "I ought to have known, Mr. Malone. And you want to talk to me a little bit, right?"

"That's right," Malone said.

"But this is no way to act, Mr. Malone," Manelli said reproachfully. "After all, we understand each other, you and me. What you should do, you should come in through channels, in the correct way, so everything it would be open and above the board."

"Through channels?" Malone said.

Manelli regarded him with a pitying glance. "You must be new on your job, Mr. Malone," he said. "Because there is an entire system built up, and you don't know about it. The way things work, we sit around and we don't see people. And then somebody comes and presents his credentials, you might say—search warrants, for instance, or subpoenas. And then we know where we are."

Malone shook his head. "This isn't that kind of call," he said. "It's more a friendly type of call."

"Mr. Malone," Manelli said. The reproach was stronger in his voice. "You must be very new at your job."

"Nevertheless," Malone said.

Manelli hesitated only a second. "Because I like you," he said, "and to teach you how things operate around here, I could do you a favor."

"Good," Malone said patiently.

"In an hour," Manelli said. "My place. Here."

The screen blanked out before Malone could even say goodbye.

Malone got up, went out to the corridor, and decided that, since he had time to kill, he might as well walk on down to Manelli's office. That, he told himself, would give him time to decide what he wanted to say.

He toyed at first with the idea of a nice bourbon and soda in a Madison Avenue bar, but he discarded that idea in a hurry. It was always possible for him to get into a tight spot and have to teleport his way out, and he didn't want to be fuzzy around the edges in case that happened. *Trotkin's* had showed him that, under enough stress, he could manage the job with quite a lot of vodka in him. But there was absolutely no sense, he told himself sadly, in taking chances.

He started off downtown along Fifth. Soon he was standing in front of the blue-and-crystal tower of the Ravell Building.

That made up his mind for him. He checked his watch, mentally flipped a coin and then cheated a little to make the answer come out right. He went inside and stepped into an elevator.

"Six," he said with decision.

Lou was sitting at the Psychical Research Society desk, talking to the tweedy Sir Lewis Carter. Malone waved at Carter, decided that conversation with Lou was out, and started to walk away. Then he realized that he couldn't have Carter thinking he was crazy. He had to figure out something to tell the man—and in a hurry, too.

Carter smiled and gestured to him. "Ah, Mr. Malone," he said. "I'm glad you brought our Lou home safely. I've heard a little about your— ah—escapade. Astounding, really."

"Not for the FBI," Malone said modestly. "We've been through too much."

"But—"

"No, really," Malone said. "We never call anything astounding any more."

"I can well imagine," Carter said. "Is there anything I can do for you?"

Malone thought fast. He had to have something, and he didn't have much time. "Why—uh—" he said, and then it came to him. "Yes, as a matter of fact you can," he said.

"Glad to be of service," Carter said. "I'm sure we can do anything you request."

"Have you got any more data on telepathic projection?" Malone said.

Sir Lewis Carter frowned. "Telepathic projection?" he said.

"The stuff—the phenomenon Cartier Taylor mentioned," Malone said, "in *Minds and Morons*. I think it was page eighty-four."

"Oh," Carter said. "Oh, yes. Of course. Well, Mr. Malone, we'll see what we can do for you."

Malone sighed. "Thanks," he said mournfully. "I guess—I guess that's all, then." He smiled at Lou, and turned the smile into a terrifying scowl when his eye caught Carter's. "Oh," Malone said. "So long. So long, everybody."

"Ken—"

This was not, he told himself sadly, either the time or the place. "Goodbye, Sir Lewis," he said. "Goodbye, Lou."

The elevator opened its doors and received him.

* * * * *

Exactly fifty-nine minutes after Cesare Manelli had hung up on him, Malone showed up in the stately and sumptuous suite that belonged, for a stiff fee every month, to the firm of Rodger, Willcoe, O'Vurr and Aoud. The girl at the desk was his old Spearmint friend.

"Mr. Manelli," Malone said. "I've got an appointment. My name is Malone and his is Manelli. He works here." That, he told himself, was an understatement; but at least he had a chance of getting his point across.

"Oh," the girl said. Her gum popped. "Certainly. Right away, Mr. Maloney."

Malone opened his mouth, then shut it again. It just wasn't worth the trouble, he thought.

The girl did things with a switchboard, then turned to him again. "Mr. Manelli's office is right down there in back," she said, pointing vaguely. "Think you can find it, Mr. Maloney?"

"I'll try," Malone promised. He went down the long corridor and stopped at an unmarked door. It was at least an even chance, he told himself, and opened the door.

The room inside appeared to be mostly desk. The gigantic slab of wood sat against the far wall of the room, in the right-hand corner and spreading over toward the center. It appeared, in the soft half-light of the room, to be waiting for somebody to walk into its lair. Malone was sure, at first sight, that this desk ate people; it was just the type: big and dark and glowering and massive.

There wasn't anybody seated behind it, which reinforced his belief. The desk had eaten its master. Now it was out of control and they would have to have it shot. Malone took a deep breath and tried not to veer.

Then he heard a voice.

"Sit down, Mr. Malone," the voice said. "How about you having a drink while we talk? If this is going to be so friendly."

The voice didn't belong to the desk. It belonged, unmistakably, to Big Cheese himself. Malone turned and saw him, sitting in the left-hand corner of the room behind a low table. There was another empty chair facing Manelli, and Malone went over and sat in it.

"A drink?" he said. "Okay. Sure."

"Bourbon and soda, isn't it?" Manelli said. He stood up.

"Your research department gets fast answers," Malone said. "Bourbon and soda it is."

"After all," Manelli said, shrugging slightly, "a person in my position, he has to make sure he knows what is what, and all the time. It's routine, what you call S. O. P. Standard Operating Procedure, they call it."

"I'm sure they do," Malone murmured politely.

"And besides," Manelli said, "you are a well-known type. I thought I knew the name when old Fred mentioned it, or I would never talk to you. You know how it is."

Malone nodded. "Well," he said, as Manelli went over to a small portable bar at the back of the room and got busy, "we're being frank, anyway."

"And why shouldn't we be frank, Mr. Malone?" Manelli said. "It's a nice, friendly conversation, and what have we got on our minds?"

For the first time, as he turned, Malone got a glimpse of something behind the structured and muscular face. There was panic there, just a tiny seed under iron control, but it showed in the eyes and in the muscles of the cheek.

"Just a nice, friendly conversation," Malone said. Manelli brought the drinks over and set them on the table.

"Take your pick," he said. "That's not what a good host should do, ask the guest to pick one, like a game; but I got into the habit. People get nervous about arsenic in the drinks. Which is silly."

"Sure it is," Malone agreed. He picked up the left-hand glass and regarded it carefully. "If you wanted to kill me, you'd need a motive and an opportunity, and you don't have either at the moment. Besides, you'd make sure to be far away when it happened." He hoped he sounded confident. He took a sip of the drink, but it tasted like bourbon and soda.

"Mr. Malone," Manelli said, "you say these things about me, and it hurts. It hurts me, right here." He pressed a hand over the checkbook side of his jacket. "I'm a legitimate businessman, and no different from any other legitimate businessman. You can't prove anything else."

"I know I can't," Malone said. "But I want to talk to you about your real business."

"This is my real business," Manelli said. "The advertising agency. I work here. Advertising is in my blood. And I don't understand the least little bit why you have to do things to me all the time."

"Do things?" Malone said. "What did I do?"

"Now, Mr. Malone," Manelli said. He took a swallow of his drink. "You said let's be frank, so I'm frank. Why not you?"

"I don't know what you're talking about," Malone said, telling part of the truth.

Manelli took another swallow of his drink, fished in a jacket pocket and brought out two cigars. "Smoke, Mr. Malone?" he said. "The very best, from Havana, Cuba. Cost me a dollar and a half each."

Malone looked with longing at the cigar. But it was okay for Manelli to smoke cigars, he thought bitterly. Manelli was a gangster, and who cared how he looked? Malone was an FBI man, and FBI men didn't smoke cigars. Particularly Havana cigars. That, he told himself with regretful firmness, was that.

"No, thanks," he said. "I never smoke on duty."

Manelli shrugged and put one cigar away. He lit the other one and dense clouds of smoke began to rise in the room. Malone breathed deeply.

"I understand you've been having troubles," he said.

Manelli nodded. "Now, you see, Mr. Malone?" he said. "You tell me you don't know what's happening, but you know I got troubles. How come, Mr. Malone? How come?"

"Because you have got troubles," Malone said. "But I have nothing to do with them." He hesitated, thought of adding: "Yet," and decided against it.

"Now, Mr. Malone," Manelli said. "You know better than that."

"I do?" Malone said.

Manelli sighed, took another swallow of his drink and dragged deeply on the cigar. "Let's take a for-instance," he said. "Now, you understand my business is advertising, Mr. Malone?"

"It's in your blood," Malone said, involuntarily.

"Right," Manelli said. "But I think about things. I like to figure things out. In a sort of a theoretical way, like a for-instance. Understand?"

"What sort of theoretical story are you going to tell me?" Malone said.

Manelli leaned back in his chair. "Let's take, for instance, some numbers runners who had some trouble the other day, got beat up and money taken from them. Maybe you read about it in the papers."

"I haven't been following the papers much," Malone said.

"That's all right," Manelli said grandly. "Maybe it wasn't *in* the papers. But anyhow, I figured out maybe that happened. I had nothing to do with this, Mr. Malone; you understand that? But I figured out how maybe it happened."

"How?" Malone said.

Manelli took another puff on his cigar. "Maybe there was an error at a racetrack—we could say Jamaica, for instance, just for laughs. And maybe two different totals were published for the pari-mutuel numbers, and both got given out. So the numbers runners got all fouled up, so they got beat up and money taken from them."

"It could have happened that way," Malone said.

"I figure maybe the FBI had something to do with this," Manelli said.

"We didn't," Malone said. "Frankly."

"And that's not all," Manelli said. "Let's say at Jamaica one day there was a race."

"All right," Malone said agreeably. "That doesn't require a whole lot of imagination."

"And let's say," Manelli went on, "that the bookies—if there are any bookies in this town; who knows?—that they got the word about who came in, win, place and show."

"Sounds natural," Malone said.

"Sure it does," Manelli said. "But there was a foul-up someplace, because the win animal was disqualified and nobody heard about it until after a lot of payoffs were made. That costs money." He stopped. "I mean it would cost money, if it happened," he finished.

"Sure," Malone said. "Certainly would."

"And you tell me it's not the FBI?" Manelli said.

"That's right," Malone said. "As a matter of fact, we're investigating things like these confusions and inefficiencies all over."

Manelli finished his drink in one long, amazed swallow. "Now, wait a minute," he said. "Let's say for a joke, like, for laughs, that I am some kind of a wheel in these things, in bookies and numbers boys and like that."

"Let's call it a syndicate," Malone said. "Just for laughs."

"Okay, then," Manelli said, with a suspicious gaze at Malone. "Whatever you call it, a man like me today, he wouldn't be some two-bit chiseler without brains. He would be a businessman, a smooth-operating smart businessman. Right?"

"Right," Malone said. "And what I want to know is: how's business?"

"You're kidding?" Manelli said.

"I'm not kidding," Malone said. "I mean it. The FBI's investigating mix-ups just like the ones you're telling me about. We want to stop them."

Manelli blinked. "You know, Mr. Malone," he said softly, "I heard about government interference in private enterprise, but don't you think this is a little too far out?"

Malone shrugged. "That's what I'm here for," he said. "Take it or leave it."

"Just so it's understood," Manelli said, "that we're talking about imaginary things. Theoretical."

"Sure," Malone said. "Imagine away."

"Well," Manelli said slowly, "you heard about this wrecked night-club in Florida? It happened maybe a month ago, in Miami?"

"I heard about it," Malone said.

"This is just a for-instance, you know," Manelli said. "But suppose there was a roulette wheel in that club. Just a wheel."

"Okay," Malone said.

"And suppose the wheel was rigged a little bit," Manelli said. "Not seriously, just a little bit."

"Fine," Malone said. "This is going to explain a wrecked club?"

"Well, sure," Manelli said. "Because something went wrong with the machinery, or maybe the operator goofed up. And number seven came up eight times in a row."

"Good old lucky seven," Malone said.

"So there was a riot," Manelli said. "Because some people had money on the number, and some people got suspicious, and like that. And there was a riot."

"And the club got wrecked," Malone said. "That's what I call bad luck."

"Luck?" Manelli said. "What does luck have to do with roulette? Somebody goofed, that's all."

"Oh," Malone said. "Sure."

"And that's the way it's been going," Manelli said. He puffed on his cigar, put it in a nearby ashtray, and blew out a great Vesuvian spout of smoke.

"Too bad," Malone said sympathetically.

"It's all over," Manelli said. "Mistakes and people making the mistakes, goofing up here and there and everyplace. There have been guys killed because they made mistakes, and nobody can afford guys being killed all the time."

"It does run into expense," Malone said.

"And time, and hiring guys to do the killing, and then they goof up, too," Manelli said. "It's terrible. Some guys have even been killed without they made any mistakes at all. Just by accident, sort of."

"Well," Malone said carefully, "you can depend on the government to do everything in its power to straighten things out."

Manelli frowned. "You mean that, Mr. Malone?"

"Of course I do," Malone said honestly. He hadn't, he reminded himself, promised to help Manelli. He had only promised to straighten things out. And he could figure out what that might mean later, when he had the time.

"All I say is, it's funny," Manelli said. "It's crazy."

"That's the way it is," Malone said.

Manelli looked at him narrowly. "Mr. Malone," he said at last, "maybe you mean it at that. Maybe you do."

"Sure I do," Malone said. "After all, the government is supposed to help its citizens."

Manelli shook his head. "Mr. Malone," he said, "you can call me Cesare. Everybody does."

"No, they don't," Malone said. "They call you Cheese. I've got a research staff too."

"So call me Cheese," Manelli said. "I don't mind."

"There's only one little trouble," Malone said. "If I called you Cheese, you'd call me Ken. And word would get around."

"I see what you mean," Manelli said.

"I don't think either one of us wants his associates to think we're friends," Malone said.

"I guess not," Manelli said. "It would cause uneasiness."

"And a certain lack of confidence," Malone said. "So suppose I go on calling you Mr. Manelli?"

"Fine," Manelli said. "And I'll call you Mr. Malone, like always."

Malone smiled and stood up. "Well, then," he said, "good-bye, Mr. Manelli."

Manelli rose, too. "Goodbye, Mr. Malone," he said. "And good luck, if you really mean what you said."

"Oh, I do," Malone said.

"Because things are terrible," Manelli said. "And they're getting worse every day. You should only know."

"Don't worry," Malone said. "Things will be straightened out pretty soon." He hoped, as he went out the door and down the corridor, that he was telling the truth there, at least. He'd sounded fairly confident, he thought, but he didn't feel quite so confident. The secretary was busy on the switchboard when he came out into the anteroom, and he went by without a greeting, his mind busy, churning and confused.

He felt as if his head were on just a little crooked. Or as if, maybe, he had a small hole in it somewhere and facts were leaking out onto the sidewalk.

If he only looked at the problem in the right way, he told himself, he would see just what was going on.

But what was the right way?

"That," Malone murmured as he hailed a cab for the ride back to 69th Street, "is the big, sixty-four-thousand-dollar question. And how much time do I have for an answer?"

11

"Boyd?" the agent-in-charge said. "He went out to talk to Mike Sand down at the ITU a while ago, and he hasn't come back yet."

"Fine," Malone said. "I'll be in my office if he wants me."

The agent-in-charge picked up a small package. "A messenger brought this," he said. "It's from the Psychical Research Society, and if it's ghosts, they're much smaller than last time."

"Dehydrated," Malone said. "Just add ectoplasm and out they come, shouting *boo* at everybody and dancing all over the world."

"Sounds wonderful," the agent-in-charge said. "Can I come to the party?"

"First," Malone said judiciously, "you'd have to be dead. Of course, I can arrange that—"

"Thanks," the agent-in-charge said, leaving in a hurry. Malone went on down to his office and opened the package. It contained more facsimiles from Sir Lewis Carter, all dealing with telepathic projection. He spent a few minutes looking them over and trying to make some connected sense out of them, and then he just sat and thought for awhile.

Finally he picked up the phone. In a few minutes he was talking to Dr. Thomas O'Connor, at Yucca Flats.

"Telepathic projection?" O'Connor said when Malone asked him the question he'd thought of. "Well, now. I should say that—no. First, Mr. Malone, tell me what evidence you have for this phenomenon."

Malone felt almost happy, as if he had done all his homework before the instructor called on him. "According to what I've been able to get from the PRS," he said, "ordinary people—people who aren't telepaths— occasionally receive some sort of messages from other people."

"I assume," O'Connor said frostily, "that you are speaking of telepathic messages?"

Malone nodded guiltily. "I didn't mean the phone," he said, "or letters or things like that. Telepathic messages, or something very like it."

"Indeed," O'Connor said. "Mr. Malone, I believe you will find that such occurrences, when accurately reported, are confined to close relatives or loved ones of the person projecting the message."

Malone thought back. "That's right," he said.

"And, further," O'Connor went on, "I think you'll find that the—ah— message so received is one indicating that the projector of such a message is in dire peril. He has, for instance, been badly injured, or is rapidly approaching death, or else he has narrowly escaped death."

"True," Malone said.

"Under such circumstances," O'Connor said coldly, "it is possible that the mind of the person projecting the communication might be capable of generating immense psionic power, thereby forcing even a non-telepath to recognize the content of the message."

"Good," Malone said. "That's wonderful, Doctor, and I—"

"But," O'Connor said sharply, "the amount of psionic energy necessary for such a feat is tremendous. Usually, it is the final burst of energy, the outpouring of all the remaining psionic force immediately before death. And if death does not occur, the person is at the least greatly weakened; his mind, if it ever does recover, needs time and rest to do so."

Malone let that sink in slowly. "Then a person couldn't do it very often," he said.

"Hardly," O'Connor said.

Malone nodded. "It's like—like giving blood to a blood bank. Giving, say, three quarts of blood. It might not kill you. But if it didn't, you'd be weak for a long time."

"Exactly," O'Connor said. "A good analogy, Mr. Malone."

Malone hated himself for it, but he felt pleased when O'Connor praised him. "Well," he said, "that winds up Cartier Taylor's theory pretty thoroughly."

"I should think so," O'Connor said. "I am surprised, Mr. Malone, that you would put any credence whatever in that man's theories. His factual data, I will admit, is fairly reliable. But his theories are— well, they are hardly worth the time it takes to read them."

"I see," Malone said. "It did seem like a good answer, though."

"It undoubtedly is a good one," O'Connor said. "It is clever and has the advantage of being simple. It is contradicted, Mr. Malone, only by the facts."

"Sure," Malone said sadly. "But—hey. Wait a minute."

"Yes?" O'Connor said.

"One person couldn't do this alone, at least, not very often and not without serious harm to himself. Right?"

"That is what I said," O'Connor agreed. "Yes, Mr. Malone."

"But how about several people?" Malone said. "I mean, well, let's look at that blood bank again. You need three quarts of blood. But one person doesn't have to give it. Suppose twelve people gave half a pint each. Suppose twenty-four people gave a quarter of a pint each. Suppose—"

"There is," O'Connor said, "a point of diminishing returns. But I do see your point, Mr. Malone." He thought for a second. "It might just be possible," he said. "At least theoretically. But it would take a great deal of mental co-ordination among the participants. They would have to be telepathic themselves, for one thing."

"Why?" Malone said, feeling stupid.

"Because they would have to mesh their thoughts closely enough to direct them properly and at the correct time." O'Connor nodded. "But, given that, I imagine that it could be done."

"Wonderful," Malone said.

"However," O'Connor said, apparently glad to throw even a little cold water on the notion, "it could not be done for very long periods of time, you realize."

"Sure," Malone said happily.

"By the way, Mr. Malone," O'Connor said. "Does this have anything to do with the hypothesis you presented to me some time ago? Mass hypnotism, as I recall—"

"No," Malone said. "I've given that idea up for good. I think this is being done on an individual basis—working on one person at a time." Then another idea hit him. "You say these people would have to be telepaths?"

"That's right," O'Connor said.

"Then wouldn't Her Majesty know about them? If they're telepaths? Or is there some kind of a mind shield or something that a telepath could work out?"

"Mind shield?" O'Connor said. "Ah, yes. Miss Thompson might be fooled by such a shield. It would have to be an exceptional one, but such things do seem to be possible. They belong to the realm of mental disciplines, of course, rather than psionics."

"Sure," Malone said. "But there could be that kind of shield?"

"There could," O'Connor said. "The mind which created the shield for itself would have to be of tremendous power and a really high order of control. A strong, sane mind might conceivably create such a block that even Miss Thompson, let us say, might believe that she was picking up a real mind, when she was only picking up surface thoughts, with the real thought hidden behind the telepathic block."

"Fine," Malone said. "Thanks. Thanks a lot, Dr. O'Connor."

"I am always happy to put my extensive knowledge of science at your disposal, Mr. Malone," O'Connor said.

Malone watched the image collapse without really seeing it. Instead, he was busily talking to himself, or rather to his other self.

"Well, now, Sir Kenneth," he said. "Let's pull all the facts together and see what happens."

"Indeed, Mr. Malone," said Sir Kenneth Malone, "it is time that we did. Proceed, Sirrah. I shall attend."

* * * * *

"Let's start from the beginning," Malone said. "We know there's confusion in all parts of the country, in all parts of the world, I guess. And we know that confusion is being caused by carefully timed accidents and errors. We also know that these errors appear to be accompanied by violent bursts of psionic static—violent energy. And we know, further, that on three specific occasions, these bursts of energy were immediately followed by a reversal of policy in the mind of the person on the receiving end."

"You mean," Sir Kenneth put in, "that they changed their minds."

"Correct," Malone said. "I refer, of course, to the firm of Brubitsch, Borbitsch and Garbitsch, Spying Done Cheap."

"Indeed," Sir Kenneth said. "Then the operators of this force, whatever it may be, have some interest in allowing these spies to confess?"

"Maybe," Malone said. "Let's leave that for later. To get back to the beginning of all this: it seems to me to follow that the accidents and errors which have caused all the confusion through the United States and Russia are caused by somebody's mind being changed at exactly the right moment. A man does something just a little differently than he decided to—or else he forgets to do it at all."

"Correct," Sir Kenneth said. "And you feel, Mr. Malone, that a telepathic command is the cause of this confusion?"

"A series of them," Malone said. "But we also know, from Dr. O'Connor, that it takes a great deal of psychic energy to perform this particular trick—more than a person can normally afford to expend."

"Marry, now," Sir Kenneth exclaimed, "such a statement does not seem to have reason in it. Changing the mind of a man seems a small thing in comparison to teleportation, or psychokinesis, or levitation. And yet it takes more power than any of these?"

Malone thought for a second. "Sure it does," he said. "I'd say it was a matter of resistance. Moving an inanimate object is pretty simple— comparatively, anyhow—because inert matter has no mental resistance."

"And moving yourself?" Sir Kenneth said.

"There is some resistance there, probably," Malone said. "But you'll remember that part of the Fueyo training system for teleportation involved overcoming your own mental resistance to the idea."

"True," Sir Kenneth said. "Quite true. Then let us say that it requires enormous power to effect these changes. What is our next step, Mr. Malone?"

"Next, Sir Kenneth," Malone said, "we have to do a little supposing. This project must be handled by a fairly large group, since no individual can work it. This large group has to be telepathic, and not only for the precise timing O'Connor specified."

"There is another reason?" Sir Kenneth said.

"There is," Malone said. "They've also got to know exactly when to make their victim change his mind. Right?"

"Absolutely," said Sir Kenneth. "Now, Sirrah, where does all this leave us? We have had the orderly presentation of the case; where, Sirrah, is your summation?"

"Coming up," Malone said. "We've got to look for a widespread organization of telepaths, with enough mental discipline to hold a mental shield that Her Majesty can't crack, and can't even recognize the existence of. We thought she'd found all the telepaths. She said so, and she obviously thought so. But she didn't. These are strong, trained—and sane."

"Aha," said Sir Kenneth.

"Her Majesty," Malone said, "found us only the crazy telepaths, the weak ones, the nuts."

"Fine," said Sir Kenneth. "And this, Mr. Malone, leaves us with only one question. Her Majesty—may God bless her—stated that she first spotted these flashes of telepathic static by listening in on our minds."

"Our mind," Malone said. "I hope."

"Very well," Sir Kenneth said. "This means that some force is being directed in this way, toward us. And how do we know that all the deduction, all the careful case-building we have done, hasn't been influenced by this group? That might mean, of course, that we are miles, or even light-years, from the solution."

Malone said: "Yeep." The sound was echoed by Sir Kenneth, and the two halves of the coruscating mind of Kenneth J. Malone were once more one.

Your Majesty, the minds thought, *I'd like to talk to you.*

Nothing happened. Evidently, Her Majesty was temporarily out of mental contact with him.

"Hell," Malone said. "Not to mention od's blood." He flipped on the visiphone and dialed Yucca Flats.

The figure that appeared on the screen was that of a tall, solidly-built man with a red face and the uniform of a Beefeater. This Tower Warder had the British royal crest embroidered on his chest, and the letters: "E. R."

"Good evening, Sir Kenneth," he said politely.

Malone had sometimes wondered what it would be like to be on the Queen's permanent, personal staff.

Evidently, it soaked in so thoroughly that one began to stay in character all the time. The little old lady's delusion was such a pleasant one that it was painlessly infectious.

"I'd like to speak to Her Majesty, Colonel Fairfax," Malone said.

"Her Majesty," Colonel Fairfax said with regret, "is asleep, sir. I understand that she has had rather a trying time, of late."

"Then I must ask you to wake her," Malone said. "I don't want to disturb her any more than you do, Colonel, but this is important."

"Her Majesty's rest," Colonel Fairfax said gently, "is also important, Sir Kenneth."

"This is more important," Malone said. "I know how you feel, but it's necessary to wake her."

The screen blanked out.

Malone sighed and began to sing softly to himself while he waited:

"The soldiers of the Queen are linked in friendly tether— And if she's off her bean, we'll all go nuts together..."

Her Majesty appeared at this point, dressed in a silken robe bearing her crest and initials (E. R., rather than R. T., of course), and wearing a silken Mother Hubbard cap on her head. "Oh, dear," she said instantly. "Are you still worried about them?"

"The flashes?" Malone said. "That's right. You tuned in on my mind right away, didn't you?"

"As soon as I got your message," she said. "I like your little song, at least, I think I do."

Malone blushed faintly. "Sorry," he said.

"Oh, don't be, Sir Kenneth," Her Majesty said. "After all, I do allow my subjects a good deal of liberty; it is theirs to make use of." She smiled at him. "Actually, I should have told you, Sir Kenneth. But it seemed so natural that I—that I forgot it."

Oh, no, Malone thought.

"I'm afraid so," Her Majesty said. "When I told you about the interference, your mind quite automatically began to build what I think of as a—as a defense against it. A shield, so to speak."

Me? Malone thought.

"Most certainly," Her Majesty said. "You know, Sir Kenneth, you have a very strong mind."

"Oh, I don't know," Malone said aloud. "Sometimes I don't feel so bright."

"I'm not talking about intelligence," Her Majesty said. "The two properties are interconnected, of course, but they are not identical. After all ... well, never mind. But you have strength of will, Sir Kenneth, and strength of purpose. As a matter of fact, you have been building your strength in the last few days."

"Really?" Malone said, surprised.

"It's become more and more difficult," Her Majesty said, "to see into the depths of your mind, during the past few days. The surface of your mind is as easy to read as ever, but it's hard to see what's going on in the depths."

"I'm not doing it deliberately," Malone said.

"In any case," Her Majesty said, "this process has been going on ever since you knew that telepathy was possible, two years ago. But in the past forty-eight hours matters have accelerated tremendously."

"That sounds good," Malone said. "Does it mean these mind-changers I've been thinking about can't get through to me?"

"What mind-changers?" the Queen said. "Oh. I see." She paused. "Well, I can't be positive about this, Sir Kenneth; it's all so new, you know. All I can tell you is that there haven't been any flashes of telepathic energy in your mind in the last forty-eight hours."

"Well," Malone said doubtfully, "that's something. And I am sorry I had to wake you, Your Majesty."

"Oh, that's perfectly all right," she said. "I know you're working hard to restore order to the realm, and it is the duty of any Sovereign to give such aid as she can to her Royal subjects."

Malone cleared his throat. "I trust," he said, "Your Majesty will ever find me a faithful servant."

Her Majesty smiled. "I'm sure I shall," she said. "Good night, Sir Kenneth."

"Good night," he said, and flipped off. At once, the phone chimed again.

He flipped the switch on. "Malone here," he said.

Boyd's face appeared on the screen. "Ken," he said fervently, "I am very glad you're still in town."

"Thanks," Malone said politely. "But what about Mike Sand? Any information?"

"Plenty," Boyd said. "I damn near didn't believe it."

"What do you mean, you didn't believe it?" Malone said. "Isn't the information any good?"

"It's good, all right," Boyd said. "It's great. He practically talked his head off to me. Gave me all his books, including secret sets. And I've put him under arrest as a material witness—at his own request."

"It sounds," Malone said, "as if Mike Sand has had a sudden and surprising change of heart."

"Doesn't it, though," Boyd said. "We can crack the ITU wide open now, and I mean really wide open."

"Same pattern?" Malone said.

"Of course it is," Boyd said. "What does it sound like? Same pattern."

"Good," Malone said. "Get on up here. I'll talk to you later."

He cut off in a hurry, leaned back in his chair and started to think. At first, he thought of a cigar. Boyd, he figured, couldn't be back in the office for some time, and nobody else would come in. He locked the door, drew out the cigar-laden box he kept in his desk in New York, and lit up with great satisfaction.

When the cloud of smoke around his head was dense enough to cut with a knife, he went back to more serious subjects. He didn't have to worry too much about his mind being spied on; if Her Majesty couldn't read his deepest thoughts, and the mind-changers weren't throwing any bolts of static in his direction, he was safe.

Now, then, he told himself—and sneezed.

He shook his head, cursed slightly, and went on.

Now, then...

There was an organization, spread all over the Western world, and with secret branches, evidently, in the Soviet Union. The organization had to be an old one, because it had to have trained telepaths of such a high degree of efficiency that they could evade Her Majesty's probing without her even being aware of the evasion. And training took time.

There was something else to consider, too. In order to organize to such a degree that they could wreak the efficient, complete havoc they were wreaking, the organization couldn't be completely secret; there are always leaks, always suspicious events, and a secret society that covered all of those up would have no time for anything else.

So the organization had to be a known one, a known group, masquerading as something else.

So far, everything made sense. Malone took another deep, grateful puff on the cigar, and frowned. Where, he wondered, did he go from here?

He reached for a pencil and a piece of paper. He headed the paper: *Organization.* Then he started putting down what he knew about it, and what he'd figured out.

1. Large
2. Old
3. Disguised

It sounded just a little like Frankenstein's Monster, so far. But what else did he know about it?

After a second's thought, he murmured: "Nothing," and took another puff.

But that wasn't quite true.

He knew one more thing about the organization. He knew they'd probably be immune to the confusion everybody else was suffering from. The organization would be—had to be—efficient. It would be composed of intelligent, superbly cooperative people, who could work together as a unit without in the least impairing their own individuality.

He reached for the list again, put down:

    4. Efficient

And looked at it. Now it didn't remind him quite so much of the Monster. But it didn't look familiar, either. Who did he know, he thought, who was large, old, disguised and efficient?

It sounded like an improbable combination. He set the list down again, clearing off some of the papers the PRS had sent him to make room for it.

Then he stopped.

The papers the PRS had sent him...

And he'd gotten them so quickly, so efficiently...

They were a large organization...

And an old one...

He tossed the cigar in the general direction of the ashtray, grabbed the phone and jabbed at buttons.

The girl who answered the phone looked familiar. She did not look very old, but she was large and she had to be disguised, Malone thought. Nobody could naturally have that many teeth.

"Psychical Research Society," she said. "Oh, Mr. Malone, good evening."

"Sir Lewis," Malone said. "Sir Lewis Carter. President. I want to talk to him. Hurry."

"Sir Lewis?" the girl said slowly. "Oh, I'm sorry, Mr. Malone, but the office is closed now for the day. And Sir Lewis has gone already. It's after six o'clock, Mr. Malone, and the office is closed."

"Home number," Malone said desperately. "I've got to."

"Well, I can do that, Mr. Malone," she said, "but it wouldn't do you any good, really. Because he went away on his vacation, and when he goes on his vacation he never tells us where. You know? He won't be back for two or three weeks."

"Oog," Malone said, and thought for less than a second. "Miss Garbitsch," he said. "Lou. Got to talk to her. Now."

"Oh, I can't do that, either, Mr. Malone," the toothy girl said. "All of the executive officers, they left already on their vacation. And that includes Miss Garbitsch, too. They just left a skeleton force here at the office."

"They're all gone?" Malone said hollowly.

"That's right," she said cheerfully. "As a matter of fact, I'm in charge now, and that's why I'm staying so late. To sort of catch up on things. You know?"

"It's very important," Malone said tensely. "You don't know where any of them went? You don't have any address?"

"None at all," she said. "I'm sorry, but that's how it is. Maybe it's strange, and maybe you'd ask questions, but I obey orders, and those're my orders. To take over until they get back. They didn't tell me where they went, and I didn't ask."

"Great," Malone said. He wanted to shoot himself.

Lou was one of them. Of course she was; that was obvious now, when he thought about it. Lou was one of the secret group that was sabotaging practically everything.

And now they'd all gone. For two weeks—or for good.

The girl's voice broke in on his thoughts.

"Oh, Mr. Malone," she said, "I'm sorry, but I just remembered. They left a note for you."

"A note?" Malone said.

"Sir Lewis said you might call," the girl said, "and he left a message. If you'll hold on a minute I'll read it to you."

Malone waited tensely. The girl found a slip of paper, blinked at it and read:

"My dear Malone, I'm afraid you are perfectly correct in your deductions; and, as you can see, that leaves us no alternative. Sorry. Miss G. sends her apologies to you, as do I." The girl looked up. "It's signed by Sir Lewis," she said. "Does that mean anything to you, Mr. Malone?"

"I'm afraid it does," Malone said bleakly. "It means entirely too much."

12

After the great mass of teeth, vaguely surrounded by a face, had faded from Malone's screen, he just sat there, looking at the dead, grey screen of the visiphone and feeling about twice as dead and at least three times as grey.

Things, he told himself, were terrible. But even that sentence, which was a good deal more cheerful than what he actually felt, didn't do anything to improve his mood. All of the evidence, after all, had been practically living on the tip of his nose for nearly twenty-four hours, and not only had he done nothing about it, but he hadn't even seen it.

Two or three times, for instance, he'd doubted the possibility of teleporting another human being. All his logic had told him it wasn't so. But, he'd thought, he and Her Majesty had teleported Lou, and so, obviously, his logic was wrong.

No, it wasn't, he thought now. There *would* be too much mental resistance, even if the person were unconscious. Teleportation of another human being *would* be impossible.

Unless, of course, the other human being was able to teleport on her own.

True, she had been no more than semiconscious. She probably couldn't have teleported on her own. But Malone and Her Majesty had, ever so kindly and ever so mistakenly, helped her, and Lou had managed to teleport to the plane.

And that wasn't all, he thought dismally. That was far from all.

"Let's take another for-instance," he said savagely, in what he thought was a caricature of the Manelli voice. In order for all three to teleport, there had to be perfect synchronization.

Otherwise, they'd have arrived either at different places, or at the same place but at different times.

And perfect synchronization on a psionic level meant telepathy. At least two of the three had to be telepathic. Her Majesty was, of course. Malone wasn't.

So Lou had to be telepathic, too.

Malone told himself bitterly to quit calling the girl Lou. After the way she'd deceived him, she didn't deserve it. Her name was Luba Garbitsch, and from now on he was going to call her Luba Garbitsch. In his own mind, anyway.

Facts came tumbling in on him like the side of a mountain, falling on a hapless traveler during a landslide. And, Malone told himself, he had never had less help in all of his ill-starred life.

Her Majesty had never, never suspected that Luba Garbitsch was anything other than the girl she pretended to be. That was negative evidence, true, and taken alone it meant nothing at all. But when you added the other facts to it, it showed, with perfect plainness, that Luba Garbitsch was the fortunate possessor of a mind shield as tough, as strong and as perfect as any Malone, O'Connor or good old Cartier Taylor had ever even thought of dreaming up.

And then, very suddenly, another fact arrived, and pushed the rest out into the black night of Malone's bitter mind. He punched hard on the intercom button and got the desk of the agent-in-charge.

"Now what's wrong?" the A-in-C said. "Ghosts got loose? Or do you want some help with a beautiful blonde heiress?"

"What would I be doing," Malone snapped, "with a beautiful blonde heiress?"

The agent-in-charge looked thoughtful. It was obvious that he had been saving his one joke up for several hours.

"You might be holding her," he suggested, "for ransom, of course."

"That's not funny," Malone said. "Nothing is funny any more."

"Oh, all right," the A-in-C said. "You Washington boys are just too good for the rest of us. What's on your mind?"

"You've got a twenty-four-hour watch on Luba Garbitsch, haven't you?" Malone said.

"Sure we have," the A-in-C said. "Boyd said—"

"Yes, I know what he said," Malone cut in. "Give me a check on those men. I want to find out where she is right now. Right this minute."

The agent-in-charge shrugged. "Sure," he said. "It's none of my business. Hang on a second."

The screen went blank, but it didn't go silent. Each of the agents, on a stakeout job like the Garbitsch one, would be carrying personal communicators, and Malone could hear the voice of the agent-in-charge as he spoke to them.

He couldn't make out all the words, and it wasn't important anyhow. He'd know soon enough, he kept telling himself; just as soon as the A-in-C came back and reported.

It seemed like about twelve years before he did.

"She's all right," he said. "Nothing to worry about; she's probably working late at her office, that's all. She hasn't gone home yet."

"Want to bet?" Malone snapped.

"Don't tempt me," the A-in-C said. "I wouldn't take your money—it's probably counterfeit, printed in Washington."

"I'll give you ten to one," Malone said.

"Ten to one, I'll take," the A-in-C said rapidly. "Ten to one is like taking candy from a traffic cop. I'm no amateur, even if I am stuck away in dull little old New York—and I know the boys I've got on stakeout. I'll check, and—"

"Let me know when you do," Malone said. "I've got some long-distance calls to make."

* * * * *

Forty-five minutes later, he had all the news he needed. Spot checks on PRS offices on the West Coast, where it wasn't closing time yet, showed that all the executive officers had suddenly felt the need of extended vacations to parts unknown.

That, if not exactly cheering news, was still welcome; Malone had more backing for his theory.

An overseas call to New Scotland Yard in London took a little more time, and several arguments with bored overseas operators who, apparently, had nothing better to do than to confuse the customers. But Malone finally managed to get Assistant Commissioner C. E. Teal, who promised to check on Malone's inquiry at once.

It seemed like years before he called back, and Malone leaped to the phone.

"Yes?" he said.

Teal, red-faced and apparently masticating a stick of gum, said: "I got C. I. D. Commander Gideon to follow up on that matter, Mr. Malone. It is rather late here, as you must realize—"

"Yes?" Malone said. "And they've all gone?"

"Why, no," Teal said, surprised. "A spot check shows that most of the executives of the London branch of the Psychical Research Society are spending quiet evenings in their homes. Our Inspector Ottermole actually spoke to Dr. Carnacki, the head of the office here."

"Oh," Malone said.

"They haven't skipped," Teal went on. "Is this in connection with anything serious, Mr. Malone?"

"Not yet," Malone said. "But I'll let you know at once if there are any further developments. Thanks very much, Mr. Teal."

"A pleasure, Mr. Malone," Teal said. "A pleasure." And then, still masticating, he switched off.

And that, Malone told himself, was definitely that. Of course the British PRS hadn't gone underground; why should they? The British police weren't on to them, as Scotland Yard showed. And, no matter what opinions Her Majesty Queen Elizabeth I might hold in the matter, the FBI had absolutely no jurisdiction in the British Isles.

Malone buried his face in his hands, thought about a cigar and decided that even a cigar might make him feel worse. Where were they? What were they doing now? What did they plan to do?

Where had they gone?

"Out of the everywhere," he said in a hollow, sepulchral voice, "into the here."

But where was the here?

He tried to make up his mind whether or not that made sense. Superficially, it sounded like plain bad English, but he wasn't sure of anything any more. Things were getting much too confused.

There was a knock at the door.

Malone, without any hope at all, called: "Come in," and the door opened.

The agent-in-charge came in, and dropped a dollar on Malone's desk.

"So you checked," Malone said.

"I checked," the A-in-C said sadly. "The boys went through the entire damned building. Not a sign of her. Not even a trace."

"There wouldn't be one," Malone said, shoving the dollar back to waiting hands. "Take the money; I knew what would happen. It was a sucker bet."

"Well, I feel like the sucker, all right," the A-in-C said. "I don't know how she did it."

"I do," Malone said quietly. "Teleportation."

The A-in-C whistled. "Well," he said, "it was a great secret as long as it was FBI property. But now, friend, all hell is going to bust loose."

"It already has," Malone said hollowly.

"Great," the A-in-C said. "What now?"

"Now," Malone said, "I am going to go back to Washington. Take care of poor little old New York for me."

He closed his eyes, and vanished.

When he opened them, he was in his Washington apartment. He went over to the big couch and sat down, feeling that if he were going to curse he might as well be comfortable while he did it. But when the air was bright blue, some minutes later, he didn't feel any better. Cursing was not the answer.

Nothing seemed to be.

What was his next move?

Where did he go from here?

The more he thought about it, the more his mind spun. He was, he realized, at an absolute, total, dead end.

Oh, there were things he could do. Malone knew that very well. He could make a lot of noise and go through a lot of waste motion—that was what it would amount to. He could have all the homes of all the missing PRS members checked. That would result, undoubtedly, in the discovery that the PRS members involved weren't in their homes. He could have their files impounded, which would clutter everything with a great many more pieces of paper, and none of the pieces of paper would do any good to him. In general, he could have the entire FBI chasing all over hell and gone—and finding nothing whatever.

No, it would be a waste of time, he told himself. That much was certain.

And, though he probably had enough evidence to get the FBI in motion, he had nowhere near enough to carry the case into court, much less make a try at getting the case to stand up in court. That was one thing he couldn't do, even if he wanted to: issue warrants for arrest on any basis whatever.

But Malone was an FBI agent, and his motto was: "There's always a way." No normal method of tracking down the PRS members, and finding their present whereabouts, was going to work. They'd been covering themselves for such an emergency, undoubtedly, for a good many years and, due to telepathy, they certainly knew enough not to leave any clues around, of any kind.

But nobody, Malone told himself, was perfect. There were clues lying around somewhere, he was sure of that; there had to be. The problem was, simply, to figure out where to look, and what to look for.

Somewhere, the clues were sitting quietly and waiting for him to find them. The thought cheered him slightly, but not very much. Instead, he went into the kitchen and started heating water for coffee. He thought there might be a long night ahead of him, and sighed gently. But there was no help for it. The work had to be done, and done quickly.

But when eight cigars had been reduced to ash, and what seemed like several gallons of coffee had sloshed their way into Malone's interior workings, his mind was as blank as a baby's. The lovely, opalescent dawn began to show in the East, and Malone swore at it. Then, haggard, red-eyed, confused, violently angry, and not one inch closer to a solution, he fell into a fitful doze on his couch.

* * * * *

When he awoke the sun was high in the sky, and outside his window the cheerful sound of traffic floated in the air. Downstairs somebody was playing a television set too loudly, and the voice reached Malone's semi-aware mind in a great tinny shout:

"And now, the makers of Bon-Ton B-Complex Bolsters—the blanket of health—present Mother Kohler's Chit-Chat Hour!"

The invisible audience screamed and howled. Malone ripped out a particularly foul oath and sat up on the couch. "That," he muttered, "is a fine thing to wake up to." He focused his eyes, with only slight difficulty, on his watch. The time was exactly noon.

"But first," the announcer burbled downstairs, "a word from Mother Kohler herself, about the brand new special B-Complex *Irradiated* Bolster you can get at your neighborhood stores..."

"Shut up," Malone said. He had wasted a lot of time doing nothing but sleeping, he told himself. This was no time to be listening to television. He got up and found, to his vague surprise, that he felt a lot better and more clear-headed than he'd been feeling. Maybe the sleep had done him some good.

He yawned, blinked and stretched, and then he padded into the bathroom, showered and shaved and put on fresh clothes. He thought about having a morning cup of coffee, but last night's dregs appeared to have taken up permanent residence in his digestive tract, and he decided against it at last. He swallowed some orange juice and toast and then, heaving a great sigh of resignation and brushing crumbs off his shirt, he teleported himself over to his office.

He was going to have to face Burris eventually, he knew.

And now was just as good, or as bad, a time as any.

Malone didn't hesitate. He punched the button on his intercom for Burris' office and then sat back, with his eyes closed, for the well-known voice.

It didn't come.

Instead, Wolf, the director's secretary, spoke up.

"Burris isn't in, Malone," he said. "He had to fly to Miami. I can get a call through to him on the plane, if it's urgent, but he'll be landing in about fifteen minutes. And he did say he'd call this afternoon."

"Oh," Malone said. "Sure. Okay. It isn't urgent." He was just as glad of the reprieve; it gave him one more chance to work matters through to a solution, and report success instead of failure. "But what's going on in Miami?" he added.

"Don't you read the papers?" Wolf asked.

Everybody, Malone reflected, seemed to be asking him that lately. "I haven't had time," he said.

"The governor of Mississippi was assassinated yesterday, at Miami Beach," Wolf said.

"Ah," Malone said. He thought about it for a second. "Frankly," he said, "this does not strike me as an irreparable loss to the nation. Not even to Mississippi."

"You express my views precisely," Wolf said.

"How about the killer?" Malone said. "I gather they haven't got him yet, or Burris wouldn't be on his way down."

"No," Wolf said. "The killer would be on his way here instead. They haven't got him, Malone. It seems Governor Flarion was walking along Collins Avenue when somebody fired at him, using a high-powered rifle with, I guess, a scope sight."

"Professional," Malone commented.

"It looks like it," Wolf said. "Nobody even heard the sniper's shot; the governor just fell over, right there in the street. And by the time his bodyguards found out what had happened, it was impossible even to be sure just which way he was facing when the shot had been fired."

"And, as I remember Collins Avenue—" Malone started.

"Right," Wolf said. "Out where Governor Flarion was taking his stroll, there's an awful lot of it to search. The boys are trying to find somebody who might have seen a man acting suspicious in any of the nearby buildings, or heard a shot, or seen anybody at all lurking or loitering anywhere remotely close to the scene."

"Lovely," Malone said. "Sounds like a nice complicated job."

"You don't know the half of it," Wolf said. "There's also the Miami Beach Chamber of Commerce. According to them, Flarion died of a heart attack, and not even in Miami Beach. The bullet and the body are supposed to be written off as just coincidences, to keep the fair name of Miami Beach unsullied."

"All I can say," Malone offered, "is good luck. This is the saddest day in American history since the assassination of Huey P. Long."

"Agreed," Wolf said. "Want me to tell Burris you called?"

"Right," Malone said. He flicked off.

Now, he asked himself, how did the assassination of Governor Nemours P. Flarion fit in with anything? Granted, good old Nemours P. had been a horrible mistake, a paranoid, self-centered, would-be dictator whose talents as a rabble-rouser and a fearmonger had somehow managed to get him elected to a governorship. Certainly nobody felt particularly unhappy about his death. But he wouldn't fit into the pattern. Malone reminded himself that that was one more thing he had to find out when he got the chance.

The trouble lay in finding an opportunity, he thought—and then he corrected himself.

Not *finding* it—*making* it. Nobody was going to hand him anything on a silver serving salver.

He punched the intercom again and got the Records office.

"Yes, sir?" a familiar voice said.

"Potter?" Malone said. "This is Malone. I want facsimiles of everything we have on the Psychical Research Society, on Sir Lewis Carter, and on Luba Vasilovna Garbitsch. Both of those last are connected with the Society."

"Right," Potter said. "They'll be up at once."

Then he punched again, and asked for the latest copy of the Washington *Post*. He gave the article on Governor Flarion one quick glance, but it didn't contain anything in the way of facts that he hadn't already had from Wolf. After that, he left it and concentrated on the more prosaic, human-interest news, the smaller stories.

FIFTH SPLINTER GROUP FORMS IN DCA BATTLE

That was an interesting one, he thought. The Daughters of Colonial Americans had about reached the point of diminishing returns in their battle over the claims of Rose Carswell Elder, a descendant of a Negro freedman named William Elder who had lived in Boston in 1776 and fought on the side of the Colonies during the Revolution. One more splinter group, Malone thought, and there'd be as many splinters as members. Rose Carswell Elder was pressing her claim for membership, and the ladies were replying by throwing crockery and hard words at each other.

Then there was the Legion of American War Veterans. The headline on this one read:

LAWV OUSTS 'ROWDIES': AID MEETING CONTINUES

The "rowdies," Malone discovered, were a large minority group that wanted the good old days of electric canes, paper hats, whistles and pretty girls. "The Legion has grown up," a spokesman told them. "This convention is being held to discuss the possibility of increased technological aid to India and Africa. There is no place for tomfoolery or high jinks."

The expulsion order had been carried by a record majority.

And then there were two items, on different pages, that seemed to contradict each other. The first was a small headline on page fourteen:

RESIGNATIONS REACH NEW HIGH IN U.S. COLLEGE FACULTIES

Teachers were apparently resigning all over the place, in virtually every department of virtually every college. That made sense. And the other item, on page three, made just as much sense:

HIGHER TAXES VOTED THROUGHOUT U.S. FOR TEACHER INCOME RISE

State and Federal Aid Also Promised in Drive to Raise Salaries Now

Apparently, teachers were resigning just as they were about to get more money than they'd ever seen before. But Malone could fit that into the pattern easily enough; it was perfectly obvious, once he thought about it.

Malone didn't have time to go through much more of the paper; the facsimile records he'd been waiting for arrived, and he put the *Post* aside and concentrated on them instead. Maybe somewhere in the records was the clue he desperately needed.

The PRS was widely spread, all right. It had branches in almost every major city in the United States, in Europe, South Africa, South America and Australia. There was even a small branch society in Greenland. True, the Communist disapproval of such non-materialistic, un-Marxian objectives as Psychical Research showed up in the fact that there were no registered branches in the Sino-Soviet bloc. But that, Malone thought, didn't really matter. Maybe in Russia they called themselves the Lenin Study Group, or the Better Borshcht League. He was fairly sure, from what he'd experienced, that the PRS had some kind of organization even behind the Iron Curtain.

Money didn't seem to be much of a problem, either. Malone checked for the supporters of the organization and found a microfilmed list that ran into the hundreds of thousands of names, most of them ordinary people who seemed to be interested in spiritualism and the like, and who donated a few dollars apiece each year to the PRS.

Besides this mass of small donations, of course, there were a few large ones, from independently wealthy men who gave support to the organization and seemed actively interested in its aims.

It wasn't an unusual picture; it was just an exceptionally big one.

Malone sighed and went on to the personal dossiers.

Sir Lewis Carter himself was a well-known astronomer and mathematician. He was a Fellow of the Royal Society, the Royal Astronomical Society and the Royal Mathematical Society. He had been knighted for his contributions in higher mathematics only two years before he had come to live in the United States. Malone went over the papers dealing with his entry into the country carefully, but they were all in order and they contained absolutely no clues he could use.

Sir Lewis' books on political and historical philosophy had been well-received, and he had also written a novel, *But Some Are More Equal,* which, for a few weeks after publication, had managed to reach the bottom of the best-seller list.

And that was that. Malone tried to figure out whether all this information did him any good at all, and he didn't have to think for very long. The answer was no. He opened the next dossier.

Luba Vasilovna Garbitsch had been born in New York. Her mother had been a woman of Irish descent named Mary O'Keefe, and had died in '68. Her father, of course, had now been revealed as a Russian agent, and was at present making his home, such as it probably was, in good old Moscow.

Malone sighed. Somewhere in the dossiers, he was sure, there was a clue, the basic clue that would tell him everything he needed to know. His prescience had never been so strong; he knew perfectly well that he was staring at the biggest, most startling and most complete disclosure of all. And he couldn't see it.

He stared at the folders for a long minute. What did they tell him? What was the clue?

And then, very slowly, the soft light of a prodigal sun illuminated his mind.

"Mr. Malone," Malone said gently, "you are a damned fool. There are times when it is necessary to discard the impossible after you have seen that the obscure is the obvious."

He wasn't sure whether that meant anything, or even whether he knew what he was saying. He was sure of only one thing: the final answer.

And it *was* obvious. Obvious as all hell.

13

There was, of course, only one thing to do, and only one place to go. Malone went downstairs without even stopping to wave farewell to the agent-in-charge, and climbed into the big, specially-built FBI Lincoln that waited for him.

"Want a driver?" one of the mechanics asked.

"No, thanks," Malone said. "This one's a solo job."

That was for sure. He drove out onto the streets and into the heavy late afternoon traffic of Washington, D. C. The Lincoln handled smoothly, but Malone didn't press his luck among the rushing cars. He wasn't in any hurry. He had all the time in the world, and he knew it. They— and, for once, Malone knew just who "they" were—would still be waiting for him when he got there.

If he got there, he thought suddenly, dodging a combination roadblock consisting of a green Plymouth making an illegal turn, a fourteen-year-old boy on a bicycle and a sweet young girl pushing a baby carriage. He managed to get past and wiped his forehead with one hand. He continued driving, even more carefully, until he was out of the city.

It took quite a lot of time. Washington traffic was getting worse and worse with every passing month, and the pedestrians were as nonchalant as ever. As Malone turned a corner, a familiar face popped into view, practically in front of his car. He swerved and got by without committing homicide, and a cheerful voice said: "Thanks, sorry."

"It's okay, Chester," Malone said. The big man skipped back to the sidewalk and watched the car go by. Malone knew him slightly, a private eye who did some work on the fringes of Washington crime; basically a nice guy, but a little too active for Malone's taste.

For a second he thought of asking the man to accompany him, but the last thing Malone needed was muscle. What he wanted was brains, and he even thought he might be developing some of those.

He was nearly sure of it by the time he finally did leave the city and get out onto the highway that went south into the depths of Virginia. And, while he drove, he began to use that brain, letting his reflexes take over most of the driving problems now that the Washington traffic tangle was behind him.

He took all his thoughts from behind the shield that had sheltered them and arrayed them neatly before him. Everything was perfectly clear; all he had to do now was explain it.

Malone had wondered, over the years, about the detectives in books. They always managed to wrap everything up in the last chapter—and that was all right. But they always had a whole crowd of suspects listening to them, too. And Malone knew perfectly well that he could never manage a set-up like that. People would be interrupting him. Things would happen. Dogs would rush in and start a fight on the floor. There would be earthquakes, or else somebody would suddenly faint and interrupt him.

But now, at long last, he realized, he had his chance.

Nobody, he thought happily, could interrupt him. And he could explain to his heart's content.

Because the members of the PRS were telepathic. And Malone, he thought cheerfully, was not.

Somebody, he was sure, would be tuned in on him as he drove toward their Virginia hiding place. And he hoped that that somebody would alert everybody else, so they could all tune in and hear his grand final explanation of everything.

And a hearty good afternoon to everybody, he thought. *A very hearty and happy and sunny good afternoon to all—and most especially to Miss Luba Garbitsch. I hope she's the one who's tuned in—or that somebody has alerted her by now, because I'd rather talk to her than to anyone else I can think of out there.*

Nothing personal, you understand. It's just that I'd like to show off a little. I don't need to hide anything from you—as a matter of plain, simple fact, I can't. Not with my shield down.

He paused then, and, in his imagination, he could almost hear Lou's voice.

"I'm listening, Kenneth," the voice said. "Go on."

Well, then, he thought. He fished around in his mind for a second, wondering exactly where to start. Then he decided, in the best traditions of the detective story, not to mention *Alice in Wonderland,* to start at the beginning.

The dear old Psychical Research Society, he thought, *had been going along for a good many years now—since the 1880's, as a matter of fact, or somewhere near there. That's a long time and a lot of research. A lot of famous and intelligent men and women have belonged to the Society. And in all that time, they've worked hard, and worked sincerely, in testing every kind of psychic phenomenon. They've worked impartially and scientifically to find out whether a given unusual incident was explicable in terms of known natural laws, or was the result of some unknown force.*

And it's hardly surprising that, after about a hundred years of work, something finally came of it.

"Not surprising at all," he imagined Lou's voice saying. "You're making things very clear, Kenneth."

Or had that been "Sir Kenneth"? Malone wasn't sure, but it didn't really matter. He spun the car around a curve in the highway, smiled gently to himself, and went on.

Naturally, to the average man in the street, the Society was just a bunch of crackpots, and the more respected and famous the people who belonged to it, the happier he was;

it just proved his superiority to them. He didn't deal with crackpot notions, did he?

No, the Society did. And nobody except the members paid much attention to what was going on.

I remember one of the book facsimiles you gave me, for instance. Some man, whose name I can't recall, wrote a great "expose" of the Society, in which he tried to prove that Sir Lewis Carter and certain other members were trying to take over the world and run it to suit themselves, making a sort of horrible dictatorship out of their power and position. At that, he wasn't really far from the truth, though he had it turned around a little. But the book shows that he has no knowledge whatever of what psionics is, or how it works. He seems to me to be just a little afraid of it, which probably adds to his ignorance. And, as a result, he got a twisted idea of what the PRS is actually doing.

He could almost hear Lou's voice again. "Yes," she was saying. "I remember the book. It was put in our reference library for its humorous aspects."

That's right, Malone thought. *It would be only funny to you. But it would be frightening and terrible to an awful lot of people simply because they wouldn't understand what the Society was all about.*

"All right," Lou's voice said helpfully. "And what *is* it all about?"

Malone settled back in the driver's seat as the car continued to spin along the road. *It seems to me,* he thought carefully, *that any telepath has to go one of two ways. Either, like Her Majesty or the others we found when we discovered her two years ago, the telepath ends up insane—or perhaps commits suicide, which is simply one step further in retreat—or else he learns to understand and control his own powers, and to understand other human beings so well that, if he actually did control the world, everyone would benefit in the long run.*

The difference between the two kinds is the difference between Her Majesty and the PRS.

"That's good thinking," he could hear Lou say.

No, it isn't, he thought; *it's no more than guessing, and it could be just as wild as you please. But there is one thing 1 do know: the way to get a better world, or anyhow the first step, is to clear the road ahead. And that means getting rid of the fools, idiots, maniacs, blockheads, morons, psychopaths, paranoids, timidity-ridden, fear-worshipers, fanatics, thieves, criminals and a whole lot more.*

"Get rid of them?" Lou's voice said.

Well, Malone thought, *I don't mean they've got to be killed or driven out of the civilized world. You've just got to get them out of any place where their influence is heavily felt on society as a whole.*

"All right," Lou's voice said pleasantly. "And how could we go about that? Do we write nasty letters to the editor?"

There's a much more effective way, Malone thought. *There's no trouble in getting rid of a man if you can make him expose himself. And you've managed that pretty well. You've thwarted their idiotic plans, made them stumble over their own fumble-mindedness, played on their neuroses, concocted errors for them to fight and, in general, rigged things in any possible way so that they'd quit, or get fired, or lose elections, or get arrested, or just generally get put out of circulation somehow.*

It's extremely effective—and it works very well.

Sometimes, you've only had to put the blocks to individuals. Sometimes whole nations have had to go. And sometimes it's been in-between, and you've managed to foul up whole organizations with misplaced papers missent messages, error, and changed minds and everything else you can think of.

As a matter of fact, it sounds like fun.

"Well," he imagined Lou saying, "it is fun, in away. But it's a deadly serious business, too."

Sure it is, Malone thought. *I think the first time that came home to me was when I saw what was happening in Russia, and compared it to what had been going on over here. Tom Boyd saw that, too, when I pointed it out to him—as you probably know if you were spying on my mind at the time.*

Not that I mind that in the least.

Come more often, by all means.

But Tom, in case you weren't listening, said: "Over here there are a lot of confused jerks and idiots... And in Russia there's a lot of confusion."

Now, that's perfectly true, and it spells out the difference. Over here, you've been confusing the jerks and the idiots, getting rid of them so the system can work properly. Over in Russia, on the other hand, you've left the jerks and the idiots all alone to do their dirty work, and you've just added to the confusion where necessary, so that the system will break down of its own weight.

"But, after all," Lou said, "things look pretty bad over here, too. Look at the papers."

Everybody, Malone thought, *has been telling me to go and look at the newspapers. And when I do look at them I find all sorts of evidence of confusion. Teachers resigning, senators and representatives goofing up bills on Congress, gang wars cluttering up the streets with cadavers and making things tough for the Sanitation Department, factional fights in various organizations. Now, all of that looks pretty horrible in the papers, but do you know something? It isn't horrible at all.*

It's pretty damn good, as a matter of fact.

The teachers who are resigning, for instance, are the nincompoops who've got to be pruned out so that competent teachers can come in. And, with the higher salaries, more and more competent men and women are going to be attracted to the job. The universities are going to be freer and better places to work in; they won't be monopolies any more.

"Monopolies?" Lou said.

In restraint of knowledge, Malone thought. *The old monopoly was in restraint of trade, and legal action helped to kill that kind. The monopoly in restraint of knowledge took a little more killing, but you're doing the job quite nicely. And not only in the schools.*

The factional fights are having the same result. Look at the AAAM, for instance. That organization is a monopoly, pure and simple. Simple, anyhow. And what the factional fights are doing to it is just breaking up the monopoly and letting knowledge free again.

And then we come to Congress. Senators and representatives are having a terrible time, some of them. There's a fight going on between Furbisher and Deeks because Deeks has discovered some evidence against Furbisher. Who's having the terrible time?

All of them?

Nope. Furbisher is. Deeks isn't.

And that's the way it's going all over. The useful, necessary legislation is going through Congress now without being cluttered up by stupid dam bills and water bills and other idiocies that simply clog the works.

And then, of course, there are the gang wars. Now, I feel as sorry for the Sanitation Department as anybody, but at least they're cleaning the streets for good now. The boys who are dying off and getting sent to hospitals and jails are just the ones who should have been sent away long ago. Everybody knows that, but nobody can prove it.

Except the PRS.

And the PRS is busy doing just what it can about that proof.

And all it takes is a few of you. I don't know how many—I don't know how many of you there really are, for that matter. But it must be a fair number to stock all your branches with "top-level" executives and the lower-level men and women who really believe in the PRS blind, and do their best to keep it working.

There are probably a lot of ways it might work, but the simplest and best way I can think of is this one: there's a clearing-house sort of set-up, and information comes in from various telepathic spies working for the PRS, about various projected activities of the imbecile contingent.

And, from this information, you figure out the best time and place for lightning to strike, and you select the kind of lightning it's going to be. Here it's a misplaced letter, there some "facts" that aren't facts, and somewhere else a dropped package of secret records. Somebody goofs—and is exposed.

Maybe it works on the local-organization level. Maybe there are teams all over the country, all ready to synchronize their minds and jab somebody in the thought processes at just the right time, in just the right way, as soon as they get the word. That's one way of doing it, maybe the best way.

There are others, but it doesn't really matter how that end of it works. The important thing is that it does work.

And, when it works, it can certainly create quite a mess. Yes-sirree, Bob. Or Lou, as the case may be.

I sure hope somebody's picking all this up, because I'd hate to have to explain it again when I get there.

Are you there, anybody?

Malone imagined he heard Lou's voice. "Yes, Ken," she said. "Yes, I'm here."

But, of course, there was no way for them to get through to him. They were telepathic, but Kenneth J. Malone wasn't he told himself sadly.

Hello, out there, he thought. *I hope you've been listening so far, because there isn't going to be too much more. But there are a couple of things that still need to be cleared up. I've got some answers, but there are others I'm going to need.*

There's Russia, for instance. It does seem to me as if your teams in Russia, whatever they're calling themselves, are having a lot more fun than the U. S. teams. For one thing they've got an easier job.

In this country, the teams are looking for ways to get rid of the blockheads, and there are a lot of them. In Russia, you don't have to get rid of the blockheads. All you have to do is clear the road for them. And you can do that by fouling up the more intelligent people.

"Intelligent people?" he could hear Lou say.

Intelligence doesn't mean good sense, Malone thought. *I don't doubt that the men who are maintaining Russia's power are intelligent men— but what they're doing is bad for the world as a whole, in the long run.*

So you foul them up, and leave the blockheads a clear field to run the country into the ground. And that's easier than fouling up the blockheads.

Sure it is.

There are fewer intelligent, active people around than there are blockheads.

Always were.

And maybe there always will be—but not if the PRS can help it.

Oh, and by the way, Malone thought. *You do know how I spotted you, don't you? You were tuned in then, weren't you?*

And I don't mean just Lou. I mean all of you.

In a world of blind men, the man who can see stands out. In a world of the insane, the sane man stands out.

And in a world where organizations are regularly being confused and fouled up—either as whole organizations, or through your attempts to get rid of individual members—a smooth-running, efficient organization stands out like a sore thumb.

Frankly, it took me longer to see it than it should have.

But I've got the answer at last—the main answer. Though, as I say, there are some others I'd like to have.

Like, for instance, Russia. And exactly what did happen that night in Moscow.

14

At this point Malone suddenly became aware of a sound that was not coming from his own mind. It was coming from somewhere behind his car, and it was a very loud sound. It was, he discovered when he looked back, the siren of a highway patrolman on a motorcycle, coming toward him at imminent risk of life and limb and waving frantically with an unbelievably free hand.

Malone glanced down at the speedometer. With a sigh, he realized that his reflexes had allowed him a little leeway, and that he was going slightly over the legal speed limit for this Virginia highway. He shook his head, eased up on the accelerator, and began to apply the brakes.

By the time he had pulled over to the side of the road, the highway patrolman was coming to a halt behind the big Lincoln. Malone watched him check the number on the rear plate and then walk slowly around to the window on the driver's side. "Can't you hurry?" Malone muttered under his breath. "All this Virginian ease is okay in its place, but—" In the meanwhile he was getting out his identification, and by the time the patrolman reached him he had it in his hand.

"I'm sorry," he said.

"Sorry?" the patrolman said, frowning. He had an open, boyish face with freckles and a pug nose. He looked like somebody's kid brother, very dependable but just a little cute. "What for?" he said.

Malone shrugged. "What else?" he said. "Speeding."

"Oh, that," the patrolman said. "Why, don't you worry about that."

"Don't worry about it?" Malone said. This particular kid brother was obviously a little nuts, and should have been put away years ago. He ground his teeth silently, but he didn't make any complaints. It was never wise, he knew, to irritate a traffic cop of any sort.

"Sure not," the patrolman said. "Why, we don't pay any attention out here until a fella hits ten miles over the posted limit. That's okay."

"Fine," Malone said cheerily. "Then I can drive on?"

"Now, just hold it a second there," the patrolman said. "Let's see your identification if you don't mind."

Malone held it out wordlessly. The patrolman, obviously intent on finding out just what kind of paper the card was made of, who had printed it and whether there were any germs on it, gave it a long, careful scrutiny. Malone shifted slightly in his seat, counted to ten and managed to say nothing.

Then the patrolman started reading the card aloud. "Kenneth J. Malone," he said in a tone of some surprise. "Special Agent of the FBI." He looked up. "That right?" he said. "What it says here?"

"That's right," Malone said. "And you can have my autograph later." He regretted the last sentence as soon as it was out of his mouth, but the patrolman didn't seem to notice.

"Then you're the man, all right," he said happily. "I caught your plate number as you went on by me, back there."

"Plate number?" Malone said. "What am I supposed to have done?" He'd overslept, he knew, but that was the only violation of even his personal code that he could think of. And it didn't seem likely that the Virginia Highway Patrol was sending out its men to arrest people who overslept.

"Why, Mr. Malone," the patrolman said with honest surprise written all over his Norman Rockwell face, "as far as I know you didn't do a thing wrong."

"But—"

"They just told us to be on the watch for a black 1973 Lincoln with your number, and see if you were driving it. They did say you'd probably be driving it."

"Good," Malone said. "And I am. And I'd like to continue doing so." He paused and then added, "But what happened?"

"Well," the patrolman said, in exactly the manner of a man starting out to tell a long, interesting story about the Wars of the Spanish Succession, "well, sir, it seems FBI Headquarters in Washington, they got in touch with the Highway Patrol Headquarters, down in Richmond, and Highway Patrol Headquarters—"

"Down in Richmond," Malone muttered resignedly.

"That's right," the patrolman said in a pleased voice. "Well, they called all the local barracks, and then we got the message on our radios." He stopped, exactly as if he thought he had finished.

Malone counted to ten again, made it twenty and then found that he was capable of speech. "What?" he said in a calm, patient voice, "was the message about?"

"Well," the patrolman said, "it seems some fella down in Washington, fella name of Thomas Boyd, they said it was, wants to talk to you pretty bad."

"He could have called me on the car phone," Malone said in what he thought was a reasonable tone of voice. "He didn't have to—"

"There's no call for yelling at me, Mr. Malone," the patrolman said reproachfully. "I only obeyed my orders, which were to locate your black 1973 Lincoln and see if you were driving it, and give you a message. That's all."

"It's enough," Malone muttered. "He didn't have to send out the militia to round me up."

"Oh, no, Mr. Malone," the patrolman said. "Not the militia. Highway Patrol. We don't rightly have any connection with the militia at all."

"Glad to hear it," Malone said. He picked up the receiver of the car phone and waited for the buzz that would show that he was connected with Communications Central in Washington.

It didn't come.

"Oh, yes," the patrolman said suddenly. "I suppose that's why this Mr. Boyd, he couldn't call you on the car telephone, Mr. Malone. The message we got, it also says that the fella at the FBI garage in Washington just forgot to plug in that phone there."

"Oh," Malone said. "Well, thanks for telling me."

"You're right welcome, Mr. Malone," the patrolman said "You can plug it in now."

"I intend to," Malone said through his teeth. He closed his eyes for a long second, and then opened them again. He saw the interested face of the patrolman looking down at him. Hurriedly, he turned away, felt underneath the dashboard until he found the dangling plug, and inserted it into its socket.

The buzz now arrived.

Malone heaved a great sigh and punched for Boyd's office. Then he looked around.

The patrolman was still standing at the car window. He was looking down at Malone with an interested, slightly blank expression.

Malone thought of several things to say, and chose the most harmless. "Thanks a lot," he told the patrolman. "I appreciate your stopping off to let me know."

"Oh, that's all right, Mr. Malone," the patrolman said. "That was my orders, to do that. And even if they weren't, it was no trouble at all. Any time. I'd always be glad to do anything for the FBI."

"Boyd here," a tinny voice from the phone said.

Malone eyed the patrolman sourly. "Malone here," he said. "What's the trouble, Tom? I—No, wait a minute."

"Ken!" Boyd's voice said. "I've been trying to—"

"Hold it a second," Malone said. He opened his mouth, and then he saw a car go by. The patrolman hadn't seen it. Malone felt sorry for the driver, but not too sorry. "Say!" he said to the patrolman.

"Yes, sir?" the patrolman said.

"That boy was really going, wasn't he?" Malone said. "He must have been doing at least ninety."

The patrolman jerked his head around to stare at the disappearing car. "Well—" he said, and then: "Yes, sir. Thank you, Mr. Malone. Thanks. I'll see you later." He raced for his machine, swung aboard and roared down the road, guiding with one hand and manipulating the controls of his radar set with the other.

Malone waved him a cheery farewell, and got back to the phone.

"Okay, Tom," he said. "Go ahead."

"Who was that you were talking to?" Boyd asked.

"Oh, just a motorcycle patrolman," Malone said. "He wanted to be helpful, so I told him to go chase a Buick."

"Why a Buick?" Boyd said, interestedly.

"Why not?" Malone said. "There happened to be one handy at the time. Now, what's on your mind?"

"I've been searching all over hell for you," Boyd said. "I wish you'd just leave some word where you were going, and then I wouldn't have to—"

"Damn it," Malone cut in. "Tom, just tell me what you want. In straightforward, simple language. It just took me ten minutes to pry a few idiotic facts out of a highway patrolman. Don't make me go through it all over again with you."

"Okay, okay," Boyd said. "Keep your pants on. But here's the dope: I just flew in from New York, and I brought all the files on the case— the stuff you left in your office in New York, remember?"

"Right," Malone said. "Thanks."

"And I think we may be able to get the Big Cheese," Boyd went on.

"Manelli?" Malone said.

"None other than the famous Cesare Antonio," Boyd said. "It seems two of his most valued lieutenants were found in a garage in Queens, practically weighted down with machine-gun bullets."

Malone thought of Manelli, complaining sadly about the high overhead of murder. "And where does that get us?" he said.

"Well," Boyd said, "whoever did the job forgot to search the bodies."

"Oh-oh," Malone said.

"Very much oh-oh," Boyd said. "They're loaded down, not only with lead, but with paper. There are documents linking Manelli right up to the International Truckers' Union—a direct tie-in with Mike Sand. And Sand now says he's tied in with the Great Lakes Transport Union in Chicago."

"This sounds like a big one," Malone said.

"You have no idea," Boyd said. "And in the middle of all this, Burris called."

"Burris?" Malone said.

"That's right," Boyd said. "He wants me to go on down to Florida and take over the investigation of the Flarion assassination. So it looks as if I'm going to miss most of the fun."

"Too bad," Malone said.

"But maybe not all," Boyd said. "It may tie in with the case we're working on. At least, that's what Burris thinks."

"Yes," Malone said. "I can see why he thinks so. Did he have any message for me, by the way?"

"Not exactly," Boyd said.

Malone blinked. "Not exactly?" he said. "What's that supposed to mean?"

"Well," Boyd said, "he says he does have something to tell you, but it'll wait until he sees you. Then, he says, he'll tell you personally."

"Great," Malone said.

"Maybe it's a surprise," Boyd said. "Maybe you're fired."

"I wouldn't have the luck," Malone said. "But if I get any leads on the Flarion job, I'll let you know right away."

"Sure," Boyd said. "Thanks. And—by the way, what are you doing now?"

"Me?" Malone said. "I'm driving."

"Yes, I know," Boyd said patiently. "To where, and why? Or is this another secret? Sometimes I think nobody loves me any more."

"Oh, don't be silly," Malone said. "The entire city of Miami Beach is awaiting your arrival with bated breath."

"But what are you doing?" Boyd said.

Malone chose his words carefully. "I'm just checking a lead," he said at last. "I don't know if it's going to pan out or not, but I thought I'd drive down to Richmond and check on a name I've got. I'll call you about it in the morning, Tom, and let you know what the result is."

"Oh," Boyd said. "Okay. Sure. So long, Ken."

"So long," Malone said. He hung up the phone, put the car into gear again and roared off down U. S. Highway Number One. He didn't feel entirely happy about the way things had gone; he'd been forced to lie to Tom Boyd, and that just wasn't right.

However, there was no help for it. It was actually better this way, he told himself hopefully. After all, the less Tom knew from now on, the better off he was going to be. The better off everyone would be.

He went on through Fredericksburg without incident, but he didn't continue on to Richmond. Instead, he turned off U. S. 1 when he reached a little town called Thornburg, which was smaller than he had believed a town could be and live. He began following a secondary road out into the countryside.

The countryside, of course, was filled with country, in the shape of hills, birds, trees, flowers, grass and other distractions to the passing motorist. It took Malone quite a bit longer than he expected to find the place he was looking for, and he finally came to the sad conclusion that country estates are just as difficult to find as houses in Brooklyn. In both cases, he thought, there was the same frantic search down what seemed to be a likely route, the same disappointment when the route turned out to lead nowhere, and the same discovery that no one had ever heard of the place and, in fact, doubted very strongly whether it even existed.

But he found it at last, rounding a curve in a narrow black-top road and spotting the house beyond a grove of trees. He recognized it instantly.

He had seen it so often that he felt as if he knew it intimately.

It was a big, rambling, Colonial-type mansion, painted a blinding and beautiful white, with a broad, pillared porch and a great carved front door. The front windows were curtained in rich purples, and before the house was a great front garden, and tall old trees. Malone half-expected Scarlett O'Hara to come tripping out of the house at any moment.

Inside it, however, if Malone were right, was not the magnetic Scarlett. Inside the house were some of the most important members of the Psychical Research Society.

But it was impossible to tell from the outside. Nothing moved on the well-kept grounds, and the windows didn't show so much as the flutter of a purple curtain. There was no sound. No cars were parked around the house, nor, Malone thought as he remembered *Gone With the Wind,* were there any horses or carriages.

The place looked deserted.

Malone thought he knew better, but it took a few minutes for him to get up enough courage to go up the long driveway. He stared at the house. It was an old one, he knew, built long before the Civil War and originally commanding a huge plantation. Now, all that remained of that vast parcel of land was the few acres that surrounded the house.

But the original family still inhabited it, proud of the house and of their part in its past. Over the years, Malone knew, they had kept it up scrupulously, and the place had been both restored and modernized on the inside without harming the classic outlines of the hundred-and-fifty-year-old structure.

A fence surrounded the estate, but the front gate was swinging open. Malone saw it and took a deep breath. Now, he told himself, or never. He drove the Lincoln through the opening slowly, alert for almost anything.

There was no disturbance. Thirty yards from the front door he pulled the car to a cautious stop and got out. He started to walk toward the building. Each step seemed to take whole minutes, and everything he had thought raced through his mind again.

Nothing seemed to move anywhere, except Malone himself.

Was he right? Were the PRS people really here? Or had he been led astray by them? Had he been manipulated as easily as they had manipulated so many others?

That was possible. But it wasn't the only possibility.

Suppose, he thought, that he was perfectly right, and that the PRS members were waiting inside. And suppose, too, that he'd misunderstood their motives.

Suppose they were just waiting for him to get a little closer.

Malone kept walking.

In just a few steps, he would be close enough so that a bullet aimed at him from the house hadn't a real chance of missing him.

And it didn't have to be bullets, either. They might have set a trap, he thought, and were waiting for him to walk right into it. Then they would hold him prisoner while they devised ways to...

To what? He didn't know. And that was even worse; it called up horrible terrors from the darkest depths of

Malone's mind. He continued to walk forward, feeling about as exposed as a restaurant lamb chop caught with its panty down.

He reached the steps that led up to the porch, and took them one at a time.

He stood on the porch. A long second passed.

He took a step toward the high, wide and handsome oaken door. Then he took another step, and another.

What was waiting for him inside?

He took a deep breath, and pressed the doorbell button.

The door swung open immediately, and Malone involuntarily stepped back.

The owner of the house smiled at him from the doorway. Malone let out his breath in one long sigh of relief.

"I was hoping it would be you," he said weakly. "May I come in?"

"Why, certainly, Malone. Come on in. We've been expecting you, you know," said Andrew J. Burris, director of the FBI.

15

Malone sat, quietly relaxed and almost completely at ease, in the depths of a huge, comfortable, old-fashioned Morris chair. Three similar chairs were clustered with his, around a squat, massive coffee table made of a single slab of dark wood set on short, curved legs. Malone looked around at the other three with a relaxed feeling of recognition: Andrew J. Burris, Sir Lewis Carter, and Luba Vasilovna Garbitsch.

"That mind shield of yours," Burris was saying, "is functioning very well. We weren't entirely sure you had actually located us until you pulled into that driveway."

"I wasn't entirely sure what I was locating," Malone said.

"And so it's over," Burris said with a satisfied air. "Everything's over."

"And just beginning," Sir Lewis put in. He drew a pipe from an inside pocket and began to fill it.

"And, of course," Burris said, "just beginning. Things do that; they go round and round in circles. It's what makes everything so confusing."

"And so much fun," Lou said, leaning back in her chair. She didn't look hostile now, Malone thought; she looked like a cat, wary but content. He decided that he liked this Lou even better than the old one. Lou, at home among her psionic colleagues, was even more than he'd ever thought she could be.

"More what?" she said suddenly. Burris jerked upright a trifle.

"What's more what?" he said. "Damn it, let's stick to one thing or the other. As soon as this thing starts mixing talk and thought it confuses me."

"Never mind," Lou said. She smiled across the table at Malone.

Malone jerked a finger under his collar.

"What made you decide to come here?" Sir Lewis said. He had the pipe lit now, and blew a cloud of fragrant smoke over the table.

Malone wondered where to start. "One of the clues," he said at last, "was the efficiency of the FBI. It hit me the same way the efficiency of the PRS had hit me, while I was looking at the batch of reports that had been run off so rapidly."

"Ah," Sir Lewis said. "The dossiers."

"Dossiers?" Burris said.

Sir Lewis puffed at his pipe. "Sorry," he said. "I thought you had been tuned in for that."

"I was busy," Burris said. "I can't tune into everything. After all, I've only got one mind."

"And two hands," Malone said at random.

"At least," Lou said. Their eyes met in a glance of perfect understanding.

"What the hell do hands have to do with it?" Burris said.

Sir Lewis shrugged. "Tune in and see," he said. "It's an old joke; but you'll never really adjust to telepathy unless you practice."

"Damn it," Burris said, "I practice. I'm always practicing. This and that and the other thing—after all, I am the director of the FBI. There's a lot to be done."

Sir Lewis puffed at his pipe again. "At any rate," he said smoothly, "Mr. Malone had requested some dossiers on us. On the PRS, myself, and Luba. They arrived very quickly. The efficiency of that arrival, and the efficiency he'd been noting about the FBI ever since he began work on this case, finally struck home to him."

"Ah," Burris said. "You see? The FBI's a full-time job. It's got to be efficient."

"Of course," Sir Lewis said soothingly.

"Anyhow," Malone said, "Sir Lewis is right. While every other branch of the government was having its troubles with the Great Confusion, the FBI was ticking along like a transistorized computer."

"A good start," Sir Lewis said.

"Darn good," Burris said. "Malone, I knew I could depend on you. You're a good man."

Malone swallowed hard. "Well, anyway," he said after a pause, "when I saw that I began to remember a few other things. Starting with a couple of years ago, when we first found Her Majesty, remember?"

"I'll never forget it," Burris said fervently. "She knighted me. Knight Commander of the Queen's Own FBI. What a moment."

"Thrilling," Malone said. "But you got to Yucca Flats for your knighting awfully quickly, a little too fast even for a modern plane."

"It had to be done," Burris said. "Anyhow, I've never really liked planes. Basically unsafe. People crash in them."

"But you wouldn't," Malone said. "You could always teleport yourself out."

"Sure," Burris said. "But that's troublesome. Why bother? Anyhow, I'd been to Yucca Flats before, so I could teleport there—a little way down the road, where I could meet my car—without any trouble."

"Anyhow, that was one thing," Malone said. "And then there was Her Majesty, when she pointed at that visiphone screen and accused you of being the telepathic spy. Remember?"

"She wasn't pointing at me," Burris said. "She was pointing at the man in the next room. How about you doing some remembering?"

"Sure she was," Malone said. "But it was just a little coincidence. And I have a hunch she felt, subconsciously, that there was something not quite right about you."

"Maybe," Burris conceded. "But that doesn't answer my question."

"It doesn't?" Malone said.

"Now look, Malone," Burris said. "None of this is proof. Not real proof. Not the kind the FBI has trained you to look for."

"But—"

"What I want to know," Burris said, "is why you came here, to my home? And in spite of everything you've said, that hasn't been tied down."

Malone frowned. After a second's thought he said, "Well... All I know is that it just seemed obvious. That's all."

"Indeed it is," Sir Lewis said. "But one of the things we'll have to teach you, my boy, is how to distinguish between a deduction from observed fact and a psionic intuition. You've been confusing them for some years now."

"I have?" Malone said.

"Sure you have," Burris said. "And, what's more—"

"Well, he's no worse than you are, Andrew," Lou said.

Burris turned. "Me?" he said in a voice of withering scorn.

"Certainly," Lou said. "After all, you've never really become used to mixtures of thought and speech. And, what's more, you've been using telepathy so long that when you try to communicate with nothing but words you only confuse yourself."

"And everybody else," Sir Lewis added.

"Hmpf," Burris said. "I'm busy all the time. I haven't got any extra time for practice."

Malone nodded, comparatively unsurprised. He'd wondered for years how a man so obviously unable to express himself clearly could run an organization like the FBI as well as he did. Having psionic abilities evidently led to drawbacks as well as advantages.

"Actually," he said, "my prescience made one mistake."

"Really?" Burris said, looking both worried and pleased about it.

"I expected the place to be full of people," Malone said. "I thought the elite corps of the PRS would be here."

"Oh," Burris said, looking crestfallen.

"Why, that was no mistake," Sir Lewis said. "As a matter of fact, they are all here. But they're quite busy at the moment; things are coning to a head, you know, and they must work quite undisturbed."

"And this," Burris added, "is a good place for it. There are sixty rooms in this house. Sixty."

"That's a lot of rooms," Malone said politely.

"A mansion," Burris said. "A positive mansion. And my family has lived here ever since—"

"I'm sure Ken isn't very interested in your family just now," Lou broke in.

"My family," Burris said with dignity, "is a very interesting family."

"I'm sure it must be," Lou said demurely. Sir Lewis choked with laughter suddenly and began waving his pipe. After a minute, Malone joined in.

"Damn it," Burris said. "Let's stick to one thing or the other. Did I say that?"

"Twice," Malone said.

"Sixty rooms," Burris said. "All built by my family. And local contractors, of course. That's enough to house sixty rooms full of people. And that number of people is a large houseful, I should think."

"It sounds like a lot," Malone said.

"It is a lot," Burris said. "All in my house. The house my family built."

"And we're grateful for it," Sir Lewis said soothingly. "We truly are."

"Good," Burris said.

"You must have had a large family," Lou said.

"A large family," Burris said, "and many guests. Many, many guests. From all over. Including famous people. General Hood slept in this house, and he slept very well indeed."

"As a matter of fact," Lou added, "he's still sleeping. They call it being dead."

"That's not funny," Burris snapped.

"Sorry," Lou said. "It was meant to be."

"I—" Burris shut his mouth and glared.

Malone was far away, thinking of the sixty rooms full of people, sitting quietly, their minds ranging into the distance, meshed together in small units. It was a picture that frightened and comforted him at the same time. He wasn't sure he liked it, but he certainly didn't dislike it, either.

After all, he told himself confusedly, too many cooks save a stitch in time.

He veered away from that sentence quickly. "Tell me," he said, "were you receiving my broadcast on the way here?"

Burris and Sir Lewis nodded. Lou started to nod, too, but stopped and looked surprised. "You mean you didn't know we were?" she said.

"How could I know?" Malone said. "After all, I was just tossing it out and hoping that somebody was on the listening end."

"But of course somebody was," Lou said. "I was."

"Good," Malone said. "But I still don't see how I was supposed to know that you—"

"I answered you, silly," Lou said. "I kept on answering you. Remember?"

Malone blinked, focused and then said, very slowly, "That was my imagination. Please tell me it was my imagination before I go nuts."

"Sorry," Lou said. "It wasn't."

"But that kind of thing," Malone said, "it takes a tremendous amount of power, doesn't it?"

"Not when the receiver is a telepath," Lou said sweetly.

Malone nodded slowly. "That," he said, "is exactly what I'm afraid of. Don't tell me—"

There was silence.

"Well?" Malone said.

"You said not to tell you," Lou said instantly.

"All right," Malone said. "I rescind the order. Am I a telepath, or am I not?"

Lou's lips didn't move. But then, they didn't have to.

The message came, unbidden, into Malone's mind.

Of course you are. That was the whole reason for Andrew's assigning you to this type of case.

"My God," Malone said softly.

Sir Lewis laid down his pipe in a handy ashtray. "Of course," he said, "you will find it difficult to pick up anyone but Lou, at first. The rapport between you two is really quite strong."

"Very strong indeed," Lou murmured. Malone found himself beginning to blush.

"It will be some time yet," Sir Lewis went on, "before you can really call yourself a telepath, my boy."

"I'll bet it will," Malone said. "Before I can call myself a telepath I'm going to have to get thoroughly used to the idea. And that's going to take a long, long time indeed."

"You only think that," Sir Lewis said. "Actually, you're used to the idea now. That was Andrew's big job."

"His big job?" Malone said. "Now, wait a minute—"

"You don't think I picked you for our first psionics case out of thin air, do you?" Burris said. "Before anything else, you had to be forced to accept the fact that such things as telepaths really existed."

"Oh, they do," Malone said. "They certainly do."

"There's me, for instance," Burris said. "But you had to be convinced. So I ordered you to go out and find one."

"Like the Bluebird of Happiness," Malone said.

Burris frowned. "What's like the Bluebird of Happiness?" he said.

"You are," Malone said.

"I am not," Burris said indignantly. "Bluebirds eat worms. My God, Malone."

"But the Bluebird," Malone said doggedly, "was right at home all the time, while everyone searched for it far away. And I had to go far away to find a telepath, when you were the one who ordered me to do it."

"Right," Burris said. "So you went and found Her Majesty. And, when you did find her, she forced acceptance on you simply by being Her Majesty and proving to you, once and for all, that she could read minds."

"Great," Malone said. "Of course, I could have got myself killed taking these lessons—"

"We were watching you," Burris said. "If anything had happened, we'd have been right on the spot."

"In time to bury the body," Malone said. "I think that's very thoughtful of you."

"We would have arrived in time to save you," Burris said. "Don't quibble. You're alive, aren't you?"

"Well," Malone said slowly, "if you're not sure, I don't know how I can convince you."

"There," Burris said triumphantly. "You see?"

Malone sighed wearily. "Okay," he said. "So you sent me out to find a telepath and to prove to me that there were such things. And I did. And then what happened?"

"You had a year," Burris said, "to get used to the idea of somebody reading your mind."

"Thanks," Malone said. "Of course, I didn't know it was you."

"It was Her Majesty too," Burris said. "Everybody."

"Good old Malone," Malone said. "The human peep-show."

"Now, that's what we mean," Sir Lewis broke in. "Subconsciously, you disliked the idea of leaving your thoughts bare to anyone, even a sweet little old lady. To some extent, you still do. But that will pass."

"Goody," Malone said.

"The residue is simply not important," Sir Lewis went on. "Your telepathic talents prove that."

"Oh, fine," Malone said. "Here I am reading minds and teleporting and all sorts of things. What will the boys back at Headquarters think now?"

"We'll get to that," Burris said. "But that first case did one more thing for you. Because you didn't like the idea of leaving your mind open, you began to develop a shield. That allowed you some sort of mental privacy."

"And then," Malone said, "I met Mike Fueyo and his little gang of teleporting juvenile delinquents."

"So that you could develop a psionic ability of your own," Burris said. "That completed your acceptance. But it took a threat to solidify that shield. That was step three. When you discovered your mind was being tampered with—"

"The shield started growing stronger," Malone said. "Sure. Her Majesty told me that, though she didn't know why."

"Right," Burris said.

"But, wait a minute," Malone said. "How could I do all that without knowing it? How would I know that some of my thoughts were safe behind a shield if I didn't know the shield existed and couldn't even tell if my mind were being read?" He paused. "Does that make sense?" he asked.

"It does," Burris said, "but it shouldn't."

"What?" Malone said.

"Two years ago, you had the answer to that one," Burris said. "Dr. O'Connor's machine. Remember why it did detect when a person's mind was being read?"

"Oh," Malone said. "Oh, sure. He said that any human being would know, subconsciously, whether his mind was being read."

"He did, indeed," Burris said. "And then we came to the fourth step: to put you in rapport with some psionicist who could teach you how to control the shield, how to raise and lower it, you might say. To learn to accept other thoughts, as well as reject them. To learn to accept your full telepathic talent. That was Lou's job."

"Lou's ... job?" Malone said. He felt his own shield go up. The thoughts behind it weren't pleasant. Lou had been ... well, hired to stay with him. She had pretended to like him; it was part of her job.

That was perfectly clear now.

Horribly clear.

"You are now on your way," Sir Lewis said, "to being a real psionicist."

"Fine," Malone said dully. "But why me? Why not, oh, Wolfe Wolf? I'd think he'd have a better chance than I would."

"My secretary," Burris said, "has talents enough of his own. But you, you're something brand-new. It's wonderful, Malone. It's exciting."

"It's a new taste thrill," Malone murmured. "Try Bon-Ton B-Complex Bolsters. Learn to eat your blanket as well as sleep with it."

"What?" Burris said.

"Never mind," Malone said. "You wouldn't understand."

"But I—"

"I know you wouldn't," Malone said, "because I don't."

Sir Lewis cleared his throat "My dear boy," he said, "you represent a breakthrough. You are an adult."

"That," Malone said testily, "is not news."

"But you are a telepathic adult," Sir Lewis said. "Many of them are capable of developing it into a useful ability. Children who have the talent may accidentally develop the ability to use it, but that almost invariably results in insanity. Without proper guidance, a child is no more capable of handling the variety of impressions it receives from adult minds than it is capable of understanding a complex piece of modern music. The effort to make a coherent whole out of the impression overstrains the mind, so to speak, and the damage is permanent."

"So here I am," Malone said, "and I'm not nuts. At least I don't think I'm nuts."

"Because you are an adult," Sir Lewis went on. "Telepathy seems to be almost impossible to develop in an adult, even difficult to test for it. A child may be tested comparatively simply; an adult, seldom or never."

He paused to relight his pipe.

"However," he went on, "the Psychical Research Society's executive board discovered a method of bringing out the ability in a talented child as far back as 1931. All of us who are sane telepaths today owe our ability to that process, which was applied to us, in each case, before the age of sixteen."

"How about me?" Malone said.

"You," Sir Lewis said, "are the first adult ever to learn the use of psionic powers from scratch."

"Oh," Malone said. "And that's why Mike Fueyo, for instance, could learn to teleport, though his older sister couldn't."

"Mike was an experiment," Sir Lewis said. "We decided to teach him teleportation without teaching him telepathy. You saw what happened."

"Sure I did," Malone said. "I had to stop it."

"We were forced to make you stop him," Sir Lewis said. "But we also let him teach you his abilities."

"So I'm an experiment," Malone said.

"A successful experiment," Sir Lewis added.

"Well," Malone said dully, "bully for me."

"Don't feel that way," Sir Lewis said. "We have—"

He stopped suddenly, and glanced at the others. Burris and Lou stood up, and Sir Lewis followed them.

"Sorry," Sir Lewis said in a different tone. "There's something important that we must take care of. Something quite urgent, I'm afraid."

"You can go on home, Malone," Burris said. "We'll talk later, but right now there's a crisis coming and we've got to help. Leave the car. I'll take care of it."

"Sure," Malone said, without moving.

Lou said, "Ken—" and stopped. Then the three of them turned and started up the long, curving staircase that led to the upstairs rooms.

Malone sat in the Morris chair for several long minutes, wishing that he were dead. Nobody made a sound. He rubbed his hands over the soft leather and tried to tell himself that he was lucky, and talented, and successful.

But he didn't care.

He closed his eyes at last, and took a deep breath.

Then he vanished.

16

Two hours passed, somehow. Bourbon and soda helped them pass, Malone discovered; he drank two highballs slowly, trying not to think about anything, and kept staring around at the walls of his apartment without really seeing anything. He felt terrible.

He made himself a third bourbon and soda and started in on it. Maybe this one would make him feel better. Maybe, he thought, he ought to break out the cigars and celebrate.

But there didn't seem to be very much to celebrate, somehow.

He felt like a guinea pig being congratulated on having successfully resisted a germ during an experiment.

He drank some more of the bourbon and soda. Guinea pigs didn't drink bourbon and soda, he told himself. He was better off than a guinea pig. He was happier than a guinea pig. But he couldn't imagine any guinea pig in the world, no matter how heartbroken, feeling any worse than Kenneth J. Malone.

He looked up. There was another guinea pig in the room.

Then he frowned. She wasn't a guinea pig. She was one off the experimenters. She was the one the guinea pig was supposed to fall in love with, so the guinea pig could be nice and telepathic and all the other experimenters could congratulate themselves. But whoever heard of a scientist falling in love with a guinea pig? It was fate. And fate was awful. Malone had often suspected it, but now he was sure. Now he saw things from the guinea pig's side, and fate was terrible.

"But Ken," the experimenter said. "It isn't like that at all."

"It is, too," Malone said. "It's even worse, but that'll have to wait. When I have some more to drink it will get worse. Watch and see."

"But Ken—" Lou hesitated, and then went on. "Don't feel sad about being an experiment. We're all experiments."

"I'm the guinea pig," Malone said. "I'm the only guinea pig. You said so."

"No, Ken," she said. "Remember, all of us in the PRS got early training when it was new and untried. Some of those methods weren't as good as we now have them; that's why a man like your boss sometimes tends to have a little trouble."

"Sure," Malone said. "But I'm your guinea pig. You made me dance through hoops and do tricks and everything just for an experiment. That's what." He took another swallow of his drink. "See?" he said. "It's getting worse already."

"No, it's not," Lou said. "It's getting better, if you'll only listen. I wasn't given this job, Ken. I volunteered for it."

"That isn't any better," Malone said morosely.

"I volunteered because I—because I liked you," Lou said. "Because I wanted to work with you, wanted to be with you."

"It's more experimenting," Malone said flatly. "More guinea-pigging around."

"It isn't, Ken," Lou said. "Believe me. Look into my mind. Believe me."

Malone tried. A second passed...

And then a long time passed, without any words at all.

"Well, well," Malone said at last. "If this is the life of a guinea pig, I'm all for it."

"I'm all for guinea pigs' rights," Lou said. "Life, Liberty and the Pursuit of Me."

"Agreed," Malone said. "How about that crisis, by the way? Are you going to have to leave suddenly again?"

Lou stretched lazily on the couch. "That's all over with, thank God," she said. "We had to get our agent out of Miami Beach, and cover his tracks at the same time."

"Tricky," Malone said.

"Very," Lou said.

"But—" Malone blinked. "Wait a minute," he said. "Your agent? You mean you had Governor Flarion killed?"

Lou nodded soberly. "We had to," she said. "That paranoid mind of his had built up a shield we simply couldn't get through. He had plans for making himself president, you know—and all the terrifying potentialities of an embryonic Hitler." She grimaced. "We don't like being forced to kill," she said, "but sometimes we've got to."

Malone thought of his own .44 Magnum, and the times he had used it, and nodded very slowly.

"There are still a couple of questions, though," he said. "For instance, there's that trip to Russia. Why *did* you make it? Was it your father?"

"Of course it was," Lou said. "We had to get him back in and make sure he was safe."

"You mean that Vasili Garbitsch is a PSR member?" Malone said, stunned.

"Well, really," Lou said. "Did you think my father would really be a spy? We had to get him back to Russia; he was needed for work in the Kremlin. That's why we nudged Boyd into making the arrest."

"And the others?" Malone said. "Brubitsch and Borbitsch?"

"Real spies," Lou said. "Bad ones, but real. Any more questions?"

"Some," Malone said. "Were you kidding about that drink in Moscow?"

She shook her head. "I wish I had been," she said. "But I was concentrating on Petkoff, who didn't know a thing about the drugged drink. I didn't catch anything else until after I'd swallowed it. And then it was too late."

"Good old Petkoff," Malone said. "Always helpful. But he was right about one thing, anyway."

"What?" Lou said.

"The FBI," Malone said. "He told us it was a secret police organization. And, by God, in a way it is!"

Lou grinned. Malone started to laugh outright. They found themselves very close and the laughter stopped, and there was some more time without words. When Malone broke free, he had a suddenly sobered expression on his face.

"Hey," he said. "What about Tom Boyd? He knows a lot but he hasn't got any talents, as far as I know, and—"

"He'll be all right," Lou said. "Andrew and the others have thought of that."

"But he knows an awful lot about the evidence I dug up."

"Andrew will give him a cover-up explanation they're working out," Lou said. "That will convince Boyd there's nothing more to worry about. Of course, we may have to change his mind about a few things, but we can do that, probably through you, since you know him best. There's nothing for you to worry over, Ken. Nothing at all."

"Good," Malone said. He leaned over and kissed her. "Because I'm not in the least worried."

Lou sighed deeply, looking off into space.

"Luba Malone," she said. "It sounds nice. And, after all, my mother was Irish. At least it sounds better than Garbitsch."

"What doesn't?" Malone said automatically. Then he blinked. "Hey, *I'm* Malone!" he said. "How could you be Malone?"

"Me?" Lou said. She caroled happily. "I'm Malone because I love you, love you with all my heart."

"That," Malone said, "does it. A woman after my own heart."

Lou made a low curtsy.

"And a woman of grace and breeding," Malone said. "Eftsoons, if that means anything."

"You know," Lou said, "I like you even better when you're being Sir Kenneth. Especially when you're talking to yourself."

"My innate gallantry and all my good qualities come out," Malone said.

"Yes," Lou said. "Indeed they do. All over the place. It's nice to go back to Elizabethan times, anyhow, in the middle of all these troubles."

"Oh, I don't know," Malone said. "There's always been trouble. In the Middle Ages, it was witches. In the Seventeenth Century, it was demons. In the Nineteenth it was revolutions. In—"

Lou cut him off with a kiss. When she broke away Malone raised his eyebrows.

"I prithee," he said, "interrupt me not. I am developing a scheme of philosophy. There have always been troubles. In the 1890's there was a Depression and panic, and the Spanish-American War—"

"All right, Sirrah," Lou said. "And then what?"

"Let's see," Malone said, reverting to 1973 for a second. "In 1903 there was the airplane, and troubles abroad."

"Yes?" Lou said. "Do go on, Sirrah. Your liege awaits your slightest word."

"Hmm," Malone said.

"That, Milord, was a very slight word indeed," Lou said. "What's after 1903?"

Malone smiled and went back to the days of the First Elizabeth happily.

"In 1914, it was enemy aliens," said Sir Kenneth Malone.

THE END

And Now a Message . . .
By Greg Fowlkes

A short Story from the upcoming Book - *Back Road to the Stars*

And Now A Message . . .

For the third time that night Jack Olsen was about to nod off over the copy of *Statistical Information Theory* that he was attempting to read. Giving it up as a bad effort, he shut the book and looked out the window of the control room at the giant bowl of the Arecibo radio telescope. Theoretically he was running the huge instrument, but in reality all the controlling was being done by the computers in the room around him. For six months he had been working eight hour shifts every night, and his job had consisted of the five minutes a shift that it took to enter the coordinates to be examined on the control console. Other than that, he was on hand only for the off chance that the monitoring programs would recognize some pattern in the radio noise, in which case an alarm would sound. So far, in the six months, it hadn't happened.

He walked over to the coffee machine in the hopes that a cup would revive him enough so that he could continue his studies. He never made it, for as if to prove the lie of his earlier thoughts, the alarm sounded. For a moment Jack was frozen, the alarm beating raucously in his ears, then he pulled himself together and flicked off the switch on the bell. With the room returned to the relative quiet of the whoosh of the cooling fans on the equipment, Jack sat down at the console and keyed in an enquiry. Within seconds the computer had replied that it was receiving a strong periodic signal on the 42 centimeter band. Further questioning showed that it was not a program malfunction but a genuine signal.

Jack picked up the phone and dialed his boss's number. It was three in the morning, but his instructions had been clear. If anything was received that could possibly be an intelligent signal, he was supposed to contact his superior immediately.

Despite the long drive through the mountains in the cool Puerto Rican night, Professor Kraft showed up with his eyes still sleepy. Shuffling over to the coffee pot by the window he poured himself a large mug before he said anything. "You'd better have something good to get me up at this hour."

"I think so," Jack said, aware that his boss's irritation was only feigned. "I've been checking with the computer since I called you. It shows a strong periodic signal with a sharp pulse every fifty milliseconds. It runs on like that for about two and a half minutes before the signal fades below the background."

"Any chance that it might be a pulsar?" Kraft asked, referring to the radio signals of rapidly rotating neutron stars. "That's within the range of periods for them. When the first one was discovered, they thought that they had received intelligent signals."

"I thought of that, so I checked the record of the broad band receiver." Jack brought out a long strip of graph paper and pointed to the evenly spaced patterns of peaks on it. "Where the narrow band shows only a single repetitive pulse, the wide band gives us this fine structure. It's far too regular to be a pulsar and much too detailed. It's more like some sort of timing signal or spacer. And in between the pulses there is another signal. It's not as repetitive as the main pulse. That's why the program doesn't bring it out. But there definitely is some sort of transmission in between. It's weaker, but I think that we can write a processing program to pick it out from the noise."

Kraft looked at the trace in his hand thoughtfully. "I hate to make snap judgements. You can be suckered in too easily that way. But it does look like some kind of artificial signal. We'll get the team working on it in the morning. Have you received any additional signals?"

"No. I've kept the dish tracking the source, but all we get on 42 cm. is background noise. It's like there was a moment of freak atmospheric conditions that opened a window, and then it shut again. Just like you get with shortwave sometimes because of the ionosphere."

"Well, we should be grateful for what we've got. I don't think I can sleep anymore tonight, so I'll keep you company. I'd like to be here if we get any more messages from our friends out there," he said, pointing with his cup towards the star filled sky that loomed over the radio telescope's antenna.

"Frustrating, isn't it?" Prof. Kraft remarked to the team of graduate students and post doctoral fellows that were working under him on the interstellar communications project. And frustrating it had been. For six months they had continuously monitored the sky searching for signs of life finally to be rewarded by a two minute snippet of extraterrestrial conversation.

Now, another six months later, they had still made no sense of the signal, nor had they received any further transmissions from that part of the sky, though they had concentrated their efforts in that direction.

"Rumors have leaked out about our discovery, and I've been getting requests for the data. I'd sure hate to have someone else steal our thunder by deciphering the signal, but if we don't make some progress soon, we're going to have to release it." He looked around the table at the young faces of his assistants. At the moment they didn't look nearly as bright and intelligent as he knew they were.

"Why don't I summarize what we've found so far in hopes that it will give us some new ideas?"

"First, we've got this repetitive pattern of pulses every twentieth of a second as regular as clockwork. So regular, in fact, that we can't decide whether they serve as breaks in the message or were just put there to attract our attention. Remember, it was these pulses that were first recognized by the computer."

"But the pulses aren't the real message. That lays in the spaces in between. We've been able to deduce that the messages are digitized and the computer has been able to enhance them so that we have a fairly error free record of them. There is some repetitive structure to them, and they do vary in some sort of progression, but beyond that, we haven't been able to get the least notion of what they mean. Anyone have something to add?"

Bill Warden, one of the post docs, spoke up. "Well, we've tried mathematical analysis on the signals and have gotten zero results. It has already been assumed that any sort of interstellar communications would be based on sort of easily recognizable mathematical progression. Like one, two three. Something like that to show that they were rational. From there you can always build up more complicated concepts."

"With this message we don't have that, which leads us to one of two assumptions. One, we have only a fragment of a broadcast, and from a very advanced lesson at that. If that's the case, I don't see much hope of our being able to decipher the message until we can receive more signals to give us a broader base to work from."

"The other alternative is that they, whoever they are, just don't think like us. Their minds work in some fashion so that this mess we have makes sense to them. If so, I don't see any hope at all. Their minds may just be too foreign for us to hold a dialog with them."

"Thank you for that optimistic note," Prof. Kraft said wryly. "For the first time mankind has received a message from another species and we can't tell whether it is a cure for cancer, a means of achieving universal peace, or a recipe for sauerbratten. Any comments?"

"If it's sauerbratten, where do we go for a tablespoon of powdered bandersnatch egg?" quipped one of the grad students. They all laughed at the joke more than it deserved. Six months of unrewarded work had left them all a little giddy. After the giggles and comments had died down, Jack Olsen coughed, trying to get their attention.

"You've got something useful to say, Jack?" Kraft asked. "You might as well tell us. I don't think anyone else has anything useful to add," he said, pointedly looking at the wisecracker.

"I've been thinking about the signal, and I remember something that I said to you the night it came in. I don't know if you recall, but I called the pulses timing signals. Now there is one type of common transmission that has the same kind of pulses, and that's television. They use the pulses to synchronize the frames. It's possible that the message in between each pulse is a picture, and the whole transmission is meant to be viewed in sequence."

"How long have you been sitting on this while the rest of us were beating our brains out?" Kraft asked.

"It just came to me," Jack said, his face flushed. "I should have thought of it earlier, but like Bill said, we've all been conditioned to look for something like one plus one equals two."

"I think that we should all have seen it," Kraft said. "It makes as much sense as anything else that's been suggested. Do you think that you can get us a picture?"

"If it's there, I should be able to pick it out using the computer," Jack answered.

"Good. Then, since it was your idea, you're in charge. Dragoon anything or anybody that you need to help you."

Five days later they were all gathered around the conference room table again, but this time there was a TV set and a video recorder on a cart at its end. From the nervous stubbing of cigarette butts and fingers drumming on the table, it was obvious that all the members of the team were in a state of anticipation.

"It took some time to figure out exactly how the signal was put together," Jack began. "After all, we didn't know how many lines there were in each frame or how many bits made up each unit of picture. In the end, I had to have the computer run through all the likely possibilities for one of the frames. It took a lot of computer time, but I've finally got some recognizable pictures."

"It turns out that the original broadcast was in color. That threw us for a while, but we finally psyched it out. The aliens must have eyes structurally different from ours; there are only two colors, not three in the signal. Which colors they are is anybody's guess. They might be ultraviolet and infrared for all we can tell. Arbitrarily, I've assigned them red and bluish green, so keep that in mind. Also, because the video recorder uses thirty frames a second instead of the twenty in the transmission, it was necessary to compress the program a bit. This means that everything you'll be seeing has been speeded up about fifty percent.

"I guess you're all more interested in seeing the tape than in listening to me." A snort from Prof. Kraft indicated agreement. Jack flicked off the lights and started the tape. For a minute the screen showed only snow, then a face became recognizable. It was a sickly chartreuse, and there was no nose between the two large, oval eyes, but it was recognizable as a face. The figures movements were quick and jerky like an old silent movie, the result of the difference in frame speed, and the picture left a lot to be desired in clarity, the product of interstellar noise, but it was a picture, the first of an alien race.

As the tape played, a weird, sings song voice came from the speaker sounding something like a Chinese chipmunk. "I forgot to mention that there was also an audio track along with the signal. Again, it's only a reconstruction and may not bear much resemblance to the original, but then, we'll never know," Jack commented. They had determined that the source of the transmission was at least several dozen light years away. It would take twice that number of years to send a message and receive a reply, by which time they would all be dead.

They continued to watch the tape. The camera had drawn back to show the alien from the waist up revealing rounded shoulders and a pair of six fingered hands. Apparently he was standing behind a low lectern or a table of some sort. The fuzzy picture and camera angle made it hard to tell which. As he, or her, or it, spoke, the alien pointed at a chart or poster suspended on the backdrop. A pattern of red and blue that hurt the eye with violent contrasts seemed to be some sort of text. The voice continued as the picture disappeared in a sea of snow and then it broke into static. The transmission had ended.

"You've done a fine job, Jack," Prof. Kraft said after they had played the tape through a half dozen times. "It's actually far better than I thought it would be, and I think we can accept any of the shortcomings that you mentioned."

"So, we've got a face and body of what certainly is a rational creature. He seemed to be giving us a lesson or lecture of some sort, though I for one don't have the faintest idea of what he was talking about. We have an idea of what they look like which I am sure will give the biologists a lot to speculate on, so I guess that we should be thankful for small favors, but I still don't see how we're going to learn any more about them without receiving further signals."

"I wouldn't hold out much hope of that," Jack interjected. "I think that it's clear now that the signal we picked up was not meant for interstellar communication. Any such signal would have been designed with much greater noise immunity. We were able to receive it only because of an accident of atmospheric conditions. It was actually just a local TV broadcast. As we haven't received anything since, those conditions must be rare."

"So," Kraft said, "we have a message of great potential import, that at the very least could provide us with insights on a totally alien culture, and no way to decipher it."

"I've got an idea," Bill said. "We've all been looking at the problem from the point of view of hardware and computer programs. That's natural because of our backgrounds, but now that we have what amounts to an artifact, maybe we should call in a specialist. We need someone who is trained in resurrecting a culture from its fragments. I suggest that we show the tape to some archeologists and get their opinions."

Convincing an archeologist to look at the tape was harder than it had sounded. Most of them were more interested in ancient rather than alien civilizations. Jack suspected that they felt out of their depth with the computers and electronics. With some pressure and pleading, a group finally agreed to view the tape, but after the showing, only one evinced any interest in following up on it.

A visiting lecturer from Norway, she was reputed to have a good background in languages, though Jack lacked the knowledge to judge her qualifications. However, as she was young, blond, and attractive, he was quite willing to spend the time required to familiarize her with the tape and the equipment they had used to come up with it. Together, they spent hours viewing the tape, studying it frame by frame attempting to pick out the slightest piece of information.

The project team had been assembled in the conference room, and this time it was the archeologist's turn to address them. For three weeks Cristina Peterson had been studying the tape almost constantly, and now she was ready to give her opinion. With the exception of Jack, who had been working closely with her, they were all, even Prof. Kraft, eagerly awaiting the report. There had been a great deal of speculation about what her findings would be.

"First," she began, "before I get your hopes up, I want to say that I have not been able to get a word for word translation of the voice on the tape. The sample of speech is just too brief for that to be possible. If the scene had contained more action, I might have been more successful, but we were not that fortunate. I have, however, been able to form a hypothesis based on the spoken word as well as visual clues such as facial expression, setting, and so on."

"An important point to remember is that the aliens, despite certain differences in appearance, are not too dissimilar from ourselves. They are bipedal, intelligent, and possess opposable thumbs. They have binocular vision and a form of color perception as well. Brain size is about the same in relationship to total body size as in humans, and I would be greatly surprised if they were much larger or smaller than ourselves. That much can be guessed on the basis of physiology from the picture and the nature of the signal. From this information, I think that we can draw the conclusion that their planet is, within limits, earthlike."

"Probably more relevant is their state of culture. They obviously have a technology and one that is recognizable in terms of our own. That we can receive their signals is proof of that. Also, they speak, they wear clothing, we can even guess at the purpose of some of the objects visible in the tape. I might add that this is more than we can do for some of the artifacts of primitive human cultures. In some ways we have more in common with the aliens than we do with the Tasadi or Bushman."

"I want you to bear in mind that these beings are not greatly different from ourselves. If we are to properly analyze the contents of the message, we must remember that they are influenced by the same drives and forces as humans." There was an uneasy shifting in their seats on the part of the team members as they took in the meaning of her statement.

"If we accept this premise, and replace the alien with a human, we can make an educated guess as to what we are seen on the tape. I'll run it again for you so that you can make the substitution." Jack tapped the switch, and for the next minute and a half they watched the now familiar scene replay itself.

"Before I give my own opinion, would anyone else like to make a guess?" Cristina asked.

Kraft looked around the room, but it appeared as though no one had the courage to be the first to put his own views forward. To break the silence he said, "It's only a guess, but to start the discussion, I'd say that the alien might be a lecturer. He's obviously standing at some sort of podium or speaker's table."

"He seems a little too impassioned for a lecturer, at least in the physical sciences," one of the grad students remarked. "I've never seen you that excited before a class." Kraft smiled at the reference to his own low keyed classroom delivery.

"Maybe it's a political science class. They get more aroused."

Bill Warden broke in, "Why a class? It looks to me more like he's a politician trying to persuade the voters. He must be up for reelection. The sign in back could be an election poster." That brought a couple of laughs and a few less than serious comments.

"We've all had a crack at it," Prof. Kraft said. "You obviously have your own interpretation, and I think that we've been kept in suspense long enough. From the look on Jack's face, it must be a good one. Let's hear it now. After all, the communication between two species is one of the most important events in human history."

She smiled at the jibe. "All your suggestions are plausible, but I've spent more time analyzing the tape than you have. I'll play it again for you and point out the features that have led me to my interpretation."

"The first thing that caught my attention was the fact that the word 'gratach' was mentioned fourteen times, an unusually high incidence in such a brief speech. Furthermore, at least four of those times the speaker pointed to the symbols on the chart behind him. I think that we can assume that 'gratach' is a name, and the symbols form the written version."

"Now here's something that I want you to see." She froze the picture on the television. "Note the artifacts on the table, a bowl filled with a substance and a box or container. There appears to be some writing on the box, but the resolution of the picture isn't good enough to allow us to make it out. However," she said as the tape began to roll again, "as the alien points to the box and says 'gratach' it is likely that the symbols again spell out the name in the chart behind the alien. Note, too, the expression on his face. Despite the lack of a nose, the face is surprisingly human, and if that expression was on a human face, it would be one of approval or pleasure."

"I think that if you put all the clues together, you can come to only one conclusion. Dr. Warden was not far off when he suggested a political campaign. The speaker is definitely trying to persuade his audience, but it is the package, not himself, that he is trying to sell."

"Oh, god," Kraft sputtered. "You can't mean it. The first communication from another planet and it's only . . ."

"Yes, I'm afraid so," Cristina said. "The first and only signal received from another world is nothing more than a breakfast food commercial."

Special Preview!

THE LAWS OF MAGIC
BY GREG FOWLKES
© 2010

Now available from The Fictional Press
www.TheFictionalPress.com

THE LAWS OF MAGIC
WITHOUT LICENSE

☆ ☆ ☆ ☆ ☆

As Egil Njalsson climbed the steps of the criminal courts building he wondered if it was really worth it. Eighteen months of practicing law on his own and here he was in his only suit, about to attend the preliminary hearing in a petty case for which with luck he would be able to recover his expenses. It wasn't even a paying client. The state would be picking up the tab for this one, and he'd ended up being the lawyer appointed by the court. At the moment it wasn't clear who would benefit most from the charity, the client or the lawyer. He hadn't had a case in three months and he'd just been eking out a living writing briefs for other lawyers. He could do that well enough. His technical background gave him a depth of knowledge most lawyers lacked when it came to cases involving points of science as well as law. If he hadn't had that he'd be starving.

He'd been thinking about that a lot lately; whether he had made the right decision giving up science and going into the law. At the time, with the aerospace industry in a depression in the early seventies, it had seemed like a good idea. Engineers were pumping gas and PhD's in physics were selling insurance. Being a lawyer had seemed like a good way to make money. A stable income, no ups and downs. He'd put in his time at law school and done well. After the grind at CalThaum, law school had been a snap. So here he was a lawyer barely making ends meet and his school mates, the ones who had stuck with science were all making it rich designing personal calculating engines and disk storage units.

He tried to put all these thoughts out of his mind as he passed through the big brass doors of the court house. After all, he did have a client to defend, and a duty to him. It wasn't easy, though. It wasn't, after all, a very important case. Just a charge of fortune telling and practicing the Art without a license. Minor offenses, probably not even any jail time involved. This wouldn't even be a trial today, just a plea and arranging of bail.

It wouldn't even have amounted to that if his client hadn't instisted on pleading not guilty. He'd met him at the county jail, an old man, one Jake Schmidts. He'd tried to talk him out of pleading not guilty, too. A guilty plea, a small fine, and they both could be done with it. His client, though, had turned out to be something of a character. So here he was.

It took an hour and a half before their case came up. The judge looked at him questioningly when he had pleaded not guilty, but thankfully had released his client on his own recognizance when he indicated he had a permanent address. It was over in five minutes.

They got the release papers and the court date from the bailiff. Egil started to head out when he noticed that his client seemed lost and disoriented by it all. "Do you have car fare home?"

"No," Schmidts said. "I didn't have any money on me when they came and arrested me. Not a cent."

"Which way do you live?"

The old man gave an address on Fair Oaks Street. It wasn't far out of his way. Neither one of them lived in the best part of town.

"I can give you a lift," Egil said.

"That's kind of you, Mr. Njalsson," Schmidts said. The mister was ironic. The arrest report hadn't given an age, just "somewhere around seventy." As far as Egil could tell that might have been off by a decade or two.

The address turned out to be a sort of second hand junk store. The operative word was junk. If the pieces in the dirty window were the best of the lot then Egil could see how Schmidts qualified as indigent.

"Thanks for the ride. I've a beer inside if you'd like."

Njalsson looked at his watch. It wasn't too early to start drinking, at least just a beer. The work at the office would wait. He had to talk to Schmidts anyway to prepare a case. Besides, the old man seemed to want to pay him back for the ride.

If anything, the shop was worse on the inside than it looked from the front. Odd bits of bric-a-brac were strewn around everywhere; most of it looking like it hadn't been moved or even dusted in twenty years. Broken down pieces of furniture were covered with moldering sheets.

The old man led him to the back and up some stairs to an apartment above the shop. The kitchen was cleaner, though still hardly spotless. Of course, Egil's own small apartment wasn't the neatest of place, either.

The refrigerator looked as old as Schmidt's, but the beer was cold. Schmidt's took out two and motioned him to a chair at the kitchen table.

"So what happens now, Mr. Njalsson?"

"The trial will be held on the date on the summons. The district attorney will call his witnesses and make his case. Then I'll make my case. The judge will then decide."

"No jury?" Schmidt's asked disappointedly.

"Not unless we've got a very strong case to present. This is a small matter. It's better left to a judge. A jury would be considered a waste of time, I'm afraid, and would probably result in a higher fine. Maybe even jail."

"So you think I'm guilty?"

"I don't think you have much of a case."

"That's different?"

"To a lawyer it is."

Schmidts snorted in disgust.

"I don't want to disillusion you, Mr. Schmidts, but you've got to face the facts. Do you have a license to practice Magic?"

"No."

"Did you tell the fortune of one Mrs. Einar Johnson?"

"Yes, and an ungrateful woman she is, too. Just because I told her the truth about that shifty salesman she thinks is going to marry her. He's just after her late husband's money."

Egil raised an eyebrow.

"It's the truth. I've been reading the cards longer than you've been alive, Mr. Njalsson, and I know what I'm doing. That salesman is the one that got her to swear out a complaint against me."

"It doesn't matter whether what you said was the truth or not. What matters is that you were practicing the Art without a license. Magic is a potentially dangerous business. It's not something that untrained people should be dealing with. That's what the law is about."

"What would you know about the Art, Mr. Lawyer?" Schmidts asked sharply.

"I know more than most, Mr. Schmidts. I studied applied metaphysics at the California Institute of Thaumaturgy for four years before going into the law. I've got a Bachelor's of Science degree. I've also got my practitioner's license from both the state of California and Wisconsin. I may not be the greatest practitioner of the Art, but I am competent enough to know what I am and am not capable of."

"So maybe you did study at a fancy school out west. Those scientists don't know everything. They think that they've discovered magic, but magic goes back. Way back. Back before Helmholtz and Gauss. Before the Egyptians and Babylonians. Magic is old, Mr. Njalsson, and the doctors and professors haven't learned half of it."

"And you have?" Egil asked sarcastically. He was getting annoyed at the old man's pretensions of knowledge. He was surprised, though, that Schmidts knew that the two physicists Helmholtz and Gauss had been instrumental in proving the scientific basis for magic.

"No. I'm no fool. I've been studying the Art all my life. I know what I know and I have a good idea of what I don't. What I do know is more than a youngster like you learns in four years at college, even if it is a fancy one."

"Look, Mr. Schmidts," Egil said. "This isn't working out. Maybe you should get yourself a different lawyer."

The old man looked at him in surprise, then shook his head. "No. I guess you were just telling me the way it is. I may not like it, but I can't fault you for telling the truth."

"Okay. Is there anything I can use in your defense?"

"Guess not."

"Well, where did you learn to tell fortunes, to read the cards?" Egil asked.

"From an old Romany woman," the old man answered.

"Where? Here in the city?"

"No, it was a long time ago. Bohemia, I think it was."

"Bohemia? You mean Czechoslovakia."

"Yes, that's what they call it now I think. Prague. I was a student there."

"A student? At a university? I thought you didn't believe in learning."

"I was younger then. I thought there were things I might learn. I was wrong."

"Did you get a degree, though? That might carry some weight, especially a foreign one."

"Wait a moment. I think I have one someplace. Let me go look." Schmidts went down to his shop. From below Egil could hear noises as if boxes were being moved around. He didn't quite know what to make of the old man's gypsy tale. Bohemia had become part of Czechoslovakia after the First World War in the breakup of the Austrian Empire.   It hadn't been a separate country since the Hapsburgs.

There were footsteps on the stairway and Schmidts showed up with a small picture frame carrying a piece of parchment.   It was certainly a degree, but not from the University of Prague.   The writing had faded with age and Egil had never learned French, but it appeared to be a doctorate granted by the Sorbonne.   It was also made out to one Jacques Krieger.

"This isn't your name."

"It was the name I was using then."

"Can you prove that?"

"Not that I can see."

"Oh well.   Maybe we can use it.   If you can find anymore old papers like this save them for me.   We might have some defense if we can prove you had an education, particularly if it was before the current examination system went into effect."

"I'll do that, Mr. Njalsson."

"Well I've got to get going now.   Can I take this with me?" the lawyer asked, holding up the sheepskin.

"Yes, if it will help."

Egil let himself out through the shop.   He dumped the diploma on the car seat next to him and started the car. While the engine was warming up he glanced down at it. The date was written in Roman numerals.   It took him a moment to figure out the year.   It was 1847.   Either the old man was lying to him or he might find himself defending him in a commitment hearing.

CLASSIC SCIENCE FICTION RESURRECTED FROM RANDALL GARRETT AND LAURENCE JANIFER WRITING AS MARK PHILLIPS

BRAIN TWISTER

Someone is reading the minds of America's space scientists at a secret base in Nevada, and FBI agent Kenneth Malone must find out whom. The problem is that the only way to find a telepathic spy is with another telepath, but Malone discovers that all telepaths are crazy. His best chance seems to be a little old lady who thinks that she's Queen Elizabeth the first. Will Malone find the spy, or will this case prove to be a real brain twister.

THE IMPOSSIBLES

FBI Agent Kenneth Malone is back with another case, this one involving a gang of car thieves that only steal Red 1972 Cadillacs. The only problem is that the thief, or thieves as the case may be, seem to have the ability to make themselves invisible. Of course that's impossible, isn't it? But with the help of the usual beautiful girl, Agent Boyd, and Queen Elizabeth I (Rose Thompson), Malone finds himself hot on the trail of the impossible.

SUPERMIND

FBI Agent Kenneth Malone faces his toughest challenge yet, discovering why the government operates so inefficiently. Is it a plot by some mastermind operating out of the Kremlin? Or is it an even deeper conspiracy whose goal is to sow confusion and chaos throughout the world. Will Malone be able to find the cause of the mysterious psychic static causing the disruption? What will he find when he faces the Supermind?

Classic Resurrected Science Fiction by Randall Garrett

Anything You Can Do...

What do you do when an alien with exceptional physical abilities crash lands on Earth and leaves a path of death and destruction in its wake? You use biological modification to create an enhanced human able to match the alien in strength and speed. But is the result still human?

Unwise Child

After two unsuccessful and seemingly random attempts on his life in the space of as many hours, Michael Raphael Gabriel finds himself called on to act as engineering officer on a new type of spacecraft designed for one mission only, to carry a giant computer to a distant destination before it can destroy the Earth. But once under way he discovers there is a murderer on board and the computer has gone crazy.

By Randall Garrett and Laurence Janifer

Pagan Passions

The Gods and Goddesses of the Ancient Greece and Rome have returned to rule Earth. William Forrester, a mortal teacher, dedicated to the pleasures of the mind, finds himself caught up in the power struggles of the immortals and seduced by the pleasures of the flesh.

Also From Resurrected Press

Science Fiction Authors Resurrected

Fyfe Resurrected - The Stories of H. B. Fyfe

Stories from the Golden Age of Science Fiction by the author of *D-99*. dealing with the interaction of humans and aliens on far off worlds in ways that were as creative as they were imaginative.

Bone Resurrected - The Stories of J. F. Bone

More stories from the Golden Age of Science Fiction. Includes "The Issahar Artifact," "Assassin," "To Choke an Ocean" and more.

Nourse Resurrected - The Stories of Alan E. Nourse

Stories from the Golden Age of Science Fiction. Includes "Contamination Crew." "Coffin Cure," "The Link," and more.

Dick Resurrected - The Early Stories of Philip K. Dick

Early stories from the author of the novels that inspired "Blade Runner," "Total Recall," and through a scanner darkly. Science Fiction Authors Resurrected

OTHER CLASSIC SCIENCE FICTION NOVELS BEING RESURRECTED SOON

TALENTS, INCORPORATED - BY MURRAY LEINSTER
When a Mekinese fleet conquers his home planet, Captain Bors turns to Talents, Incorporated for help using their collection of individuals with unusual abilities to defeat the enemy and save the galaxy.

THE PIRATES OF ERSATZ - BY MURRAY LEINSTER
Bran Hodden just wanted to be an electronic engineer and marry a delightful girl. But when he's framed by the powers on Walden he's forced to turn back to his family's trade, piracy. Also published as The Pirates of Zan.

EMPIRE - BY CLIFFORD SIMAK
Spencer Chambers and Interplanetary Power owned the Solar System because they controlled the source of power. It fell to Russell Page and Harry Wilson to challenge that control if they had to cross the universe to do it.

NIGHT OF THE LONG KNIVES - THE CREATURE FROM THE CLEVELAND DEPTHS - BY FRITZ LEIBER
Two classic novellas set in the not too distant future from a classic master of science fiction.

ARMAGEDDON - 2419 A.D. - THE AIR LORDS OF HAN - BY PHILLIP FRANCIS NOWLAN
The two novels that introduced the world to that intrepid hero of the 25th Century, Buck Rogers. Buck Rogers must save the world from the clutches of the insidious Han.

Other Classic Resurrected Science Fiction
Edited by Greg Fowlkes

RESURRECTED MARTIANS
Classic Stories about Mars and Martians from the Golden Age of Science Fiction

RESURRECTED ALIENS
Classic Stories of Aliens and Alien Encounters from the Golden Age of Science Fiction

RESURRECTED FLYING SAUCERS
Classic Stories of Flying Saucers and Alien Invasions from the Golden Age of Science Fiction

RESURRECTED ROBOTS
Classic Stories of Robots, Cyborgs and Androids from the Golden Age of Science Fiction

RESURRECTED SPACE SHIPS -
Classic Stories of Space Ships from the Golden Age of Science Fiction

RESURRECTED TIME TRAVEL
Classic Stories of Time Travel from the Golden Age of Science Fiction

RESURRECTED DIMENSIONS
Classic Stories of other Dimensions from the Golden Age of Science Fiction

RESURRECTED FUTURES
Classic Stories of the Far Future from the Golden Age of Science Fiction

RESURRECTED MAD SCIENTISTS
Classic Stories of Mad Scientists and their Creations from the Golden Age of Science Fiction

RESURRECTED MONSTERS
Classic Stories of Monsters and Mayhem from the Golden Age of Science Fiction

The Fictional Detective
by Greg Fowlkes

Who killed Ezekial O. Handler?

A beautiful dame, a hard-boiled private eye – and a dead body.

It started like any other case. When a famous writer dies in a mysterious car crash, private detective Frank Slade is called in to find answers, but all he finds is more questions. Who killed Ezekial Handler? Who is Janet Nielsen and why is she so interested in finding out? Who is leaving the neatly typed clues? And as Slade tries to find answers to these questions he starts to wonder if the ultimate answer will threaten his very existence.

Read about it in
The Fictional Detective

Visit www.thefictionaldetective.com

About Resurrected Press

A division of Intrepid Ink, LLC, Resurrected Press is dedicated to bringing high quality, vintage books back into publication. See our entire catalogue and find out more at www.ResurrectedPress.com.

About Intrepid Ink, LLC

Intrepid Ink, LLC provides full publishing services to authors of fiction and non-fiction books, eBooks and websites. From editing to formatting, from publishing to marketing, Intrepid Ink gets your creative works into the hands of the people who want to read them. Find out more at www.IntrepidInk.com.

www.ingramcontent.com/pod-product-compliance
Lightning Source LLC
Chambersburg PA
CBHW061131200626
46817CB00016B/712